AUTUMN SPRING

Visit us at www.boldstrokesbooks.com

By the Author

The Storm

First Tango in Paris

Autumn Spring

AUTUMN SPRING

by
Shelley Thrasher

2015

AUTUMN SPRING

© 2015 By Shelley Thrasher. All Rights Reserved.

ISBN 13: 978-1-62639-365-3

This Trade Paperback Original Is Published By
Bold Strokes Books, Inc.
P.O. Box 249
Valley Falls, NY 12185

First Edition: August 2015

THIS IS A WORK OF FICTION. NAMES, CHARACTERS, PLACES, AND INCIDENTS ARE THE PRODUCT OF THE AUTHOR'S IMAGINATION OR ARE USED FICTITIOUSLY. ANY RESEMBLANCE TO ACTUAL PERSONS, LIVING OR DEAD, BUSINESS ESTABLISHMENTS, EVENTS, OR LOCALES IS ENTIRELY COINCIDENTAL.

THIS BOOK, OR PARTS THEREOF, MAY NOT BE REPRODUCED IN ANY FORM WITHOUT PERMISSION.

___

CREDITS
Editor: Ruth Sternglantz
Production Design: Susan Ramundo
Cover Design By Sheri (graphicartist2020@hotmail.com)

Acknowledgments

Many thanks to Ruth for helping me get this one off the ground, Justine for critiquing my early efforts, Sheri for creating the beautiful cover, Rad for publishing my novel, and Connie for being there during the entire process. Thanks to all of you—you know who you are—for letting me memorialize you in this story.

Dedication

For my sister—a grandmother extraordinaire; my mom—
a distinguished senior citizen; the NWAs—my old friends;
and TAG and Jewel members—my new friends.

You're the best.

Or if thy mistress some rich anger shows,
Emprison her soft hand, and let her rave,
And feed deep, deep upon her peerless eyes.
　　　—"Ode on Melancholy," John Keats

Where are the songs of spring? Ay, Where are they?
Think not of them, thou hast thy music too…
　　　—"To Autumn," John Keats

If Winter comes, can Spring be far behind?
　　　—"Ode to the West Wind," Percy Bysshe Shelley

Chapter One

Bree Principal slung her legs over the side of her girlhood bed and rushed to lower the window she'd left open last night. Shivering, she almost slipped on the slick floor. Damn. She wasn't eighteen any longer. She certainly didn't want to fall and end up in assisted living like her mother had recently.

The huge weeping willow outside was still green, she noticed, as she closed the window. The old tree's long, slender leaves hung waiting for the first frost to make them blaze like a yellow-gold fire. She'd forgotten how beautiful the willow was, and would become.

She dashed into the bathroom and threw on some makeup, then ran a brush through her hair. What a wreck. She hadn't slept well last night, her body still humming from flinging as many clothes as she could grab into a couple of suitcases and rushing to O'Hare. Of course her flight had been late, but it'd taken only two and a half hours in the air to reach Dallas. Then she'd had to rent a car and drive almost that long southeast to her hometown, deep in the piney woods of East Texas.

Her black jeans lay where she'd tossed them onto a chair last night, and she pulled a white University of Chicago sweatshirt out of her still-packed suitcase. She had to go meet the woman her mother seemed so impressed with when they talked on the phone last night.

Speeding up South Main, Bree admired the familiar old two-story houses lining the street. Huge trees shaded them, and their yards were raked clean of the leaves and pine straw that had already fallen. Yellow and orange plants dotted their neat flower beds, though the first frost of the season would kill them. Pumpkins, stacked three or four tall, decorated some of the front porches, and one home even featured a dummy dressed as a witch, wearing black and stirring a large cauldron.

How many times had she and Ann cruised this street? Ann loved the expensive houses and always talked about how she planned to live in the biggest one of the lot someday. Bree hadn't found anything wrong with Ann's parents' home in the country, but Ann had always itched to be a city girl.

Ann smoothed her long, straight blond hair back from her chiseled face. "Let's go see who's sitting on the square tonight."

"Oh, it's probably just the same old guys," Bree said. "They're all so uncool."

"But I want to see if anybody new shows up."

"Why don't we drive back home and eat some ice cream instead? I'm hot." Bree wasn't in the mood to share. This was her last summer at home, one of her last Saturday nights with Ann before she went away to college.

"Don't be such a drag. I might meet somebody special."

Ann inched a little closer, almost near enough for Bree to touch the bare skin that Ann's red off-the-shoulder dress revealed.

"Okay. If that's what you want. But don't say I didn't warn you."

Bree gunned the motor of her brand-new Rangoon Red Mustang, the best graduation present in the world.

She jerked herself back from 1964 to the present and took a left instead of driving uptown like Ann had persuaded her to do that night more than fifty years ago. If only she'd ignored Ann's request and turned around. Maybe they'd still be together now instead of—Bree shook her head. She and Ann were both long past the cruising stage.

Instead, she parked in front of Silverado, a large white building that resembled a compound and occupied the spot where the Youth Center she and Ann used to frequent once stood. She needed to forget about the past and act her age. It wouldn't be all that long before she'd be living in a place like Silverado herself.

❖

Linda Morton climbed out of bed at six a.m. and meandered into her office. What a great night's sleep. As she sat down on the carpeted floor, folding her legs and resting her hands in her lap, she heard the small clock on the wall. *Tick, tick, tick.*

She closed her eyes and breathed in, her stomach ballooning. In and out. In and out. The ticking sound slowly morphed into the *whoosh* of blood flowing through her arms, her chest, her thighs. As she let herself relax and visualized one of her most cherished memories, her breathing and heartbeat slowed, and her head dropped forward.

Linda sat between her parents in a battered pickup, her dad steering it down a country road canopied by trees bursting with new leaves. How green and lush everything was. He stopped at a gate made of welded iron rods, and her mom jumped out and opened it, then pulled it closed behind them. They passed an ancient barn made of logs and a new large red one, crammed with bales of hay, a rusty tractor, and assorted farm implements. Following two dirt ruts through a field covered with crimson clover, cows grazing in the distance, they slowly approached her favorite spot.

Other vehicles had already parked in the grove sheltered by old cedar trees. Car doors slammed, and Linda leaped out of their old Chevrolet and ran to meet her favorite cousin. Her uncles and her mother's mother, sisters, brothers, and their families tossed horseshoes, which clanked when one of them hit the metal stake at either end of their throwing area. Her mother, aunts, and grandmother spread lunch out on the weathered picnic table, where they'd all gather later to eat. Linda and her cousins swung on old tires tied to ropes hanging from branches overhead. The sun shone in the clear blue sky, and a gentle breeze kept them cool.

After lunch, Linda picked berries with her grandmother. They wandered over the hundred-acre farm, stooping to pluck sweet dewberries from low-growing vines and larger blackberries from thickets. As they strolled along, her grandmother taught her the name of every tree, bush, and plant they passed and described each one's healing powers. Bluebirds, cardinals, and sparrows flitted about, serenading them on this cloudless Mother's Day.

Safe and relaxed in her favorite mental space, Linda focused on her breathing again. In and out. In and out. Slowly she lowered her hands to either side of her body and placed her palms on the soft carpet. Dropping her head forward, her spine curving as she bowed, she let herself sink downward—into the floor, through the carpet and concrete, spiraling into the earth far below her.

Small white roots emerged from the sides of her feet, ankles, hips, and hands. They wormed down into the ground and eventually reached a vast pool of bright white light. The light permeated her white roots and traveled up, up, up into her, like water through drinking straws. The light warmed and energized her, filled her like clear liquid in a glass, circulating through her every vein.

Linda raised her hands and clasped them together in her lap. As she gradually straightened, she imagined herself glowing like an old-fashioned incandescent bulb. She directed the heat and strength of the light at the negativity lurking inside her, visualized the light dissolving it like fog on a misty morning. She was the sun, she was life.

Her meditation almost complete, Linda deliberately placed her palms on the floor again and let the swirling light and energy washing through her flow back deep into the earth. Part of her went with it, but part of it stayed with her. She was at one with the universe.

She heard the clock tick again. After several more deep breaths, she rose from her sitting position, invigorated and ready to face a new day.

❖

Bree pushed through the double plate-glass door at Silverado, signed in at the front desk, and strode down the first hallway to the left. She rapped on the door decorated with a wreath of colorful autumn foliage, then entered the room.

"Hey, Sarah," she called. "Ready for your appointment?" Paintings covered practically every wall of the sitting area, a large portrait of Bree's dead brother Brett hanging directly behind her mother's recliner. It dominated the small space and made her hurt inside when she looked at it.

"Be ready before long." The familiar voice evidently came from the bathroom. "The nurse won't be here for a while. Grab a seat."

Bree looked around. What would it be like to move from a huge two-story house to this tiny place? "Okay. But you don't want to keep her waiting, do you?" Bree shook her head. Her mother had always been late for everything. Bree prided herself on being early for her obligations, especially as the curator of a prestigious museum in Chicago. The people she dealt with there were usually all business, and time meant money.

The minutes ticked by, and Bree stared from the closed bathroom door to the front door of her mother's small apartment. She felt like she was at a racetrack, anticipating the starting gun and wondering which horse would appear out of the gate first—her mother or the woman taking care of her.

Finally, she jumped up and strode over to the bathroom door. "Are you okay? Need any help?"

Bree had no idea how to deal with an older person in this situation.

"I'm fine," her mother called. "I told you to sit down and relax for a change. And stop worrying. I'll be ready on time."

Bree paced for a few minutes, then walked over to a sliding glass door. At least Sarah had a good view. The leaves of a few trees in the manicured open area outside had begun to turn yellow and red, but they wouldn't reach their full glory for another month. She focused on the dead ones already littering the ground and told herself to calm down.

Sarah had brought her easel and some canvases and paints. Bree stared at a work in progress that sat on the easel. Her mother had already captured the throng of slender branches of the huge willow at home, stripped bare, as it was every winter. Was that how she felt right now in this new environment?

Her paintings were usually much more colorful than this, though the ones right after Brett was killed had been filled with beige and gray. After several years, Sarah had finally begun to use more color, hinting that her grief had subsided a bit. But the dull tones had returned.

Bree frowned. At least, in this place, her mother had a nice view, plenty of people to socialize with, and someone to dispense her medicine and check on her regularly. And she could spend as long as she wanted painting, instead of worrying about tending to a large house.

"Here I am. Told you I'd be ready on time."

Finally, Sarah appeared. Her iron-gray hair was cut in a flattering style, though she looked more stooped than the last time Bree had seen her. Pushing a walker, she wore a decent pair of pants and her painter's smock. At least she wasn't letting herself go.

"It's good to see you, Bree. Thanks for coming, but you really didn't need to."

"I wanted to." Bree gave her a quick half hug, then glanced at her watch.

"My nurse is never here exactly when I expect her"—Sarah shrugged—"but she always seems to be here when I need her."

Bree looked down at the woman she'd known so long yet didn't think she'd ever understand. Sarah's eyes, which usually shifted from blue to green to hazel, had lost some of their clarity, just as Bree feared Sarah had. Well, at ninety, she had to have weakened some.

Her mother maneuvered her bright-red walker over to her recliner and eased into it.

"Hey, I like your new wheels." Bree had tried to convince her to use a cane for years but never succeeded. Sarah had always insisted she didn't need it, but all those falls at home must have finally persuaded her.

Her mother pushed the walker to one side. "It's all the rage among my new set of friends."

Bree tried to copy her light tone. "Maybe you can organize some races in these long hallways. The other residents could place bets." She chuckled, but Sarah's chilly expression made her stop.

"You've watched that old sci-fi movie *Cocoon* too many times. We don't have a fountain of youth. Not even a swimming pool. People live as best they can here, and then they die."

Bree thudded down on a nearby hard chair. How could Sarah face her own death so calmly? She'd never fully accepted the loss of her only son almost sixty years ago.

Someone knocked softly on the door.

"Come on in. It's open," Sarah called.

A woman peeked through first—short white hair feathering around her face and round eyes assessing the situation. Then she burst through the door—graceful, Pillsbury-doughboy plump, soft and sweet, and…well…edible, like an enticing dessert. And she glowed as if someone had turned the three-way bulb in a lamp from 50 watts to 150.

"Bree, remember Linda Morton?" Sarah asked, but Bree could barely speak. She was letting her eyes adjust to the heightened brightness.

"Linda. I'd never have recognized you." She blinked, then swallowed. Just Ann's little sister, she told herself—no one to get excited about. "I can't believe it. After all these years."

Linda beamed even more brightly and dropped her bag of medical supplies onto a low table. "How the heck are you doing, Bree?"

"Can't complain. How about you?" Bree tried to regain her breath from the surprise of seeing Ann's sister and the force of Linda's bear hug.

"Never better. Spending time with only a few special people like your mom out here at Silverado is a real treat."

Sarah seemed to regard them as actors in a play she was directing. What was she up to?

"What have you done with yourself all these years, girl?" Bree asked.

Linda shrugged. "Got married. Raised kids and now grandkids. Always somebody to take care of or something to do at the church or in town. You know the routine."

Bree rolled her neck to work out the effects of Linda's hug and the litany of her dull life. A typical straight woman. How predictable. "Actually, I don't. My routine's never included anything like that."

"Sorry. I didn't think. You've had an exciting career and traveled all over the world." Linda looked up at her as if seeing her clearly for the first time since she'd arrived. "You were always different, special."

"Don't you mean I was the weirdo who'd never have fit in here?"

"Of course not." Linda rubbed one temple. "You disappointed all your old friends when you left and never visited us. Especially Ann."

"Ha. You've got to be kidding." Bree hated herself for asking about Ann, but she had to know. "How's she doing?"

"Your mother hasn't kept you up to date?"

"No. Why should she? Besides, I never asked."

Sarah had leaned back in her chair and closed her eyes. Was she napping or listening?

"Ann—well, she's still Ann. Been married five times."

Bree couldn't believe that news of Ann could still make her heart feel like a ripe tomato someone had just squeezed.

"Five times? Wow. Sounds like Liz Taylor. Or those Kardashians."

Linda smiled with what looked like sympathy. Did she know what had gone on between Ann and her? She'd been so young back then, barely a teenager.

"Yes. And she's still beautiful, in her special blond-haired, blue-eyed way."

The news squeezed Bree's heart harder. "Has she lived here all this time?" She didn't really want to know where Ann had lived, but she couldn't stop asking questions.

"No. She's jumped around from New Orleans to Atlanta and New York."

Linda's factual tone helped Bree digest the news she'd avoided for so many years.

"She usually comes back home between husbands," Linda added.

"Really? So where does she live now?" Questions kept on popping into her mind.

"Here. At the old home place. She's having it remodeled."

"Currently not married, eh?" Bree couldn't tamp down the excitement rising in her belly, though she knew she was just making herself vulnerable to more disappointment. You'd think she'd have learned something over so many years, but apparently not.

She opened her mouth, about to ask something else about Ann, but Linda turned to Sarah. "So, Mrs. Principal, how about you? Is your leg feeling better?"

Sarah stretched her right leg out, and Linda dropped to her knees in front of her like the teenager Bree remembered always hanging around when she visited Ann. Pushing up Sarah's pants leg, Linda began to unwrap the dressing that covered the entire calf.

Bree stared at it and gasped. "My God. I had no idea how badly you'd hurt yourself. It looks like somebody hacked all the skin off with a meat cleaver! Why aren't you in the hospital?"

Linda glanced up at her, her eyes soft. "It looks worse than it is. I've been dressing it every day, and it's improving."

"Are you crazy? She needs a doctor's care. That bandage is bloody. And those bruises—Who's her doctor? I'm calling him right now."

"Calm down, Bree." Linda removed the bloody dressing, which made Bree nauseous. "He treated her in the emergency room and dismissed her. Carolyn takes her to see him regularly." She smiled up at her patient. "Her leg should improve in several weeks. Especially if she keeps using her walker."

Sarah glanced at them and hung her head.

Bree jumped up. "I'm not so sure about that. I still intend to talk to that doctor myself and make sure my mother's receiving the right care."

Sarah straightened and stared at her. "That's enough, Bree. You need to go home and get some sleep."

"But—"

"Linda's taking good care of me, and I'm tired of listening to you fuss over me. Hurry up. I want to work on my painting."

"All right." Bree strode over to the door. "When you two finish, Linda, I'll meet you in the hall and walk you out."

Frustrated, she waved to Sarah as she left the room. "I'll let you get on with your painting. See you later today."

She was fed up with her mother regarding her as a child.

CHAPTER TWO

Linda had had a hard time focusing on Mrs. Principal with Bree still in the room. Strange how fifty years of experience could vanish in a few minutes and she could revert to being a tongue-tied freshman.

At least Bree had remembered her, though she'd seemed so much more eager to talk about Ann than about her. But why should Bree notice her—her friend's unexciting younger sister who'd never excelled in anything?

Mrs. Principal interrupted Linda's musing. "She hasn't changed all that much, has she?"

Linda secured the new bandage on Mrs. Principal's leg. "No. She's as tall and thin and impatient as always, don't you think?"

Mrs. Principal chuckled. "Yes. And still a know-it-all, if you let her. I've always thought of her as all lines and not enough color."

Linda smoothed down Mrs. Principal's pants leg and returned her supplies to her bag. "I'm not sure what you mean."

"Of course you do. You're an intelligent, educated woman. And I've told you—call me Sarah instead of Mrs. Principal. You haven't been my student in more than fifty years." Mrs. Principal—no—Sarah shook her head.

Linda closed her bag with a snap that seemed to fragment the past. As a medical professional, a specialist, no less, she had no business letting her memories of an eighteen-year-old hotshot or her sixth-grade art teacher awe her like they just had.

"Thanks, Sarah. I'll do just that. And I'll think about what you said about Bree's lines and color." She stood up. "Take care of yourself and enjoy your painting. The one you're working on should be as impressive as all these others." She glanced around the room. "See you tomorrow morning. Same time, or as close to it as we can manage."

Sarah smiled briefly. "'Bye, Linda. Enjoy your visit with Bree."

Linda waved. "Thanks." She didn't look forward to dealing with Bree, but the prospect intrigued her.

❖

Linda spotted Bree standing near the receptionist's desk perusing a pamphlet. The overhead light glinted off the silver streak in the bangs of her blunt-cut black hair. Still naturally dark or artificially colored by a talented stylist?

Linda strode toward Bree, nervous. She'd dealt with patients' families for years. This one was no different.

"What's the deal with Sarah? Will she really be okay?"

Bree's demanding tone and frown could have stopped a train, but Linda kept moving. Family members usually considered doctors the only ones who knew anything. And they often transferred their own fear or guilt onto nurses or aides.

Grasping Bree's elbow briefly, she steered her outside to a private spot. "Assisted-living facilities thrive on gossip even more than most small-town churches and beauty shops do."

As they sat down on a secluded bench, Bree put a distance between them. "Nice day," she said, her shoulders dropping a fraction after they'd sat in silence for a few seconds.

"Yes." Linda lassoed her internal butterflies and let their momentum guide her. "Don't worry. Your mother's leg should heal completely." She wanted to rest a hand on Bree's knee or otherwise touch her again, but something stopped her natural inclination.

"It looks like someone dragged her down an asphalt road. I had no idea." Bree's voice sounded as steely as her silver streak looked. "Are you certain I shouldn't put her in the hospital instead of depending on an aide like you to bandage her wounds?"

The professional in Linda trumped the high-school freshman. "You think I'm just an aide, Bree?"

"Of course. Aide, nurse. What's the difference? Don't you people practically run these places? Cuts down on the costs, I'm sure."

"That's possibly true, but I'm a retired professional, working for your mother as a favor."

Bree tossed her head. "If I thought I could find somebody reliable, I'd hire a couple of qualified nurses to stay with her at home around the clock. But she didn't consult me."

"Really? Well, you couldn't afford to employ me in that capacity, but I'd assumed you helped her decide to make this move."

"No."

Linda took a deep breath. Bree seemed more hurt than angry.

"She just called me yesterday and told me her whereabouts, and why."

"Oh. I'm sorry." That explained the anger and guilt. "But don't take it personally. At least she finally called you."

Bree frowned. "I'm glad I have a lot of unused vacation time."

Linda picked at a fleck of paint on the arm of the bench where they sat. Bree was obviously out of control, and Linda had to stop herself from touching her. If Ann were here, she might make Bree feel better with a hug or even a kiss. "You know how proud she is. She didn't want to worry you."

Bree bristled. "Worry me? Of course she worried me. And now to see her in a place like this, with people like you taking care of her—"

Linda gripped the bench's metal arm and kept her voice calm. "People like me? Just a minute, Bree. I'm an RN, a wound-care specialist."

Yet Bree kept scowling, as if she either hadn't heard what Linda said or didn't care. She seemed almost as upset as she'd been that long-ago day Ann had started dating the star football player she eventually married.

Linda took a chance and gripped Bree's arm, which didn't feel much different from the metal one she clung to with her other hand. "Listen to me. Didn't you hear what I said? I'm as much a specialist in my field as you are in yours, with almost as much experience."

When Bree became emotional like this, she lost her power of reasoning.

You have to choose between me and that football player, Bree had screamed at Ann.

Linda would never forget overhearing that argument.

But now Bree's gray eyes looked like dry ice as she slowly swung her head toward Linda. "Are you kidding me? I spent years in some of the best universities in the country to reach my position. Where did you do your training? At a local community college?"

Bree obviously hadn't matured emotionally since high school, and Linda still didn't know how to respond to her, to help her through such an extreme reaction. She pulled her hand away from Bree's arm and clung to the cool metal support to steady herself. She could do this.

Taking an even deeper breath, she chose her words carefully. "In the '70s I lived near DC and got my master's at the Johns Hopkins University School of Nursing. I already had a BS from one of your alma maters—UT Austin. I'm fully certified to give your mother the best care possible."

Bree's eyes finally lost a little of their steam. "Really? Interesting. I didn't realize you'd ever left this area."

Good. At least she'd made a little progress. Linda nodded. "Yes, I did. I wanted to see the world too."

Bree shrugged and let the straight line of her back bend a bit. "What made you become a nurse?"

Linda sighed. Maybe Bree would finally calm down. "I wanted to do something that made a difference."

Bree's eyes seemed to melt a fraction. "I owe you an apology. So I don't need to worry so much about Sarah? She'll really heal okay?"

"Yes. She will. I'll take good care of her." Linda glanced at her watch and got up. "So good to see you, Bree. I have another appointment, but surely we'll run into each other again."

"Sure. 'Bye now." Bree grinned mechanically, exactly like she had at eighteen. Then she stood and strolled toward her car as if nothing had happened between them.

Linda slid into her little Honda, exhausted and relieved to have survived that uncomfortable encounter. Evidently, nothing about Bree had changed except her age.

Chapter Three

Remembering her mother's empty refrigerator, Bree stopped by Kroger and stocked up on basic necessities to snack on or prepare quickly. She didn't like to waste her time in the kitchen, but she was starving.

After she finished lugging her brimming bags of groceries into the kitchen and restocking the fridge and the pantry, she heard someone at the back door. Only one person knocked like that. "Coming," she called.

And she was right. There stood Carolyn, her arms open wide for a welcome hug. Carolyn, who had lived next door to her parents as long as Bree could remember, was the only person in town Bree had kept in touch with all these years.

Stepping into Carolyn's arms, she sighed with relief, then finally backed away. "Thanks for helping Sarah through the big move."

Carolyn held up her hands and shook her head.

"Don't deny it. She couldn't have done it without you."

"She made me promise not to call you." Carolyn draped an arm around Bree and guided her to the back-porch swing.

Bree gazed at the willow tree with its drooping branches. "You don't need to explain. She keeps her feelings wrapped around her as tight as the bark on that old tree."

"Yep. She's an independent old cuss."

Carolyn tightened her grip on Bree and pulled her close again. "But let's talk about you. How was your flight?"

"Predictable." She squeezed Carolyn's liver-spotted hand. "Too crowded and no food." She frowned. "I'd kill for the days of empty seats and edible meals and enough legroom to stretch out. It's so bad now I'm tempted to retire."

Carolyn laughed. "They didn't feed you between O'Hare and DFW?"

Bree stood up and stuck out her lower lip like she had as a child. "Nothing edible. And I didn't see anything but fast-food places on my drive from Dallas. Then I rushed over to visit Sarah first thing this morning."

"We'll have to take care of that." Carolyn levered herself up from the swing.

Bree grinned. "When I finally thought about eating, I remembered nobody can make an omelet like you can." Surely Carolyn would take the bait, and the wait would surely be worth it.

Carolyn wrapped her arm around Bree's waist. "Now there's the Bree Principal I know and love. Didn't take long for you to finagle me into cooking for you. How about a vegetable one?"

Bree held up both hands dramatically. "I thought you'd never ask. Sounds fabulous."

They both laughed and walked through the back door side by side. It actually felt good to be home.

Bree finished her omelet and orange juice. "God, how delicious. You're the world's greatest neighbor and cook." She batted her eyelids in her best Southern-belle imitation. "I declare. Why couldn't you have been gay? I'd have enticed you to come be my partner in Chicago."

"And made me miss the chance to live with my parents in this idyllic small town?" Carolyn gestured for Bree to stay seated while she rinsed her dishes.

Bree scowled. "Didn't you want a life of your own? I'd have gone nuts after a week."

Carolyn finally sat down across the kitchen table from her and poured them each a cup of strong black coffee. "I did have a life of my own." Carolyn frowned. "I couldn't help it that both my husbands turned out to be unfaithful bums."

Bree didn't know what to say. Was Carolyn still bitter about her divorces?

Carolyn grinned. "Look at me. Who wouldn't want to see me first thing every morning?"

Bree studied Carolyn's height and rather horsey, asymmetrical features. She didn't see anything unattractive about her, but she'd never been able to convince Carolyn to believe her. She reached across the table and laced her fingers through Carolyn's. "You know I'm one of your biggest admirers. You should have kept looking till you found a man worth your while."

"Flattery will get you everywhere."

"I know."

"Did I mention I'm glad you're home?"

Bree let go of Carolyn and traced a line on the kitchen table with her finger. "I never thought I'd say this, but I am too."

They sat in comfortable silence. Finally, Bree said, "Guess who I was reminiscing about on my way to visit Sarah."

"No telling. Who?" Carolyn's eyes shone as she lifted her pottery mug to her lips.

"Ann White. I hadn't thought about her in forever. And then at Silverado this morning, I heard she's back in town. Is that right?"

Carolyn took a sip of the steaming liquid, then slowly lowered her mug and nodded. "As a matter of fact, I saw her out at Wild Iris just the other day."

"Wild Iris? What's that?" So Ann really was here. That meant she wasn't married, for now.

"It's the in place in town, out on the highway. A trendy flower and gift shop right in the same building with this great little lunch and take-out café. We'll have to go there sometime."

"Huh?" Bree couldn't remember what she'd asked Carolyn, much less process her answer. "Oh, sure."

"Are you okay?" Carolyn stared at her. "You look like you've seen a ghost."

"I have," Bree murmured, still trying to absorb the news about Ann.

Carolyn cupped the back of one ear. "What'd you say? I haven't put my hearing aids in yet."

"Oh, nothing." She'd been so upset about her mother earlier she'd pushed Linda's news about Ann being in town aside. But now it roared back. Had she just received a second chance with the one woman who'd ever meant anything to her?

Bree couldn't think about much of anything but Ann during the rest of her conversation with Carolyn. But she finally got her head on straight again as they walked out into the backyard. "By the way, do you know Linda White, Ann's little sister?"

Carolyn stopped and stared at Bree. "You mean Linda Morton? Of course. We're both master gardeners and see each other a lot around town. Why?"

"She's the one dressing Sarah's leg. And Sarah made sure I met her this morning."

"Why, that old fox."

"Who's an old fox?"

"Your mother. Who else?"

"What do you mean?"

"Linda's one of the most interesting women in town. Plus, she's a fabulous cook and a pillar of her church and the community."

"Interesting? Are you slipping drugs into your coffee? She's in her midsixties and told me she's married and has kids and grandkids."

A sly grin stretched Carolyn's mouth. "She used to be married. But now she's not."

"What do you mean?"

"Well, before one of our master gardeners' meetings several months ago, somebody said they saw her picture on Facebook."

"So? That's not very thrilling news."

Carolyn lowered her voice. "She was in Tyler, playing some kind of game with a lot of other women with really short hair. If you know what I mean."

"That's ridiculous. Almost every woman I know has short hair."

"But do they play something called Gay Monopoly?" Carolyn smiled like she'd just originated the theory of evolution.

"So what if she enjoys the company of lesbians, if that's what they are. Some straight people do, don't they?" Bree stared pointedly at Carolyn, who finally nodded.

"Yes, if they've known 'em all their lives. But I don't think of you as a lesbian. To me, you'll always be the little girl next door who can never get enough to eat." Her affection glowed in her eyes.

"Then I rest my case." Bree was getting tired. Sarah always said Carolyn could talk the ears off a donkey.

"Linda Morton may keep her nose clean, but her daughter who lives up North doesn't. She even brings her girlfriend home with her on holidays, and they sleep in the same bed. People whisper about her up a storm." Carolyn always loved to have the last word.

"Good for her." Bree walked Carolyn to the back gate.

"The apple doesn't fall far from the tree. That's what I always say. Maybe you can find out if I'm right."

Maybe. But I'd rather rip out my tongue than add anything to the gossip mill. "Thanks a million for the omelet, Carolyn. I have to return my rental car, and then I plan to treat myself to a nap before I go visit Sarah again. See you later."

So Ann's not married and is here in town, Linda might be a lesbian, and her daughter's definitely one, Bree thought as she sauntered back toward the house. This visit might be a lot more interesting than she'd expected.

❖

Ann White teed off on the fifth hole and hit a perfect drive. What a beautiful October day. She stuck her club into her bag and stood beside her golf cart as her current boyfriend, Carl Paul, swung at his ball.

His shot dribbled down the fairway, and Ann cringed as the thin young man who'd just driven up shook his head and said, "Better luck next time, Pops."

Ann frowned at the smart aleck, who promptly gave her the eye. She poufed up her bleached-blond hair and stared him down. The nerve of some guys. She could be his grandmother. Besides, that ship had already sailed more times than she cared to count, and she'd stayed in all the first-class staterooms.

She slid into her cart and waited for Carl. He finally climbed in and slumped beside her. Poor thing. He was just trying to please her.

He'd spent most of his life indoors, playing with stocks and bonds instead of golf balls.

"Don't pay any attention to that jerk, dear. You have something he'll never have."

Carl looked up. "What's that?"

"Me."

He brightened as she steered them down the fairway to their balls. She'd play with some of her female acquaintances from now on instead of torture poor Carl again. She had more important plans for him. She smiled with satisfaction.

Linda hunched over her steering wheel and sped faster than usual down the familiar winding country road. Being around Bree had shredded the mellow mood her daily visualization exercise had created. The canopy of oaks, sweet gums, and pines stretching over the pavement soothed her a bit, but she still felt on edge.

She took a right onto a gravel road and drove as fast as she dared over the hills dotted with trees. Their beauty continued to work their magic, so by the time she pulled into the large parking area in front of her aunt Sandy's dome home, she'd slowed her speed and was breathing less heavily than when she left Silverado.

Bree had asked reasonable questions, she kept telling herself. Of course she was concerned about her mother. Otherwise she probably wouldn't have questioned Linda's qualifications.

"Good morning, sunshine," Sandy said as she strolled down her driveway toward Linda, two golden retrievers dancing around her. "Thought we might have a frost last night but guess we'll have to wait a while longer for the leaves to start changing." Her long silver hair gleamed in the sunlight, and in her jeans and lightweight purple plaid flannel shirt, she didn't look or act like a typical seventy-five-year-old.

Linda climbed out of her blue CR-V and popped her trunk open. "Brought you something for our celebration tomorrow night." She pointed toward a piece of orange cloth, plus three yellow pumpkins and a cornucopia she'd just bought at a local produce stand.

"Aw. How sweet." Sandy unfolded the cloth and inspected it. "Did you make this?"

"Yes. Thought you needed a new one."

Sandy strode over to a nearby shed and grabbed the handles of a rusty old wheelbarrow. "It'll look great on the altar. Thanks." She stacked the largest pumpkin in the wheelbarrow and motioned for Linda to carry the cornucopia inside.

Sandy had obviously begun to prepare for her big event tomorrow night. A cauldron near the front door contained dried cornstalks, several large ears still attached to them, probably from Sandy's garden. A dazzling arrangement of leaves and acorns sat on the rough-hewn mantel, where Linda placed the cornucopia—full of squash, miniature pumpkins, turnips, and apples—on the other end of it. The altar held the skull of a cow, as well as several orange and black candles. Linda placed the new cloth on a nearby chair. She'd let Sandy replace the old one with it.

Sandy put the large pumpkin in an undecorated corner and stared at her. "Why so down in the mouth?" She bent and petted Zoe, one of the retrievers, who stood beside her and gazed at her with clear adoration.

"You don't miss much, do you?"

"Not when it comes to you."

Linda shrugged. "Someone I used to know a long time ago just shook me up. I'll get over it."

Sandy threw an arm around her shoulder as they walked outside again. "Come help me carry in those other two pumpkins, and then you can tell me all about it."

"It's not important, but I appreciate you noticing." Linda snuggled into her aunt, who radiated strength. "Just being here's already made me feel better. What do you want me to bring for the celebration tomorrow night?"

"Nothing besides what the group's already planned. A picture of someone special who's passed away, their favorite dish, and something negative you'd like to resolve."

After they'd carried the remaining pumpkins inside, Linda put hers on Sandy's cluttered kitchen table. "I've thought about the things we're supposed to bring for our ceremony but haven't had time to finish getting everything ready." She washed her hands in the sink. "I'll be here about eight thirty, after my grandkids finish trick-or-treating."

"Fine. We'll start eating about nine. Don't be too late." Sandy kissed Linda's cheek. "Have a good day. And thanks again for all the decorations."

As Linda slid into her Honda, she felt so much more relaxed than when she got here. What would she do without Sandy?

❖

"This beef stew's great," Bree said. "Thanks for waking me up and forcing me to come share it with you, Carolyn."

"No problem. I hate to eat alone."

Bree dished herself another bowlful from the Crock-Pot that sat in the middle of Carolyn's dining-room table. "I'll be happy to keep you company at mealtime as long as I'm here." She buttered a third piece of homemade cornbread. "If I keep this up, though, I'll have to buy two tickets when I fly back to Chicago, to fit myself into those tiny airline seats."

Carolyn chuckled. "I know you better than that. You'll be so busy while you're here, you'll burn off anything I can come up with to feed you."

"What do you think I'll find to do except visit Sarah? And even she doesn't act like she wants me to hang around her much. Some things never change."

"She'll probably act independent until the day she dies." Carolyn scraped the last of the stew from her vintage Fiestaware bowl and leaned back in her chair. "She really does need you right now though. This can't be an easy transition. I'm glad she still has her painting."

"Yes. Though I used to be jealous of it." Bree gazed at the Crock-Pot but decided to forego a third helping and shoved her own bowl away.

"Jealous? Why?"

"Between it and her teaching and Dad, she didn't have enough time to pay attention to me."

"I never knew that. You were usually busier than she was, always rushing from one activity to the next."

Bree slumped. "I had to do something to occupy myself. But now, back here in this place, I'm probably at as much of a loss as Sarah is. I don't really know anybody in town anymore, except you. I only shop when I need or want something—not that this place has many stores. And I'm definitely not into church activities. Any ideas?"

Carolyn gathered their bowls and silverware. "Yes, as a matter of fact."

Bree straightened her back. "What do you have in mind?"

"How about going to a sort of Halloween celebration tomorrow night?"

"And do what? Bob for apples and scream with the kids when a slimy hand grabs me in a house of horrors?"

Carolyn grinned. "Not exactly what I had in mind. This is a small, intimate gathering of women in our age range. No kids, no slimy hands. You might fit right in."

"Fit in at a social event here?" Bree frowned. "I never did when I was growing up. Why should I hope to now?"

"Times and places change. People change. You never know." Carolyn smiled mysteriously.

"Sure. I'll give it a whirl. But I won't get my hopes up. Do I need to take anything?"

"Yes. And one of them requires cooking."

"Ugh. Go by yourself. I'd rather spend Halloween alone."

Carolyn put her hands on her waist. "You can't wiggle out of my invitation that easy. Think it over and let me know in the morning."

Bree raised a brow.

"All you need's a picture of a person in your life who's passed over and his or her favorite dish. Plus, you have to make it yourself. That's not too hard, is it? Just don't use meat. Oh, and think of a bad habit you'd like to break."

As Carolyn carried their dishes into the kitchen, Bree picked up a damp sponge and wiped off the table where they'd just eaten. Then she took the mustard-colored salt and pepper shakers into the kitchen and set them on the counter. "No meat, eh? Now you've made me curious."

"So you want to go?"

"I'll think about it and let you know tomorrow. But right now, how about a few games of Scrabble?" She looked forward to the satisfaction of beating Carolyn, like she always did.

Chapter Four

Linda scooped the last of the baked sweet potatoes from their skins and plopped them into a large mixing bowl. Her dad had loved sweet-potato casserole, so she'd decided to take it to the celebration tonight. The back door banged.

"Granny, can I help?" Riley, her youngest grandchild, rarely slowed down except when it came to cooking.

"Sure. How about getting me some butter and brown sugar?"

Riley brought them and stood beside her at the Corian counter. "Can I stir 'em in? I like to watch the butter melt."

"Of course. I'll go round up the other ingredients. Here." Linda handed her a potato masher, noticing how Riley's hair almost matched the orange sweet potatoes. Just like her own, once. And freckles covered Riley's cheeks too, like hers at that age. Hopefully they didn't embarrass Riley as much as hers had.

Riley finally made the lumpy orange mixture smooth.

"Here. Add the salt and vanilla, and then we'll be almost through," Linda said.

Riley carefully measured the ingredients and mixed them in, then gazed up at her. "Can I chop the nuts too?"

"Sure. And I'll get a Pyrex dish and some marshmallows."

Soon, she slid the casserole into the preheated oven, and Riley headed toward the back door. "See you later, Granny. I'm going out to play again."

Linda sighed as she watched her leave. How she wished her reclusive grandmother had spent more time with her. Her mother had made her feel special, but her mother's mother had rarely socialized, except for picnics. Poor Ann hadn't even had a real grandmother and had lost her mother at such an early age. She must have really felt bad about that.

Oh. She'd forgotten she needed to call Ann. As she ran water into the sink, she punched in Ann's phone number and put her on speaker.

"Hey. How's it going, sis?"

She listened patiently as Ann complained about her usual aches and pains, all the while washing and drying the mixing bowl and utensils she'd used.

"Hope you feel better soon. Say, I don't want to bother you, but can I look through that basket of old family pictures we found in Mom's house after the funeral? I can run by and pick it up in an hour or so, when I take the kids home." Ann was agreeable.

Linda wiped the saffron-colored countertop clean. "Okay. See you after while."

She clicked the phone off. The casserole would be done in half an hour, so she had time to put away the puzzles and games her grandchildren had left scattered around the family room. It warmed her inside to act like the grandmother she wished she'd had.

Sitting on the couch, Bree flipped through the scrapbooks her mother had assembled. She'd recorded the first twelve years of Bree's life in detail: her first word, her first tooth, her first step, her first birthday party. But then her mother had condensed the rest of the almost-seventy years of Bree's existence into one volume.

Of course, Bree's twin brother Brett had shared an equal amount of space with her in the first scrapbooks. Until the accident…

She gazed at the dark-haired boy who she'd spent her first twelve birthdays with. In this photo he stood resting his hand on the green Olivetti typewriter he'd pestered their father for. Brett wanted to learn to type, he'd said, because a banker should be able to.

At twelve, Bree had wanted to become a sculptor and, in a picture of her taken just after the one of Brett, she stood with her hand on the potter's wheel their parents had given her. She'd craved to learn to throw a pot and could hardly wait to set up her new present.

A knock sounded on the back door. "Ready to go, Bree?" Carolyn called.

After carefully sliding the old photo of her brother from the four small black corners that held it, Bree slipped it into an envelope. "Just a minute. I'd have been ready on time, but I had to look for a recipe."

"A recipe. You actually cooked something? By the way, you better grab a jacket," Carolyn said as she strode into the den. "It's nippy, and we'll probably stay out pretty late."

"Sure. Just wait till you see the apple pie I made. I'm not totally helpless in the kitchen."

"I'll like to see the scene of the crime for myself, thank you very much." Carolyn walked into the kitchen. "Well, I'll be a monkey's uncle," she called. "Are you sure you made this? It looks almost edible." She emerged carrying the pie in its covered plastic container, treating it like a crown jewel.

"Don't drop it." Bree pulled on an old black leather jacket she hadn't worn since high school, amazed her mother hadn't donated it to Goodwill a long time ago. It fit a little snugly across her breasts, but she managed to zip it. Its soft leather still felt supple, though it had lost its oily, tallow smell, and she flipped up the collar just like she used to.

Carolyn stared. "Wow. You look great. And you can even cook. I can't imagine why you've never found a good woman to settle down with."

"Thanks, I think, but I'm fine on my own." She headed for the back door. "Are you ready? My stomach's growling. Do all your parties start this late?"

"Nope. This one's special. You'll see what I mean."

Why all the mystery? Bree shrugged, already bored before she got there, though the food would surely be worth her time. What else could interest her about a group of little old small-town ladies getting together on Halloween?

❖

Linda gently closed her front door behind the final trick-or-treater and turned to the straw basket of old photos she'd rummaged through periodically, when she wasn't holding out a jack-o'-lantern full of candy to neighborhood children dressed up as Spider-Man, Elsa, and other characters, celebrities, and creatures. She searched through the basket for a good picture of her dad, but almost at the bottom of the container, she discovered a mystifying photo.

A young woman not that much older than Linda's oldest grandson stood beside a man in his forties. Even in the blurry shot he conveyed an air of sophistication most of the local men lacked. Did his posture, the way he held himself, his facial expression, or the world-weary look in his eyes create this impression?

On the back of the picture someone had scrawled only *Patrick, 1949*. Though she'd never seen this photo before, it made her pause, made her remember a confused confession her mother had made. *Your father isn't who you think he is.* Her mother had been dying, in hospice, and Linda had assumed that her mother's fractured tale about a tall redheaded stranger who'd walked into the drugstore where she worked and swept her off her feet was the Alzheimer's talking, the horrible disease that had robbed her mother of her memories and herself.

Linda never brought up the subject again and didn't want to believe it, and she never discussed it with her dad. And she'd almost forgotten the strange confession, but tonight she stared at the photo. *His name was Patrick. And he left me you.* Had her mother been telling the truth?

She shook her head. She couldn't face this right now. She was already late to Sandy's big event, so she tossed the photo back into the old basket. She picked up the one she'd finally chosen, of her dad in his best suit, and grabbed his favorite dish, the sweet-potato casserole she and Riley had made. Whoever this Patrick turned out to be, she knew who her father was.

CHAPTER FIVE

Carolyn steered her big black Lincoln Town Car through town and headed northeast on the highway, taking a right onto a country road. Bree gazed out the window at the moon—full four or five days ago but now losing its size and brightness.

"New car? It sure rides smoother than my old '64 Mustang," she said, "though I'm glad Sarah kept it." The sun had set more than two hours earlier, and the number of cars and trucks full of trick-or-treaters had dwindled considerably.

"Yep. It's a valuable antique now. Your folks thought as much of that car as you did. Had a mechanic check it out regularly, kept it in the garage, and one of them drove it at least once a month during all that time you were gone." Carolyn glanced over at her. "In fact, your mom asked me to drive it after she went to Silverado, but now you can take care of it yourself."

"Thanks. What else do you secretly do for her?"

Carolyn shrugged. "Oh, this and that. We'll discuss it later." She slowed for a curve, then sped up again. "I bought this Lincoln a couple of months ago. Have to have a brand-new one every two years, just like Daddy did." She kept her foot steady and sure on the gas pedal.

"Do you miss your folks a lot?" Bree felt awkward asking such an obvious question, but today she couldn't keep her mind off the people in her life she'd lost.

Carolyn took her eyes away from the road for half a second. "Of course. Oh, I got tired of taking care of them, especially near the end." She sighed. "Everybody does, I imagine."

"So they both stayed at home until they died?" Bree couldn't imagine living with her parents as long as Carolyn had.

"Sure did. They tended to me when I was little, so I looked after them." She slowed down and turned into a long driveway. "Seemed like the right thing to do."

"You don't regret it?"

"Not a minute of it. We loved each other. Simple as that."

Bree gazed out at the waning moon again. "Sometimes I wish my life were that easy."

"I didn't say easy. We sure had our ups and downs." Carolyn shrugged. "I said simple. We all did what we had to and enjoyed ourselves in the process."

"Well, I envy you. My life has been rather complicated, and I'm not sure how much I've enjoyed it." A thread of uneasiness twined around Bree as she thought of her mother and her new situation. How much longer did she or Bree have to enjoy her life in the simple ways Carolyn described?

Carolyn drove down the dark, silent country road for several minutes, as steady as the phases of the moon and the twinkle of the stars. Bree stared at the tree-pierced horizon they drifted past. What would her life have been like if she'd stayed here, not spent so much time away at school and totally involved in her career?

She tried to visualize herself living at home with her mother but couldn't picture it. She had enough trouble taking care of herself and had no clue how to tend to an aging parent. She'd discuss the possibility with Sarah but thought she'd do better where she was, with professional help. Just so she had the best.

She looked around as Carolyn turned into a familiar-looking driveway. "Say. Didn't Sandy Porter used to live in this area? I remember coming out here with Sarah to buy eggs and fresh vegetables from Sandy's mother. What a strange woman, but she had the best produce in town."

"You're right. She was strange, but you're about to find out what made you think so." Carolyn laughed.

Bree peered through the windshield at the rounded house in the distance. "This doesn't look anything like I remember it."

"That's because Sandy had her mother's old house torn down and built herself a dome home on the site."

"I thought she left here right after she graduated. I don't ever remember seeing her except as a kid."

Carolyn pulled up beside a couple of other cars in the driveway. "That's right. Sandy went out to Oregon and California, then moved back to this area about ten years ago. She's Linda Morton's aunt, you know. Linda's mother's sister."

Bree tensed. "So will Linda be here tonight?"

Carolyn shifted her Lincoln into park. "In living color. And you should know something else."

"What? Is this a group of lesbians, present company excluded?" Bree laughed.

Carolyn killed the engine. "No. This is a coven of witches, and we're here to celebrate Samhain."

Bree stared. "Say that again."

"You heard me. Now pick your jaw up off my new leather upholstery and let's get ourselves inside."

Linda walked through the door, and Sandy announced, "Here she is, finally."

"Sorry I'm late," she said. "Two of my grandsons wanted to hang around after they finished trick-or-treating, and I've missed so much of their childhood, I didn't have the heart to rush them away."

"No problem. We understand, except we've eaten almost all the hors d'oeuvres." Sandy and the other women in the living room nodded.

All except a visitor, who stood next to Carolyn. Why was Bree Principal here? And wearing her old black leather jacket, no less, which stirred unwelcome memories. Around Bree, Linda wanted to be the person she'd become, not the girl she'd been.

Linda hurried over to the punch bowl and dipped out a cup full of the red punch Sandy always fixed for gatherings like this one. As she sipped the cinnamon-flavored drink and studied Bree, she wished she had something a little stronger.

Bree looked a little more relaxed tonight, as if being with someone as down-to-earth as Carolyn had rubbed off on her. Good. She must have had time to rest too.

Linda walked over to her and held out her hand. "Nice to see you again. How's it going?"

Bree's handshake felt strong and forceful, like that of a businessman or someone used to dealing with the public. Linda usually hugged the women she knew, especially those in the various groups she belonged to. As word had obviously trickled from mouth to mouth about her new friends in Tyler, some of her acquaintances had stiffened when she touched them. But after a while they'd evidently realized she didn't intend to make a move on them or their daughters and had greeted her as usual.

Bree responded, "Okay, though it's still a shock to my system." Bree glanced at the other women, who stood around chatting and eating deviled eggs, raw vegetables, and other finger food. "Of course, learning that I just crashed a coven celebration here in town is a jolt, but I'll adjust. In fact, things around here just got a lot more interesting than I ever expected them to." Her eyes gleamed like gray quartz.

Linda refused to let Bree's unexpected appearance ruin her night. In fact, her obvious delight with their secret group made Linda feel much more positive toward Bree than she had yesterday.

❖

"Okay, everyone," Sandy announced. "Now that we're all here, I want to welcome you to our fourth yearly celebration of Samhain. And a special welcome to Bree Principal, our guest. Carolyn invited her, so she must be good people."

Bree vaguely recognized a few of the women from long ago but noticed several strangers. Who would ever have pegged these women as Wiccans? They ranged in age from their sixties to their early nineties, she assumed, and looked like average grandmothers or society women.

"It's good to be here," she said. "I don't know how long I'll be in town, but judging by this group, it should be a fascinating stay."

"You've got that right." Sandy spoke up again. "California and Oregon don't have a thing on us."

Visions of what might happen tonight almost short-circuited Bree's imagination.

Would they strip naked later and run wildly through the woods behind Sandy's house, shouting gibberish at the waning moon as their breasts flopped and their hair flew in the chilly night air?

No. It was too cold, and they were all too old for such an undertaking. They'd come down with the flu, or at least the sniffles.

Perhaps they'd keep their clothes on and merely have a ritual outside, around a roaring fire. Bree foresaw them pulling on long black robes and processing solemnly down a winding path into the dark woods, each carrying a blazing torch aloft. Once they reached their destination, they'd encircle a huge pile of dry firewood and toss their torches into it. Flames would *whoosh* skyward, smoke billowing toward the heavens, and weird Celtic-sounding music would burst from an unknown source.

In a booming voice, Sandy would lead them in a series of strange incantations, commanding the spirits of the dead to appear and mingle among them. A cloud of mist would rise, and they'd shiver in unison as their dearly departed materialized, greeting them from the Other Side with condolences and blessings.

But wouldn't that type of smoke burn their eyes and make their clothes stink? And would Sandy's voice actually boom?

Bree shook her head clear of her musings in time to hear Sandy declare, "It's late. Let's get this party started. Food first, then business, I always say."

Now that sounded like a real East Texan, witch or not, Bree thought.

"Come on." Carolyn took her hand. "I brought our dishes in while you were getting acquainted, so everything's ready. I'm hungry. How about you?"

Bree followed Carolyn's lead. At least she could be certain the food would be delicious.

❖

Candlelight bathed the orange-speckled Formica dining table, covered with a variety of casseroles and desserts. "Join hands and form a circle," Sandy said, and they gathered around the table. Linda stood directly across from Bree and, distracted, barely heard the words.

"We have all brought the fruits of the harvest that our loved ones favored."

Sandy's long white hair shone in the flickering candlelight, and the silver streak in Bree's blazed like lightning.

"As we enter this dark time of the year, tonight we feel the presence of those who have gone before us."

While Sandy spoke, Linda struggled to ignore Bree and focus on her dead parents, especially her dad.

"Let us commune with them and each other, so we can walk with their wisdom and strength to guide us as we journey through the coming darkness together."

This was a solemn undertaking, Linda tried to remind herself, not a frivolous social event.

"Now, let's eat." Sandy's final words broke the spell and freed Linda to indulge herself in the sight of Bree, who was actually more beautiful now than in high school. She'd ripened like an exotic piece of fruit.

As Linda heaped her paper plate with fried squash, fruit salad, turnip fritters, scalloped corn, and other dishes the group members had brought, she couldn't quit glancing at Bree. She'd taken off her black leather jacket, thank goodness, but Linda had trouble dealing with some of the memories it stirred up.

She saw Bree, eighteen and lovely in an androgynous way, sitting at the dinner table with her family. She talked eagerly with her father about cars and complimented her mother's cooking. She discussed football and baseball with Linda's two brothers and charmed Ann in an understated way that perhaps only Linda had noticed.

Shaking her head to dislodge the distracting recollections, she overheard Bree say, "I don't usually cook much, but I did make an apple pie this afternoon to honor my brother."

Linda didn't remember Bree's twin brother Brett, but she knew he'd died in an accident. Ann had been in the same sixth-grade class with both Bree and Brett that year. Back then, Linda had never known anyone who had lost a close family member or any kids who'd died, so that memory had stuck.

As Linda watched Bree circulate around the group of women here tonight, she let go of her irritation from their encounter yesterday at Silverado. She hadn't been Bree's friend; Ann had. Of course Bree was interested in her. And Bree couldn't read minds. How could she know Linda's professional status?

Don't hold on to something so trivial, she told herself. Let go of your bruised pride and plunge yourself into the new phase of the year we're entering, like Sandy just reminded us.

❖

Bree chatted automatically with a woman she'd just introduced herself to, yet eyed Linda, who seemed deep in thought. Suddenly the image of a solemn-eyed, scrawny teenager flashed through her mind. Linda had rarely said much during Bree's frequent overnight visits with Ann their senior year in high school, and Bree had never tried to get to know her.

Not that she'd had much of a chance. Ann had always demanded everyone's attention, with her glossy long blond hair and porcelain complexion. The boys flocked around her, competing for her time. Bree had felt privileged to be the one to share her bed practically every Friday night after they came home from a party or a double date.

Bree remembered the Whites' typical three-bedroom home well. She and Ann had slept together in the double bed Ann usually shared with Linda. Occasionally Bree had felt bad about making Linda sleep on the living-room sofa, but not bad enough to stop coming over every Friday. After all, Linda had the bed to herself practically every Saturday night, which Ann usually spent with Bree.

Curling up beside Ann in that small bed had been the highlight of each week that year—listening to her talk about what they'd done that evening, then waking up with her arms wrapped around Ann. She could almost feel Ann's warm, pliant body, so soft and perfumed. Sometimes Bree hadn't slept at all. She hadn't wanted to miss a second of being that close to Ann, so she'd simply lain there quietly listening to Ann breathe.

"Ann said to tell you hello."

Caught up in her memories, Bree hadn't realized that Linda was standing beside her now, instead of the woman Bree had been chatting with.

"Ann?" A surge of longing engulfed Bree. She'd spent so many years trying to forget her high-school flame. Strange how one simple sentence could rekindle all the longing she thought had burned up and left only ashes.

"Yes. You asked about her yesterday, so when I saw her this afternoon, I mentioned that I'd seen you."

"And what did she say?"

"Not as much as I thought she would. She just said to tell you hello. Is that some kind of code word?"

Was Linda kidding? Bree couldn't be sure. "Code? Of course not. I'm surprised Ann bothered to say anything to me, even after so long. We didn't exactly part on friendly terms."

Linda gazed at her with a question in her eyes. "You really are out of touch, aren't you? You actually never heard about those times Ann tried to commit suicide?"

"Suicide? No. Mother rarely gossips, but surely she'd have told me something like that."

Linda took a bite of squash from the plate she stood juggling. "We tried to keep it quiet. And your mother's not known as the most sociable person in town. But surely Carolyn would have let you know."

Bree dropped into a nearby chair, put her plate on a small table beside her, and picked up her glass of cider from it. "Carolyn and I tried not to talk about home during her yearly visit. Besides, I'm not sure she knew how close Ann and I once were. She lived in Austin or Houston when Ann and I spent so much time together." She shoved her hand through her silver bangs. "Why would Ann try to kill herself? She had everything she could possibly want, didn't she?"

"Everything but you," Linda murmured, though in the middle of so many conversations, Bree wondered if she'd heard her right.

"She didn't want *me*. She wanted a man—told me a million times she'd never be complete without the right one. And apparently she proved her point, several times."

Linda shrugged. "Obviously she hasn't found the right one yet. But you have to give her credit for trying. Maybe this one will work out."

Bree sat there motionless, then picked up her plate again and tried the casserole she'd seen Linda bring in. "Umm, what great sweet potatoes. I recall seeing you work beside your mother in the kitchen, but she practically had to threaten to ground Ann to get her to even set the table."

Linda's smile seemed bittersweet. "Yes. I'm surprised you remembered. You, and almost everyone else, always treated Ann like a member of royalty. I'm not surprised she expected everyone to regard her like that for the rest of her life. It must have shocked her when she woke up with a husband or three who demanded that she wait on him, instead of vice versa."

"Poor Ann," Bree said.

"Yes. Most of the time I feel sorry for her too. Now that you're finally back, maybe you can help her get her shit together."

Linda turned and walked away, and Bree felt pulled. Should she follow her or sit here and indulge herself in memories of Ann?

CHAPTER SIX

L inda threw her dirty plate into a large black plastic bag in Sandy's kitchen. Then she rinsed her hands and gazed out the window above the kitchen sink at the three-quarters-full moon.

Like the moon, she'd lived more than half of her life too, and what had she done with it? Had a crush on Bree, become a nurse, married and divorced her husband, tended to three children and four grandchildren, and discovered she was a lesbian who *still* had a crush on Bree after all these years. Why had she turned the conversation to Ann instead of talking to Bree like one adult to another?

"Oh, there you are," Sandy said from behind her. "Everyone's finishing dessert. Come on. We're about to share our pictures."

After Linda settled into her usual place, she glanced around. The eight members of her coven, plus Bree, sat in a circle in Sandy's cozy living room. Instead of conversation, a pleasant silence engulfed them. Each of them gazed at the photo she held and seemed to commune with it, so Linda pulled her own picture from her pocket and looked at the familiar face of her dad.

Sandy initiated the ritual. "Each of you has brought a photograph of a departed loved one to dwell on."

Linda's dad wore a starched white shirt in this picture, as he'd done almost every day as owner of a small grocery store, seeming as proud as the president of the local bank. Linda could still smell the fresh, clean scent of the starch her mother had made from cornstarch and boiling water. Her dad's clear eyes shone like he'd just finished telling them about an interesting customer.

"If and when you feel the desire, feel free to share your picture and your thoughts about the person you're connecting with."

Linda let her photo lie in her lap as she focused on it. Her dad's brown hair had become gray before he died, not pure white like hers had. Her mother's had turned gray too.

Her dad's clear eyes settled on her in his usual calm, non-judgmental way. He'd always helped her with her homework, explaining the logic behind a puzzling word problem in math or how a basic science concept applied to her everyday life. Her memories of him comforted her, and she looked up and began to speak.

"I had three older siblings, two brothers and a sister," she told the group. "We had the same father, whose picture I brought with me tonight, but I was my mother's only child." She handed the shot to the woman who sat next to her, who then passed it on. "He could have favored his children by his first wife, or he could have favored me, but he didn't. He treated us all as equals, and we tried to do the same," Linda said, "though I'm not sure we always succeeded."

She thought briefly of Ann, whose beauty had always set her apart from the rest of them. Glancing at Bree, she sensed her thinking the same thing.

As the women passed the photo around the circle, some of them shared memories of her dad, while others who hadn't known him simply commented on his appearance. As Bree looked at it she said, "Every time I visited, he went around the table and asked each of us what we'd learned in school that day. And if it wasn't a school day, he wanted to know what we planned to do or had done to make that day worth living." She smiled at Linda. "I guess that impressed me because during meals with my parents, we rarely talked. Each of us usually took a book to the dinner table and read while we ate."

Sandy spoke up next. "Because Linda's mother was my older sister, I visited them sometimes. If I ever quarreled with one of Linda's older brothers, her dad always intervened and made us kiss and make up. He was a good man, a peacemaker."

When the picture finally reached Linda again, she gazed at it once more, filled with the contentment she'd always experienced after she spent time with this special man in her life.

Her own husband had always treated her as kindly as her father had, but the fire between them had burned out so many years ago, their divorce shouldn't have surprised either of them. Had that fire ever actually existed except in her fantasies? Or had she confused it with the way she'd always felt about Bree?

❖

Bree listened as the women shared memories of people they'd lost. One woman spoke about losing her six-year-old daughter, and Bree couldn't imagine living with such pain. Another described her mother and how she'd almost cheered when the old woman died. They'd quarreled and nagged each other her entire life, the speaker said, but now she missed her and hoped she could replace all those bad memories with the few remaining good ones.

Bree shared her photo last, her heart thundering as she bared herself to these acquaintances and strangers. "My brother, Brett, was killed in a hunting accident when he was twelve." She took a deep breath. "If you don't know me, you need to realize that we were twins. As the only children in our family, we did everything together." She willed her voice to quit shaking. "We'd rarely been apart before the day he died."

The others sat calmly as Bree handed her photo of Brett to the woman next to her. It was like sharing her brother for the first time since she'd lost him. The woman took the picture and cradled it in her hands.

"That accident changed my life forever," Bree managed to say, but no more words would come as the group members, commenting, slowly passed the photo around the circle and finally returned it to her.

At last, Sandy nodded and said, "Let's go outside."

Bree jumped up, eager to distract herself from the pain that recalling Brett's death still caused.

❖

Outside in the crisp night air, the moon and stars glittered until the smoke from Sandy's fire pit shrouded the women with a gauzy veil.

Linda stood between Sandy and Bree as they encircled the pit and watched the oak limbs flare with heat and light. Then the burning wood settled into a steady glow in the night's blackness. The pines on the horizon speared the sky, just as Bree's earlier words about her photo had stabbed the soft spaces inside Linda.

By the time Bree began to visit Ann on a regular basis, five years had passed since Brett's death. Bree had never mentioned him during all those visits, so for her to say tonight that his death had changed her life forever saddened Linda, as did Bree's sorrowful expression and her sudden choked silence.

Standing close to Bree, she grasped her arm. "I'm sure Ann would love to see you. Why don't you drop by the old home place? I don't think she's gotten out much lately. It's not like her to seclude herself."

Bree covered Linda's hand with her own, and its warmth made Linda shiver, though she wore a heavy sweater and stood near the fire.

Bree squeezed her hand, then whispered, "Thanks, Linda. I'll do that."

Linda squeezed back, hoping she hadn't just encouraged Bree to do something that would hurt all of them, especially her.

❖

Sandy's voice broke the silence of the night. "Right now, at midnight, the spirits of the loved ones we have remembered and commemorated gather near at hand." She opened her arms wide. "I invite you to communicate with them by burning the piece of paper on which you've written a resolution for the coming year."

Bree had spent much of the afternoon pondering what to write, and now she was glad she'd completed the strange request. She really should think about retiring. At nearly seventy she'd lost some of her former energy and enthusiasm for her job.

Her mind wandered. This sedate ceremony felt more real to her than the scenarios she'd imagined earlier. She didn't want to run naked through the woods. She didn't even want to carry a burning torch and help ignite a huge bonfire, accompanied by weird music. She wanted to sit around a cozy fire like this one and share herself with others who thought and felt like she did.

Right here, with old friends and new ones, in the town where she'd spent the first part of her life, she could plan a new beginning and perhaps finally fit in.

When her turn came, she tossed her folded piece of paper into the pit. She had written, *I resolve to quit being involved with inappropriate women.*

In silence, she watched the fire consume her words. Perhaps Linda's wise father had inspired Linda to suggest that she visit Ann. She wanted to resolve that situation, which had haunted her almost her entire adult life.

❖

Ann spent Halloween evening with Carl at Bernard's, an expensive restaurant in Tyler.

"You haven't told anyone we're dating, have you?" she asked him as she cut into one of the stuffed mushrooms they shared.

"No. If anyone asks, I just say we're old friends. Why?"

"I don't want Linda to know."

Carl glanced around the secluded area where Ann had chosen to sit. "Why not?"

"Oh, Little Miss Perfect already feels sorry for me because I haven't found the right man. Also because I get down in the dumps about that fact occasionally."

Carl had a great smile, as well as clear eyes and a serene, accepting nature. He reached over the small table and placed his hand over one of hers. "Have you now?"

"Have I now what?" The mushroom she'd just bit into tasted a little dry.

He didn't let her obvious pique faze his mellow mood. "Found the right man."

She tried another bite, including more of the moist stuffing for a change. "Maybe." She winked at him. "I'm trying to decide."

He removed his hand and leisurely ate the rest of his portion of the appetizer. "No rush," he murmured. "I want you to make sure you know what you want this time around."

She took a larger bite. "Hmm. Delicious," she said. "And thanks for the wonderful evening. Happy Halloween."

Carl's patience delighted her as thoroughly as these stuffed mushrooms finally had. He might just be the one.

CHAPTER SEVEN

B ree stared out her bedroom window at the old willow tree. Its leaves, beginning to turn gold, shone in the sun of the clear day that spread out before her. What would she do on this beautiful autumn Sunday in a small town?

Carolyn had invited her to Sunday school and church, but Bree hadn't attended a church in years, except for an occasional wedding. Though the coven and its Samhain rituals had intrigued her, traditional religion had never offered her a satisfying spiritual experience.

Sundays in Chicago, she'd enjoyed going to various restaurants where people congregated for brunch. She could read the morning newspaper there, alone or occasionally with a friend, and never feel lonely.

Her mother planned to attend the church services held for the residents at Silverado, so Bree was on her own this morning. She could play a word game on her phone, but that didn't appeal to her. She prepared herself a healthy breakfast, but eating it didn't take long. Now what would she do?

Back in her bedroom, as she ran a comb through her hair, the smell of smoke from last night's Samhain fire assailed her. She needed a good long bath, so she stripped off her sleep shirt and padded to the bathroom.

Lying in the white porcelain tub, the warm water enveloping her, she remembered the words she'd written yesterday and then burned last night. *Inappropriate women* seemed a bit vague, she decided, so she tried to refine her resolution.

She didn't want to become involved with any more women she didn't really care about. Not that she hadn't always enjoyed loving other women and feeling an outburst of emotions, for as long as the thrill of being with a new woman remained. But suddenly that way of life—always chasing the new, never the permanent—seemed unsatisfying.

Her thoughts spun and then congealed. If she wanted to change her ways, she needed to begin with the woman who had first seriously interested her, Ann.

She toweled off and dressed, then punched in the number that had always made her heart beat a little faster in high school and beyond.

"Ann?" she asked, when the familiar voice answered.

"Who's this?" Ann's voice was sharp, impatient.

She took a deep breath. "It's Bree."

"Bree Principal?"

"Yes."

Ann laughed harshly. "You haven't tried to get in touch for fifty years. Why bother to call now?"

"Forget it. I'll leave you alone for another fifty."

"Now, you know you don't want to do that." Bree nearly hung up but hesitated at the seductive tone she remembered. "Why did you come back?"

"To see about my mother." Bree swallowed her anger and let herself soften toward this woman who once could persuade her to do whatever she wanted. "When I heard you lived here, I couldn't resist calling." Bree couldn't keep her old flirtatious manner from surfacing.

Silence. Then Ann's laugh sounded more pleasant. "I'm glad you did."

"What's been going on? Rumor says you've traveled to Timbuktu and back, with how many husbands by now?"

"Only five, but none of them as much fun as you were." Ann's voice turned wistful. "We used to have some good times, didn't we?"

"If you want to call them that." Bree had never gotten enough of Ann. None of the women she'd known since had spun the magic like Ann had. "You certainly made my life interesting."

"And I might again. Think of all our experiences. At least we could entertain each other by sharing stories."

"We could try."

"What are you doing today?"

"Nothing."

"Well, what are you waiting for? How about we do nothing together?"

Bree didn't hesitate. "My place or yours?"

"Mine."

"See you soon."

Linda pulled off the new orange blouse and black slacks she'd worn to Sunday school and replaced them with a sweatshirt and jeans. She'd enjoyed the discussion she and the class of adult women she taught had become involved in this morning. Using various scriptures from the Old Testament that touched on the subject of hope had provoked a lot of personal stories and different opinions about how to deal with dark moments in life.

But now she had to get busy. Her older son's wife had invited her over for a big Sunday dinner, and she'd promised to take a pecan pie for dessert.

It didn't take long to stir the ingredients together and pour the mixture into a crust she'd made earlier. As she worked, she kept seeing Bree's pained expression when she couldn't continue to talk about the death of her twin brother. And what had Bree written on the piece of paper she'd tossed into their ritual fire last night?

Why had Linda suggested that Bree pay Ann a visit? Of course, they'd been close all those years ago, and obviously something major had happened between them to end that friendship. During the summer after they graduated from high school, they'd suddenly quit spending time with each other.

Linda had questioned Ann, but, as usual, Ann had ignored her and told her to mind her own business. So why, after all these years, did Linda decide to help them become friends again?

Would she ever quit feeling guilty that Ann hadn't had a real mother, instead of the stepmother she'd obviously never accepted? Maybe if Linda hadn't come along, Ann would have been a happy only daughter. Guilt could make you do some silly things.

❖

Bree drove the five miles into the country she remembered so well, but many of the trees she passed had either grown into giants or been cleared to make way for the new drilling sites springing up around East Texas during the past ten years. Her parents had grown up in the area during the Great Depression, when countless people had become millionaires overnight because of the oil and gas wells discovered on their property.

A huge new service center on the main highway testified to the upswing in the industry, though the decrease in gasoline prices recently seemed to have temporarily depressed its resurgence.

Regardless of the changes in the economy, the Whites' home looked practically the same. Granted, the large circular driveway wasn't still dotted with cars pulling in and out. One or another of Ann's brothers had always been coming or going somewhere, usually with a couple of his friends in tow, or a boy had sat pleading with Ann to go out with him, which she often did. Bree had always felt privileged and proud to be able to spend so much private time with Ann.

And there Ann stood, just like old times. Bree parked her Mustang and watched Ann walk across the front porch and sit in the white swing hanging from the ceiling, where she used to entertain her admirers. Bree's stomach felt queasy, and the uneasy sensation traveled up to her chest. Her breasts tingled, and her heart raced like the engine of her Mustang had as she'd steered it here.

"Ann," she called, but Ann just sat pushing the swing slowly with her feet, enticing her like the proverbial spider in the middle of her web.

Bree felt Ann's eyes on her as she climbed the three steps of the front porch. She was glad she'd decided to wear the new steel-gray shirt she'd bought just before she left Chicago. It complemented her eyes and the silver streak in her hair, and her new designer jeans were just one size larger than the ones she'd worn in high school. She'd even had her hair trimmed before she left the city the other day, so she wasn't too worried about her appearance.

"My, don't you look good enough to eat," Ann said and held out her hand like she expected Bree to kiss it.

"You too." Bree squeezed Ann's hand—still white and delicate, with no trace of the brownish age spots Bree had noticed on Linda's hands last night. Though it did feel a bit puffy and unused.

"Oh, you're just saying that to be nice," Ann said, clearly inviting Bree to compliment her on her still-youthful appearance.

"No, I'm not. Seriously, you look great. How have you done it?"

Ann settled back into the swing and patted the wooden slats beside her. "You'd be amazed what a few nips and tucks, and a lot of money, can accomplish."

"That's what some of my friends tell me."

"I bet they do. So you're still up to your old tricks." She took one of Bree's hands and examined it as if she were a fortune-teller.

Bree grinned. "Can't say I've ever had any complaints."

Ann placed Bree's right hand on her thigh and sighed. "During all the time we haven't seen each other, I've found myself thinking about this strong hand at the strangest times."

Bree couldn't resist. "Like when?"

"Like when one of my husbands was sticking it into me too quickly, instead of building up to it an inch at a time, like you used to."

A perverse pride filled Bree. "Like you enticed me to, you mean. But I have to hand it to you, Ann. You were a wonderful teacher. The best."

"You better believe it, honey." Ann beamed. "I knew you were destined for great things, both in and out of bed. I hear you've turned that little art museum where you've worked forever into a world-famous showplace."

"Yep. It's been quite a ride. But what about you? What have you done with yourself for the past fifty years?"

"Oh, you know. A husband here, a million dollars there."

"So which do you prefer? The men or the money?"

Ann rested her chin on her hand. "Hmm. The money's hard to beat. I even learned enough to do a little day-trading. To keep myself in new shoes and purses, you know."

"That probably takes a fortune." Bree pulled her hand away from Ann's thigh, where Ann had placed it. "What about the men?"

"Each marriage was fun while it lasted." Ann's expression was difficult to decipher. "But I never found anyone to take your place."

The words landed like a body blow, and Bree took a minute to regain her breath. "Apparently you weren't looking in the right place." She pushed the swing into motion with her feet.

"What do you mean?" Ann appeared truly clueless.

"Haven't you ever really seen me?" Bree couldn't keep her bitterness from tingeing her words. "I'm a woman, in case you've never noticed."

Ann stared. "But that would make me…a lesbian." She said the word as if it were a cow patty.

Bree couldn't believe Ann could so blindly dismiss that they'd once been lovers. At least Bree had made love to her. She'd certainly seemed to enjoy it at the time. "Yeah, and…?"

"But I'm not one."

How could Ann deny everything Bree had given her, the beautiful moments they'd spent together? "Let's review this situation. You've had five husbands and probably quite a few lovers. Correct?"

"Yes."

"And none of them has ever satisfied you like I have. Or so you just said."

Ann nodded.

"And I'm a woman."

Again, Ann nodded, but more hesitantly.

"I'm not a woman?" Bree began to boil inside.

"I've never really thought of you as one. I know, you look like one. But somehow you don't seem like it."

Bree abruptly stopped the motion of the swing and jumped out of it. "What do you mean?" She faced Ann, hands on her hips. She felt like slugging someone. "No one has ever said that to me before."

"Well, I just did. You've always seemed like a man to me. No, maybe a boy when we used to be together. But now you act like a man. Confident, assertive, competitive, taking what you want, like you did with me until I had to find someone to fall in love with so you'd stay away."

Ann cringed. She appeared almost frightened.

"So that's what happened. That's why you kept on seeing that damn football player and informed me right before I left for college that you intended to marry him."

"Yes. That's the only way I could get you to leave me alone. And I did marry him, eventually." Ann stood up too. "Look at you. You haven't changed a bit. You think you can swoop back into town like a big shot and start up with me again." She glanced out at the road and seemed to become calmer. "You better go now."

"Why? Because you think I'll carry you inside and take what I supposedly want from you right now?" Bree laughed without an ounce of humor. "Is that what you want me to do? You always did, didn't you? You're the one who always invited me over and teased me and—"

"No." Ann's mouth quivered, but then she tightened her cheek muscles. "Read my lips. I am not a lesbian."

A big silver Cadillac drove up and stopped. Bree watched a white-haired man climb out. "No. I suppose you're not. And I'm glad. Sorry I bothered you. Good-bye."

Ann straightened her crumpled face into a smile and spoke as her probable suitor neared. "It was great seeing you, Bree. Come again."

Bree jumped into her red Mustang and peeled out of the gravel driveway as if she were still a teenager. God damn Ann White. She'd hurt her for the last time.

❖

Linda stopped by Sandy's house on her way back from lunch with her older son and his family. The sound of barking dogs greeted her as she knocked and then pushed through the front door and set a foil-covered paper plate on the dining table. "Brought you a piece of pecan pie," she called.

"Thanks. Eat a big meal with one of your kids?" Sandy called.

"Yes." Linda petted each of the dogs that had bounded toward her, barking like they hadn't seen her in years.

"After all those years of kitchen duty, it must be a relief for you not to have to cook every day."

Linda walked into the living room, the dogs trying to jump up on her. "Yes, it is. Though once in a while I do miss having company at mealtimes."

"Down, girls." Sandy gave her a knowing look. "But it's nice to fix whatever you want, whenever you want, isn't it?"

"It certainly is."

Sandy had evidently slept late, because she was still in her pajamas, reading the Sunday paper, a lit cigarette in the ashtray next to her worn Microfiber recliner. Zoe and Cowboy, her two golden retrievers, pushed against Linda affectionately as she petted them again, then finally stretched out on the floor, one on either side of Sandy.

"How many times have you tried to stop smoking?" Linda asked as she sat on the couch.

Sandy shrugged. "Too many to count. I've quit promising myself that I would, because apparently I like it too much."

"Obviously that's not what you wrote on the slip of paper you burned last night."

"No. I gave up on that one a long time ago. I wrote that I'd start helping you find a good woman to settle down with."

"And why do you think I want your help?" Sandy was an avid matchmaker and would try to help the pope find a mate if she could.

"I saw the way you looked at Bree last night and figured someone like her might make your life a little more exciting and enjoyable."

Suddenly nervous, Linda jumped up, walked over to the refrigerator, and pulled out a bottle of water. "How did I look at her, and why don't you consider my life exciting and enjoyable?"

"You seemed like you really care for her, despite that sophisticated, big-city air she uses to keep people away. Especially when she made that comment about the effect of her brother's death on her."

"Yeah. That's one reason I stopped by." Linda slowly screwed the lid off the plastic bottle. "What do you remember about that? Were you still in town when it happened?"

Sandy took a drag from her cigarette. "Yes, I was. Let's see. I must have been about seventeen or eighteen, but I was so wrapped up in myself and my friends I didn't pay much attention."

"Surely you remember something." Linda downed a third of the bottle.

"It was definitely an accident, I recall. Happened while he and his dad were out hunting deer with friends, the weekend before Thanksgiving."

"How terrible."

"Yes. Practically the whole town turned out for his funeral. Bree and her mother looked like they were in shock for months afterward. Not that I saw them all that often, but I did run into them in town once in a while." Smoke curled above Sandy's head.

"Any idea what Bree meant last night when she said it changed her life forever?"

"None. Sorry. But you know how self-absorbed most teenagers are. All I could think about back then were boys and getting out of town as soon as I graduated."

"You certainly got what you wanted, didn't you?" Linda grinned, then took another long drink of water and sat back down. Cowboy opened his eyes and gazed at her lazily, then closed them.

"That I did." Sandy looked thoughtful. "And I enjoyed every minute of it. That's one reason I want to help you find someone."

"And why's what?"

"I don't think you've enjoyed your life enough up to now. I've had my heart smashed and broken more hearts than you can shake a stick at. Now I'm ready to live with Cowboy and Zoe and feed off the past. Getting old's my reward for wringing as much as I have out of life."

"You don't think I've had my heart broken?" Linda emptied her bottle and set it on the end table with a crunch.

"Huh. That ex-husband of yours is a caricature. Older man is afraid he's missed out, younger woman flatters him, and he jumps for her like a fish on a worm. You should be glad to be rid of him. Now maybe you can hook up with somebody interesting, and the right gender for a change."

Linda couldn't help but laugh. The end of her marriage had quit bothering her sooner than she thought it would, but she just couldn't seem to find something to take its place. And maybe Sandy was right. Bree did stir things in her that she hadn't felt in a long time, if ever. Getting involved might be good for both of them.

"So how do you suggest I put my heart out there for Bree to crush?" she asked. "Because you know she will. A lot worse than my ex did." Linda shook her head. "No. Discussing this is a waste of time. Bree would never be interested in me."

Sandy didn't say a word, just settled back into her chair and picked up her newspaper.

"In fact, last night I told Bree she should go visit Ann," Linda said.

Sandy sat up again and rustled the newspaper she held. "Why on earth would you do that?"

"I want her to be happy. I want Ann to be happy."

"What about you?" Sandy scowled. "I think Bree might be able to make you happy."

"Not until she breaks whatever spell Ann has cast on her." Linda suddenly felt like she'd fallen into a dry, dark well and could barely see the sunlight far above her. Bree would never break Ann's spell.

Bree stopped by the local Dairy Queen and ordered a chili-cheese dog with fries for lunch. The familiar smell of greasy burgers had tempted her to indulge herself. After all, she'd eaten a bowl of oatmeal and fruit earlier, and that feast last night at Sandy's and the few meals she'd had with Carolyn had been low-fat and nutritious. Her encounter with Ann had made her crave comfort food, but to salve her conscience, she ordered a Diet Coke as well.

As she took a bite of her hot dog, Linda slid into the bright-red booth across from her. "Saw your car and stopped. How are you after our wild party last night?"

"Shocked, in a good way. I never dreamed of getting involved with a coven in my hometown." She was whispering. "I thought it'd be a typical Halloween get-together."

Linda chuckled. "Don't underestimate the women around here. We have all types of groups to keep ourselves busy."

"Such as?" Bree took another bite, trying to keep the chili from dripping onto her hand.

"Church, with all its activities, such as singing in the choir, bell ringing, and Bible study."

"Of course." Bree shrugged. Church obviously filled the needs of a lot of people. To each her own.

"We have book clubs, a gourmet-cooking group, bridge, golf, tennis, mahjong, master gardeners, plus—"

Bree held up a hand. "That's enough. I get the picture."

"Sorry. Didn't mean to bore you."

"You didn't. I'd simply forgotten what life in a small town is like."

Linda took a sip of her Lemonade Chiller in its clear plastic cup. "Yes. That's easy to do. I was so busy with my family I didn't pay attention to the various clubs. Then one day I looked around and my children were grown."

"Do they still live here?" Bree asked politely.

"The two boys do. But they're long since married and have wives to take care of them."

"Two boys? I thought you had a daughter." She wasn't going to mention Carolyn's gossip.

"Just one. She's my youngest and lives out of state. She usually visits a couple of times a year."

"Grandchildren?" Bree held back a yawn.

"Four. Three boys and a girl. They belong to my sons, so I can spend a lot of time with them, now. After I came out to my oldest, he refused to let me see his two boys for a year or so."

"That's cold." Bree shivered. After last night at Sandy's, she'd momentarily forgotten how intolerant people in this area could be. "Is he okay with you now?"

Linda's smile looked strained. "He's trying."

"Trying?"

"Yes. At least he's speaking to me. And when I ate with him and his family today, he acted almost like he used to."

"Ouch. That must be rough."

Linda's cheek muscles relaxed a fraction. "The concept of same-sex love is just so foreign to some people. Apparently it takes a while for them to realize I haven't turned into a raging monster who tries to pick up unwary straight women in rest-area bathrooms."

Bree laughed, and Linda's eyes brightened. "I can't visualize you doing that. But I'm glad he's getting his head together."

Linda's domestic scene didn't exactly fascinate Bree, but she was vaguely curious. It was odd to think of Ann's quiet kid sister as a capable, self-assured grandmother trying to make a drastic midlife change. And it was even stranger to find her rather attractive, too, in an understated way that usually didn't interest Bree.

"Been to see Ann yet?" Linda asked, apparently tired of discussing her own private life.

Bree finished her hot dog and wiped some chili from the corner of her mouth. "Yes. I just got back. She hasn't changed much, has she?"

"How do you mean?"

"She's still beautiful."

Linda sighed. "Yes. She is that."

"With a little help from plastic surgeons, she confessed."

"None but the best. In Dallas, mostly."

"Last night you mentioned suicide. What happened?" Bree focused on the red DQ emblem on Linda's cup but couldn't keep the concern from her voice.

"I'm sure you know what a private person Ann has always been." Linda took another drink of lemonade, as if considering how much to reveal.

"Yes. She always seemed to share a lot more of herself than she actually did."

"She hasn't confided in me a lot. That's one reason I wanted you to go see her." She stirred the frozen lemonade with her straw. "But I suspect getting older and beginning to lose her looks was a major cause."

Bree nodded. "Must be hard on someone who's always relied on her appearance to help her get what she wants."

"You mean men."

Bree had to face facts. "Yes. From what I've heard, she's had more than her share of them."

"For sure. All types. Rugged, gentle, businessmen, ranchers."

"Quite a variety."

"Yes. But they all have one thing in common."

"What's that?"

"Money."

Bree laughed uneasily and cleared her throat. "You're not accusing your sister of being mercenary, are you?"

"No. I wouldn't use that word. But she is used to the good life, and she's spent all her energy finding the best way to have it. Most men are suckers for a pretty face."

"Do I detect a hint of bitterness?"

"Probably. My ex left me for a younger, prettier woman several years ago." Linda shrugged. "So yes. You're right. But mainly I feel sorry for Ann. Do you think you can help her?"

"Me? We lost touch right after high school. Why would you think I could have any influence on her?"

"She always seemed so crazy about you."

"Are we talking about the same person?"

Linda nodded. "She never listened to anyone the way she did to you. All we heard around the house for a year or so was Bree said this or Bree thinks that."

"Really?"

"Really."

Linda wouldn't lie about something like this, would she? Bree wanted to believe her.

"Actually, I finally got tired of hearing her talk about you so much. But that summer before you went away to college, she got so upset. Things were never the same between you two after that, were they?"

"No. Her infatuation with that football player she'd just met did us in." Bree's heart felt like a football that someone had battered with a sledge hammer. That terrible summer had been almost as painful as Brett's death.

Linda's eyes were shining. "Maybe this time you can help her find whatever she's looking for."

Bree took a long drink of her Diet Coke. Ann had never seemed to pay attention to anything she said. And then she'd made the choice that had almost killed Bree. "Thanks for sharing, and for asking me to help. But if I ever did have any influence over Ann, I lost it a long time ago. Sorry."

Linda just stared at her, seeming disappointed.

"I truly am sorry." Bree glanced at her watch. "Look. I need to go visit Sarah. Good to see you. Maybe we'll run into each other at Silverado again." She stood before she said anything hurtful about Ann that she might regret later. Then she shoved her trash into the bin, pushed the heavy glass door open, and walked out of the Dairy Queen.

If her mother were doing better, Bree would be on a plane to Chicago in a few hours. This town was even smaller than she remembered, and she didn't want to have any more to do with it than she had to.

❖

Linda slowly finished her lemonade slush and waved to the server as she left. Bree had seemed upset and rather defensive while they discussed Ann. Why? Had they been more than just friends?

Linda had planned to go home and read a novel by one of her favorite authors, then watch a classic movie she'd recorded. On Sunday afternoons and nights she tried to do whatever she pleased. However, today she decided to go visit Ann and see if she could find some answers.

As she turned into the circular driveway to her childhood home, she spotted Ann in her usual spot on the front porch.

"Hi, Linda," Ann called, and waved. Then she waited as Linda parked and climbed the front steps.

Ann almost always expected visitors to come to her where she lounged in the white porch swing. Did she visualize their home as having tall white Greek columns and herself as a Southern belle?

"How are you?" Linda sat down in a nearby rocking chair. "Nice afternoon, eh?"

"It certainly is." Ann's eyes glittered. "Guess who dropped by earlier."

Linda simply raised an eyebrow.

"Bree Principal. She's back in town. Can you believe it?" Ann looked as if she'd just announced the arrival of the president of the United States.

"Oh yes. I ran into her at Silverado the other day. She was visiting her mother."

Ann's face fell. "And you didn't tell me?"

Linda was in a quandary, as she usually was when she tried to spare Ann's feelings. Damned if you do and damned if you don't applied all too often when it came to Ann. She'd lied to Bree. She hadn't really told Ann that Bree was back in town. But at the coven get-together, for some reason it had seemed important for Ann and Bree to have a good long talk.

So she kept right on lying. "Since you two haven't spoken in fifty years, I didn't think you'd care one way or the other."

"I didn't. It was like hearing from a ghost. How did she even know I was in town?" She stared at Linda with narrowed eyes.

Linda opened her own eyes as wide as she could, caught between protesting her innocence and confessing the truth. Lying wasn't her strong suit.

"Carolyn probably told her," Ann muttered, to Linda's relief. "She's the only one who's stayed in touch with Bree and has probably talked all kinds of trash about me. I'd bet my last dollar on it."

Linda didn't say another word. It was Sunday, after all, and still Samhain for some Wiccan groups, two days she tried to honor by being totally honest. After all, she'd just wanted to help Ann, not upset her.

Ann looked down at her left hand, then over at Linda. "Hey, you. Come over here and sit next to me." She patted the empty space beside her on the swing. "Look what I just got."

Linda didn't hesitate, and when she was settled, Ann held out her hand. "Carl Paul was just over here. You know him. The most eligible bachelor in town."

The diamond on Ann's ring finger was even larger than the other five in her collection. "Wow. That's a monster," Linda said. "So he popped the question this afternoon? I didn't even know you two were dating."

Ann held up her hand and let the solitaire catch the light. "We didn't want to advertise. You know how people around here talk."

"I certainly do. But hey, congratulations. I heard he'd sworn off women."

"He hadn't met me then." Ann beamed like she'd just won a million dollars. "We're flying to Hawaii in a few days to get married. Be gone until right before Thanksgiving. Can you look after the place while we're away?" She motioned to the house and surrounding acreage.

Linda took a deep breath. *Here we go again.* "Don't you think we should put it on the market?" she asked. "After all, you'll be living with your new husband now, won't you?"

"Yes, of course. His house is one of the biggest and nicest in town. But you never can tell. I like to have this place to fall back on in case things don't work out. And I've almost finished having it remodeled."

Linda usually had to supervise the unending stream of repairmen and other workers who kept their family home and acreage in good condition. She was getting tired of being responsible for two homes. "Why don't you just rent an apartment if things don't go the way you want them to?"

Ann looked as if Linda had suggested they spit on their father's grave. "Get rid of Daddy's place? Why, it's been in his family for years. He'd have a fit."

"He's dead, Ann. I don't think he'd care if we sold it."

Ann practically stomped her foot. "That shows how much you know. He loved this place. He'd never want us to sell. Why, when I think of—"

"Okay. Calm down. Go ahead and enjoy your trip to Hawaii. I'll take care of things."

Ann's breathing began to slow, and she settled back into the swing. "Thanks. At least I can always count on you."

Linda got up. "Congratulations, again, Ann. I hope things work out for you this go-round."

Ann rose too and gave her a rare hug. "Thanks, little sis. Me too."

Linda couldn't erase Ann's wistful expression from her mind as she slowly drove home. And she hadn't learned anything about Ann and Bree's puzzling relationship. Maybe she should try to forget it and focus on what *she* wanted for a change.

The radical thought immediately made her feel a little better.

Chapter Eight

Bree pushed through the front door of Silverado and walked past several small groups of people. Apparently a lot of family members visited on Sunday afternoon, and Bree was glad she'd come.

She knocked, surprised by her mother's welcome. "Oh, hello. Good to see you."

"I'm glad." Her mother's welcome cemented a question she'd pondered. "I've decided to stay in town awhile."

Her mother smiled. "Fine. But don't you need to get back to Chicago soon? The museum won't run itself without you."

"They can manage, at least short-term. Besides, I may just decide to retire and settle down here." Bree laughed to herself. As if she'd ever fit in. Never had, never would.

"Fine. But you better think long and hard before you do something you might regret."

Sarah had always given her this contradictory message: *This is a wonderful place to live, but would it suit you?*

"Don't worry. I will. Having a good afternoon?"

Sarah glanced around the room with a strange expression. "It's okay." She seemed distracted. "Did I take my blood-pressure pill?"

"Isn't that one reason you moved here? So an aide can make sure you take your medicine regularly?"

"Oh. That's right. I forgot. My memory's not what it used to be." Sarah gazed at her small sitting area that flowed into her tiny bedroom as if suddenly realizing where she was. "I was driving myself crazy trying to keep up with all those pills."

Her mother had rarely been sick. How could she have changed so quickly during the past year or so? Maybe the shock of the fall, and the preceding ones, had affected her more than anyone realized. Surely she'd revert to her old self when her wound healed.

Sarah glanced down at her leg. "It's nice not to be responsible for anything or anybody."

"Do you like it here?"

Sarah shrugged. "The food's not always what I want, but I can tolerate just about anything. And if I don't want company I can close my door."

"Do you know a lot of the residents?"

"Yes. Three of the women I taught with live here, and we play bridge almost every day."

"That's great." A bubble of relief filled Bree.

Sarah smiled again. "We girls laugh and have such a good time."

"Sounds like fun. Maybe I'll get a room here too."

Sarah stared at her. "Ha. You have a lot of good years left. I just hope you're not too bored and lonely staying in our big house all by yourself."

"Don't worry, I'm fine. In fact, Carolyn took me to a party last night, out at Sandy Porter's, and guess who I ran into."

Sarah radiated interest. "Linda Morton."

"How'd you know?"

"Sandy is Linda's aunt, and they're in the same coven. They celebrated Samhain, right?"

"I thought they kept that a deep, dark secret."

"They do, from the townspeople so narrow-minded they'd burn them at the stake." Sarah stood and limped over to her easel, resting heavily on her walker.

"I should have known Carolyn would tell you."

Sarah grinned like a kid. "I even went with her last year."

"You did? What did you think?"

"I found it pleasant. Healthy food and good company." Sarah gazed at her easel, then picked up a small jar of paint and a brush. "They stayed up later than I'm used to, though," Sarah said. "I almost fell asleep outside around that fire." She added a touch of color to her latest painting, then stepped back as if studying its effect.

Bree laughed. "You're something else."

"Thanks. You are too. But I'm glad you mentioned Linda. I want you to do something." She added another bit of blue to the sky in the stark black-and-white painting of their willow tree.

"What?"

Again, Sarah stood back and examined her painting. "The other day when Linda came in, you acted more interested in Ann than in her. I think you hurt her feelings."

"But Ann was my friend, not her. Back then, Linda barely said a word to me, so I never gave her a second thought."

Sarah screwed the lid back on the paint jar and rinsed her brush in the small sink near her bed. "That's exactly right. She's never stood out in a crowd. You could have knocked me over with a paintbrush when she married Mike Morton."

"Mike Morton. He was a year younger than me, I think."

"Yes. And nice enough. Took her some interesting places overseas and seemed to treat her well. They raised some good kids."

"She told me a little about them."

Sarah nodded absently. "Linda and Mike never seemed to be right for each other. They went through the motions, but—"

"What do you mean?" Since when had Sarah become a marriage counselor?

"I'm not sure who was at fault, but it almost relieved me when he started running around on her."

"Sarah! Why would you say such a thing?"

"I think they needed to get a divorce."

When had her mother started participating in the local gossip yet having such liberal thoughts? "That's possible. Linda told me almost the same thing not an hour ago, at the Dairy Queen."

"She did? How did you happen to run into her there?"

"I guess she saw my car and stopped. Wanted to know if I'd seen Ann yet, like she asked me to last night."

"I should have known. She's too nice for her own good. And did you?"

"Did I what?"

"Go see Ann, silly." Her mother sat down in her velour La-Z-Boy again and extended the footrest.

"Yes. I drove out to their old house."

Sarah sighed as if she'd been standing for hours. "How'd that go?"

"Kinda awkward. Apparently she's angling to catch husband number six."

"I'm not surprised. She's a lot like her dad."

Bree couldn't decipher her mother's cynical expression. "Her dad? Why, just last night, Linda told us how wonderful he was."

"He was, to Ann and the boys. And, on the surface, to Linda too." She frowned. "Linda's never even realized she was the Cinderella in that family."

"Cinderella? What are you saying?" Did her mother really have her meds straightened out? Bree needed to ask the aide if she'd been talking crazy lately.

"I knew Linda's mother before she married Mr. White. She confided some things that helped me understand their family dynamics."

"Why are you just now letting me know?"

"Because Linda's mother made me vow not to breathe a word. Besides, it's not my place to warn Linda or dig up skeletons, and I don't want to seem like a meddling old woman. But since you're here now, I need you to do something."

Sarah rarely asked for a favor. "Okay. If I can."

"I guess Carolyn told you Linda's started associating with a group of homosexuals in Tyler."

"Yes." Associating with homosexuals. Well, at least her mother's attitude was modern even if her vocabulary wasn't.

"Since you've been a lesbian so long, can you help her meet a nice girl before you leave? I'd help her, but I don't have any idea where to look."

Bree could barely speak. "I guess I could try, though you may have underestimated her."

Sarah lowered her leg rest and leaned forward in her easy chair. "Promise me you won't take advantage of her." Her eyes blazed. "I don't think you would, but if you do, you'll have to answer to me." Sarah had shifted into full teacher mode.

"Yes, ma'am." Carolyn had implied that Sarah wanted to fix *her* up with Linda. Boy, had she ever been wrong. Sarah clearly didn't expect Bree to move back to this area or become seriously involved with anyone here.

At least Sarah had been direct for a change.

❖

The ringing of the telephone startled Linda. Had she fallen asleep watching *Doctor Zhivago*? She loved its exotic settings, beautiful music, and gorgeous women. She understood sleeping through a Sunday-afternoon football game, but *Doctor Zhivago*?

She slowly pulled herself to a sitting position on her worn leather sofa and reached for the phone. "Hello."

"Hi, Granny," a familiar voice said. "Ready for a game of The Farmer?"

"Sure." She'd promised Riley she'd play with her later this afternoon, but she'd forgotten. "Let me run get my laptop and I'll be all set."

"Bet you fell asleep watching an old movie, didn't you?"

"Now how did you know that?"

Riley laughed. "I just did."

"Okay. Be back in a minute." On her way to her office, Linda grabbed a bottle of water. Sometimes their sessions could last quite some time, and she didn't want to have to get up again.

"Okay. Here I am." She set her laptop on her kitchen table and sat down for game time with Riley.

After an hour or so, Riley finally said, "I better go do my homework, Granny. I've put it off all weekend."

"I should think so. Your dad used to do the same thing."

Riley giggled and repeated with her, "The longer you put it off, the more it seems like you have to do."

"That's right. Now you have a good night, and be good at school. I enjoyed playing with you. Love you."

"Me too. See you soon."

Wide-awake after their game, Linda realized she hadn't eaten anything since lunch except her lemonade drink at the DQ. She devoured a bowl of Cheerios topped with banana slices and blueberries, then spotted the piece of pecan pie she'd brought home.

Her son and his wife had said they were on a diet, though they'd eaten a generous slice each. She tried to talk herself out of indulging in another piece for the day but didn't have any luck.

Had Bree eaten much tonight? If so, what? Something quick like the hot dog and fries she'd had at the Dairy Queen, or did she usually prepare healthy food for herself? Did she have a long-time partner waiting back in Chicago, who cooked for her, or was she a confirmed single person? Maybe Linda should invite her to the women's dinner Tuesday night in Tyler. That way she could satisfy some of her curiosity about Bree and keep tabs on her diet.

As she rinsed her bowl and spoon, the phone rang again. Speak of the devil. Maybe it was Bree.

"Hi, Mom. How's it going?" her daughter Maureen said.

"Fine. Did you have a good Halloween weekend in Chicago?"

"I'll say. We went to a smashing party last night." She imitated her partner's native British accent.

"I did too, after all the trick-or-treaters finished their rounds. Wish you could have seen the grandkids. Riley dressed as Rapunzel. With her long red hair and wearing a medieval-looking dress, she looked so cute."

"She's ten now, isn't she?" Maureen asked. "She'll be grown before you know it."

"Yes, time flies. I'm retiring completely soon, and I don't know what I'll do with myself."

"You'll find something, Mom. Like always."

They chatted awhile longer about the promotion Maureen's partner Terry had just gotten and other news.

"Well, give Terry a hug for me. Love you, Maureen," Linda finally said. "I'm really looking forward to seeing you Thanksgiving."

"Me too, Mom. Can't wait."

Maureen's happiness pleased Linda, even though her daughter stayed so wrapped up in her career and life in Chicago, she rarely visited home.

Linda glanced at the clock. Almost time to watch tonight's episode of her favorite TV series. She settled into her easy chair for a mindless hour. Then, after the show ended, she picked up the phone again. "Hello, Bree?" she said. "It's Linda. Sorry to call so late. Am I bothering you?"

"Linda? Oh, hi. No, it's not late, and you're certainly not bothering me. My social schedule has slowed way down since I got here."

"That's why I called." She cleared her throat nervously. "Do you have plans for Tuesday night?"

Bree chuckled. "I'm not sure. Let me check my calendar." She paused a beat. "Luckily that night's free. Have something in mind?"

"Yes. I belong to an organization in Tyler called TAG—Tyler Area Gays."

"Uh, yes?"

"The first Tuesday night of every month, we meet at a restaurant over there to eat together and catch up on what's going on." There. She'd asked her. "Oh, just the women." Bree would probably find their social activities around here boring and beneath her.

"Are you inviting me to go?" Bree asked gently.

"Yes. If you'd like to." Linda wished she'd never called, that—

"Thanks. Really. I'm interested in what the women in this area are up to."

"Yeah? What if I pick you up about five? We'll meet the group at six for Asian food. Okay with you?"

"One of my favorites. And thanks, Linda. You're a pal."

"Thanks for going. I hope you find my friends interesting."

"I'm sure I will."

"'Bye, now. See you then."

"'Bye."

Still nervous, Linda clicked off. If that's all she and Bree could manage to say on the phone, what would they talk about on the drive to and from dinner Tuesday night?

CHAPTER NINE

Mildly curious about the dinner Linda had invited her to, Bree dressed in her best pair of jeans and pulled on a lightweight black-and-white sweater. Then she picked up her old leather jacket in case the temperature dropped later.

She spotted Linda in her little Honda as soon as she pulled into the driveway and strolled on out. At least she'd meet some local lesbians tonight.

Chatting about the welcome cool weather, they drove past the turnoff to Sandy's house, which reminded Bree of the recent Samhain celebration. "I don't know much about Wicca," she said idly. "Can you explain the basics?"

Linda kept her eyes on the road. "I haven't been involved all that long, but I'm beginning to realize Mother taught me a few things, maybe without even knowing it."

"Your mother was a witch?"

Linda laughed. "I'm not sure. The label might have horrified her. But she always warned me to never say or do anything to harm a living creature. If I did, she said, my action would come back to hurt me."

"How does that fit in Wicca?"

"You know how most religions have a long list of rules?"

"Yeah. Don't sleep with people of the same gender and do give generously to the church fund."

Linda laughed. "That's an oversimplication if I ever heard one."

"But you have to admit it's true. Churches want to interfere with our personal liberties and draw a salary to do it."

"You may be right." Linda nodded. "Most faiths seem to be guilty of that shortcoming."

"So is Wicca any different?"

"As far as I can tell, *Do no harm* is Wicca's only rule. It's apparently more of a lifestyle than an organized religion like we're used to."

"What about those animals out there?" Bree pointed at a herd of cattle.

"What do you mean?"

"I like hamburgers. But I sure have to harm one of those cows to have one."

Linda glanced at the pasture as they passed. "That's another thing Mom used to tell me—to thank the animal that died so I could eat."

"Sounds like an American Indian thing. Respect for the earth."

Linda simply gazed at the road unwinding before them. "Yes. It all boils down to your attitude and your intent."

"What do you mean?"

"If you respect someone or something, you seldom harm it."

"How's that?"

"Let's say you're in love with somebody."

"Okay." Bree immediately thought about Ann.

"One day you wake up and realize how much she hates to go sailing, though she's been going with you. But you can't imagine life without being out on the water."

"That's a rather far-fetched example, but okay."

"Do you insist she continue to sail with you, or do you respect the fact that she dislikes it and join a sailing club—tell her she doesn't have to go with you anymore?"

"If I loved her enough, I'd probably quit sailing and do something she prefers."

"Wow. That's a surprise."

"Why? Did you think I'd insist she learn to like it?"

"No. And I didn't mean to get personal. But a lot of people with forceful personalities would."

"And your point is?" Bree couldn't soften her tone.

"Wicca's only rule makes you decide for yourself how to act in every situation you encounter."

"That's a lot of work."

"Yes, but it puts you in charge of your life."

"Instead of relying on some God to tell you what to do and think. Yeah, makes sense to me."

Linda glanced at Bree. "Say, I've been trying to put my finger on what's different about you, and I finally know. You don't talk the way you used to."

Bree bristled and leaned forward in her seat. "What do you mean?"

"You've lost your East Texas drawl."

"You mean I don't sound like a hick anymore?"

Linda gripped the steering wheel harder and half turned toward Bree. "Do you think I sound like one?"

Bree let her shoulders relax and rested back against the seat again. "No. Your voice is soothing, like a glass of sweet milk."

Linda grinned. "Thanks. I like your new sound, but it's just different—faster and crisper, I guess you'd say."

"Well, I like it, and I worked hard to cultivate it. Maybe I'll tell you why someday."

Linda looked surprised, but Bree didn't care. She wasn't ready for Linda to judge her choices.

Bree stared out at a familiar building surrounded by distinctive low rock walls and dredged up the name of the small community they'd just reached. Joinerville—that was it. Named for the man who discovered oil in East Texas during the Great Depression.

"Didn't they build this school for the children in all those families that moved here during the oil boom?" Bree felt more comfortable discussing history than the personal topics Linda was trying to introduce.

"Yeah. My dad went to school here," Linda said. "And the schoolhouse that exploded back then isn't far."

Bree began to calm down. "My dad mentioned that explosion once. He and the rest of the high-school football team in town left spring training and drove over to help pull bodies from the rubble."

Linda suddenly looked sad. "The worst public-school disaster in American history. It's still hard to imagine almost three hundred students and teachers dying because of a natural-gas leak."

"That's true. Wonder why we didn't know more about it when we were kids?"

"People didn't want to even think about it, much less discuss it. Still in shock, I guess." Linda shook her head, her expression still solemn. "The survivors have just recently begun to get together to share their memories and put things in perspective."

As they passed vast fields dotted with pine trees, cows, and oil pumps, Bree thought about the day in 1957 her brother died. She'd been at home, sleeping late on the Saturday before Thanksgiving.

"Bree, wake up." Her mother shook her shoulder. "Something's happened."

Bree opened her eyes. Tears ran down her mother's cheeks. She'd never seen her cry before now. "What's happened?"

She sat up in bed and stared at her mother, then at the large willow tree outside her window. Its limbs drooped down bare and barren, stripped of the yellow leaves that had covered it since the first frost in early November. It seemed as if the leaves had fallen overnight.

"It's Brett." Her mother sat on the bed beside her, closed her eyes for a minute, then sighed and seemed to force the words from her mouth. "He's dead."

"Dead!" He'd gone deer hunting early that morning with their dad and a few friends. "No. He can't be. He didn't even like to hunt."

Her mother sat rigid beside her, squeezing her hands together so hard Bree hoped she didn't break all the bones in them. "I know. That makes his death even harder. Damn guns and men trying to prove they're men."

Bree had wished her mother would cry some more, but she'd just sat there like a statue, dried tears on her face, as if she'd turned to stone. So Bree did the same.

"What are you thinking so hard about, Bree?"

The voice jolted her back to the woman beside her. Linda. She must think she was a clod, sitting here ignoring her. "Sorry. This stretch of road brought back some unpleasant memories. What were we talking about?"

Linda looked relieved, as if she'd been worried about Bree. "Just some local history. It's all in the past, though. That was a long time ago. Let me tell you a little about some of the women you'll meet at the dinner. Okay?"

"Sure. I need all the help I can get. I can usually remember people's names if I'm doing business with them, but in purely social settings, I'm not so great."

"I wouldn't say that. The Bree I used to know always did everything well, no matter where it took place."

Bree grinned. "Thanks. I'll do my best. And I appreciate the kind words."

She gazed at Linda. She really was considerate, with more to offer than Bree had suspected. She began to warm to the idea of getting to know Linda better, even if she was a little too nosy.

As they neared the city, the sun had almost set. They passed the sprawling University of Texas at Tyler campus on their right, then turned left on the loop that circled Tyler. Another quick right turn led them to Cheng's China Bistro.

"This is new, isn't it?" Bree asked as they stood before the large, squared-off entryway made of whitish-yellow rectangles of Austin stone.

Linda pulled open one of the double doors, each with an oval glass inset. "Three or four years old, I think. I've eaten here a couple of times with the group. We like it because it's not crowded and they give us a private room."

In the dim interior, Linda spotted one of her friends, who immediately walked toward them.

"Bree, this is Lou Anne, the woman who keeps this group running."

They exchanged greetings, and then Bree glanced over at the bar. "Love the sign."

Linda read the white block letters on the wall above a large display of liquor bottles: Wine is Bottled Poetry. "That's strange. I've never noticed it."

Lou Anne nodded, her earrings dangling. "Neither have I. Maybe it's new, or maybe we just haven't paid attention to it."

Bree shrugged. "Strangers see differently than residents do. That's the sign I'd put up in my restaurant, if I ever opened one."

"Oh, do you cook?" Lou Anne lit up, evidently hoping for a kindred spirit.

"You've got to be kidding. But I do love to eat other people's creations, which has to count for something."

Standing side by side, Lou Anne looked like a delicate bird in contrast to Bree, who was probably six inches taller than she was.

Lou Anne glanced at the front door as another group member walked in. "Why don't you two go on back? I'll be there as soon as everyone gets here."

"I like the wood sculpture of the tree," Bree said as they strolled down the corridor toward the back of the restaurant.

"Yes. This place has a pleasant atmosphere. Here we are. Just through the door to the left."

Six members of the group already sat around a long table covered with a white tablecloth and dishes. "Hey, y'all. We have a visitor," Linda announced. "This is Bree Principal—prodigal daughter. She just came to her senses after fifty years in exile from East Texas."

What had possessed her to introduce Bree to everyone in such a silly way? Everyone probably thought she'd lost her mind.

"That's exactly right. I can't imagine why I've stayed away so long," Bree said. "If I'd known about you all, I'd have at least visited more often."

Relieved, Linda introduced Bree to each woman individually. Finally she said, "This is Kay, Lou Anne's partner. They have quite a story and are sharing it all over this part of the country."

"Hmm. Can't wait to hear it," Bree said smoothly, and sat down next to Kay.

Just then Lou Anne came in with the final member of the group tonight and sat across from them.

Linda took a deep breath of anticipation. Hopefully Bree would enjoy being with these women half as much as she did.

❖

"I understand you're the curator of a museum in Chicago," Lou Anne said as Bree dipped a piece of wonton into a clear pink sauce.

Savoring the combination of sweet and salty, Bree took her time answering. "Yes. It's a wonderful job. I have to do everything from negotiating with art sellers all over the world to getting my hands dirty preparing pieces for exhibits. I love every minute of it."

"Quite a shock to be back here, I bet," Kay said, her eyes bright and lively. She looked several years younger than Lou Anne, perhaps in her midsixties.

"A little. But Chicago has never really felt like home." Bree had never verbalized that feeling before tonight and was a little shocked that she had now. "I've always considered it a place to work and sleep."

Lou Anne nodded like she understood, so Bree continued. "I live close to the museum and don't venture out of my neighborhood all that often, except when I have to fly somewhere for business. My work has dominated my life."

"Are you part of a group like this?" Lou Anne seemed to want to bypass social chitchat and jump right into meaty topics.

"No." Bree shook her head. "Various gay and lesbian organizations do exist in the city, of course, but I've never joined any of them."

"But you do know people there, don't you?" Lou Anne certainly listened well. Bree understood why Linda liked her.

"Oh yes. I socialize mostly with various museum administrators and University of Chicago faculty members—some gay, but mostly straight."

"Of course," Linda said. "It sucks to be a minority."

Lou Anne dipped a wonton into her sauce but didn't put it in her mouth right away. "It's not so bad. I'll tell you what sucks."

Kay quirked a brow. "What?"

"When the majority think gays are sinners who are going to hell."

The woman sitting next to Lou Anne nodded so vigorously Bree could almost hear her thinking, *Amen, sister*.

"How long have you two been together?" Bree asked Lou Anne and Kay.

"Ten years, now, isn't it, dear?" Kay said, and Lou Anne smiled her agreement.

"Did you know each other long before you got together?"

Just then two waitresses appeared and asked for their drink orders.

"A glass of chardonnay," Bree immediately said, surprised when most of the others requested either iced tea or water. "No one except Karen and Jolie and me saw the sign about wine being bottled poetry?"

A tall, elegant woman, who'd just walked into the room, raised a wineglass. "I saw it. In fact, I picked up a glass from the bar on my way in." She strolled over to Bree and held out her other hand. "Tonda. I'm a defense attorney here in town. And you are?"

Bree rose and shook her hand. "Bree, visiting from Chicago, though I grew up around here."

Tonda made the rounds and lingered near Linda, whispered something to her, then found an empty chair.

Someone in the group picked up their conversation about wine. "This was a dry county for so long, most of us aren't in the habit of drinking alcohol out at a restaurant."

"Oh yes. I forgot about that archaic law." Bree grinned. "I bet most people in Chicago wouldn't even know the term dry county."

"Believe me, it's never been very dry here," Tonda said. "The liquor stores in the neighboring wet counties sure hate to lose all their customers from Tyler."

"And a lot of those customers are so-called pillars of the church," Lou Anne said. "That's one thing that really bothers me. Drinking on the sly is okay, but loving another woman isn't."

Kay reached across the table and took Lou Anne's hand. "No, dear. If we don't publicly admit to anybody that we love each other, they'll be just fine with us."

Lou Anne gazed at Kay with affection shining in her eyes. "That's exactly right. But I'm determined to tell the world about us *and* keep on going to the Baptist church just like we always have."

Bree admired Lou Anne and Kay. Not many people had their courage. Even though Bree felt no need to be part of organized religion, she respected these two women for taking a stand for what they believed in.

And, to her surprise, she envied their relationship. Was it too late to find someone who made her eyes glow as much as theirs did?

❖

"Did you find Lou Anne and Kay interesting?" Linda asked Bree as they drove back home in the dark. In some spots the tree-lined highway made her feel as if they were the only two people in the world, speeding through a tunnel. But then the lights of a house or another vehicle would break the intimate spell.

"Yes. But I never got to hear their story. All I know is they seem very much in love."

Linda dimmed her headlights as a car approached. "For starters, they were both married to men for quite some time and have several children—Lou Anne has four and Kay has two."

"That seems to be a trend around here." Bree obviously didn't mean to hurt Linda's feelings, but the remark stung. She immediately went rigid.

"Yes. When you live somewhere as repressive as this area, it's easy to bury your true feelings so deep you don't realize they're there for a very long time. It's a little different for kids today, but for our generation and those before us…" She half shrugged.

Bree touched her forearm, as if in apology, and Linda let her tense shoulders fall.

"I know. Why do you think I left?" Bree said softly and removed her hand.

Linda took a deep breath. She needed to focus on driving, not on how much she wished Bree had left her hand where it was. Being alone with her like this was a dream come true. "I've wondered about that, a lot."

"That's another story for another time." Bree stared straight ahead, as if walling herself up.

Linda tried to recapture their earlier closeness. "You're right. We were talking about Lou Anne and Kay, weren't we?"

"Yes. I'm aware that many of the women in the area—and men— of our generation denied or weren't even aware of their attraction to the same sex."

"Exactly. I had no clue about myself." Linda glanced at Bree, who was still staring at the road stretching ahead of them, lit only by their headlights. "Or if I did, I totally ignored the feeling or rationalized it as a crush I'd outgrow."

Bree turned back to her. "I can certainly understand. But how do Lou Anne and Kay differ from you or any of the other women around here who've experienced the same thing?"

Linda paused at the four-way stop in Joinerville and watched a big truck cross the intersection. As she accelerated, she said, "Because they're not placing the blame onto their exes, like so many women do. They're standing up and accepting responsibility for their feelings and their actions."

"I'm not sure what you mean. Blame for what?" Bree shifted in her seat and turned her entire body toward Linda.

"Take me, for example. Most people in town blame Mike, my ex, for our divorce because he had an affair."

"Shouldn't they?"

Linda slowed down as they entered the city limits and passed the high school on their left. "To some extent, yes."

"To some extent?"

She mused as she drove past the city park and the large cemetery where her parents lay buried. "Yes. Our marriage died a long time before he started having an affair."

"Why?"

"Obviously because I'm gay." They entered the large intersection near town, where five highways came together, and Linda thought about how her own life had once intersected with Bree's and now might do so again. At least she hoped it would.

"So you're totally responsible for the failure of your marriage?"

Bree's blunt question startled Linda. "I've never admitted this to anyone, but yes. I am."

"Aren't you being a little hard on yourself?"

And again, Bree's hand lightly touched her forearm.

Linda pulled up in Bree's driveway and killed the engine to signal her reluctance for their conversation to end. "Maybe I'm being a bit harsh. But who else can I blame? I'm the one who said yes when he proposed."

"And why did you do that?" Bree's tone was intense.

"I was young and inexperienced. He was handsome and able to provide for me and the children I thought I wanted to have. Society said women should get married and reproduce." That was as honest as Linda could be.

"So you wanted kids?"

"Of course. I never questioned that part of marriage. I wanted what my parents had. They always seemed so happy, though they never seemed passionately in love. I thought their kind of happiness would be enough."

"And it wasn't?"

Bree's front-porch light shone brightly, like the future Linda had fantasized about when she first married. "No. At first all the excitement of moving around and traveling to exotic places I'd dreamed of kept us connected. But after we settled down and started a family, I sensed something was missing."

Linda gazed out the car window at the half-full moon. Tomorrow it would be less than half full, and the next night even smaller. She'd felt that way back then. And the feeling had grown until now she thought of herself as only a sliver of a person when it came to personal relationships.

"Like what?"

"I couldn't put my finger on it. At first I thought the children had caused the problem."

"Why them?"

Linda loved Bree's sympathetic questions. She usually listened to others but rarely talked about herself. "They took up so much of my time and energy I didn't have much left for Mike. He became more involved in his job and took more business trips."

"And?"

"I'd get angry at times because he was able to still fly here and there, and I couldn't."

Bree pulled her leather jacket tighter around her. "Why didn't you get a sitter and go with him?"

"I did, but when I was away, I couldn't keep the children out of my mind."

"Not exactly conducive to a romantic getaway, eh?"

"That's right. I'd worry about them so much it became pointless to leave them." Linda paused and stared at Bree. She hadn't thought about those years in a long time. "But why am I telling you all this?"

"Because I'm interested. I could just as easily have had the same experience you did."

Linda laughed. "You? No way. You always knew yourself and were never afraid to do exactly what you wanted to, even if it made people talk."

Bree shrugged, as if she didn't want to respond to that remark. "So that's why you got married and stayed married? So people wouldn't gossip about you?"

"I suppose so." Linda held up both hands. "I'm a coward. I admit it."

Bree blew out a heavy breath, as if disagreeing. "When you were younger, did having children with a woman ever cross your mind?"

"No, never."

"What about having sex with a woman?"

"Yes. Absolutely. I fantasized about that quite a bit, from an early age."

"Why didn't you? Have sex, I mean?"

Linda thought back about some of the women she'd had crushes on—her brothers' girlfriends, Ann's friends…Bree. "Most of them weren't available."

"You mean your teachers, or older and married women?"

"Yes. All of the above. Or they talked about boys all the time and would have been horrified if they'd known I thought about them the same way they thought about boys."

"So you never had any physical encounters with girls your age?"

Linda was glad Bree couldn't see how deep the blush that suddenly heated her face was. "Well. I remember, in the fifth grade, how some of the girls I ran around with would touch each other."

"Did you enjoy it?"

"Oh God." Linda feared her face would burst into flames. "I can't believe we're discussing this. But yes, I did."

"Didn't that give you a clue about yourself?"

"No. Not at all." Linda shook her head. "I quit associating with those girls and made a whole new set of friends."

Bree sighed. "And that made you feel better about yourself?"

Linda remembered how she'd begun to get wrapped up in her homework and other after-school activities about that time. "Yes, but in a few years all my friends and I started dating, and I totally failed at that."

"How?"

Bree appeared determined to see this subject through to the end, so Linda relaxed and just let herself enjoy talking about herself. "I couldn't think of anything to say to boys on the phone, much less on a date. They didn't seem to see me as pretty, much less sexy, so I began to view myself as ugly and undesirable."

"And?"

"Finally, in high school, some of my friends and I started fooling around sexually like we had in fifth grade. You know, experimenting."

"Yeah. Remember how, before the pill, everybody avoided having sex with boys because they were afraid they'd get pregnant?"

"I sure do."

"So experimenting with other girls was safe but didn't mean anything?" Bree sounded skeptical.

"Mostly. We had to do something with all those hormones."

Bree chuckled. "That's for sure. You never fell for any of those girls?"

"No. Not like I did for the ones I'd had crushes on and fantasized about having sex with."

"The unavailable ones?" Bree seemed to be trying to understand.

"Right. Maybe I wanted to keep them on the pedestal I'd put them on."

Suddenly Linda was ready for this conversation to end.

"So you married Mike because he paid attention to you and made you feel safe."

"That's about it."

"And I'm sure you were the only one in your age group who did anything like that," Bree added, her tone ironic.

Linda laughed, feeling uneasy. "Thanks for trying to make me feel better. And thanks for listening, but I better go. It's getting late."

Bree opened the car door. "Say, what's the story on Tonda, the woman who came in late? Why don't you come in and tell me what you have going on with her? Besides, you still haven't told me much about Lou Anne and Kay."

"I'd love to, but I really need to leave. It's late, and I'm a little tired." She moved around in her seat, which was becoming rather hard after all this time. "Besides, you've given me a lot to think about." Linda turned the key to start the engine. "But let's get together again, soon. I enjoyed being with you tonight."

"It's a date. This has been enlightening. Thanks for asking me to tag along."

Bree stood in the driveway and waved as Linda pulled away. Linda waved back. What a relief to discuss her failed marriage with Bree. It had made her feel better about herself. But she wasn't ready to talk about Tonda yet. That was too new.

She noticed the half moon again as it emerged from a bank of clouds. Its sudden brightness startled her from her thoughts. What would her life have been like if she'd become seriously involved with someone like Bree or Tonda instead of Mike?

CHAPTER TEN

Beep-beep. Beep-beep. Bree put her hands over her ears after she woke from a deep sleep. What the—? If she ignored the sound, maybe it'd stop.

She glanced over at her clock: 2:42. She went to the bathroom, then tried to go back to sleep, but after ten minutes, she tossed back the covers. *Beep-beep, beep-beep.* What could it be?

Maybe some type of alarm, coming from the attic? Back in Chicago she'd just phone her apartment's twenty-four-hour emergency number, and someone would come make the obnoxious sound go away. But right now she was in an old house, responsible for taking care of whatever problem cropped up.

Reluctantly, she slid from her warm bed and felt the cold floor. Well, by Texas standards it was cold for early November. By Chicago standards, it was cool. But she could manage. Slipping on some tennis shoes, she headed for the attic.

Yep. The closer she got to the attic door, the more insistent the beep sounded—patient and regular. She wanted to strangle the damn thing.

At least she remembered where the attic door was, having once stored suitcases and Christmas ornaments in its cavernous space.

Inside the attic, the beep was louder. She flipped on one light switch, then another, trying to figure out where the sound was coming from.

Part of the space was floored with plywood, but that luxury soon ended. She stared at a tangle of huge silver ducts, what looked like water hoses, and various types of wires and pipes stretched over bare rafters. And between the rafters lay insulation. Plus, the infernal beeps seemed to be coming from the opposite side of the attic, which wasn't lit or floored.

Cursing, Bree went back downstairs and located a flashlight, took a drink of water, and, on a whim, grabbed a handful of paper towels. Then she trudged up to the attic again and stepped from one rafter to another until she reached the other side of the huge space, guided by the beep. She felt like Dante on his famous journey.

A large white tank loomed ahead, a pulsating red light faintly illuminating it. And in the beam of her flashlight she suddenly detected a light switch. Yes. Now she could see again, and the sight wasn't pretty. The water heater looked fairly new, but a tiny white tank perched behind it like a pack on a hiker's back spewed a steady stream of water into the air. Oh, shit. That's exactly why she'd lived in rental property all these years.

She examined the still-beeping little box and found the off button. At last, blessed silence. But now she had to stop the leak. Bucket, she thought, and some way to divert the water into it. Turn off the water heater first, she told herself. Reading the directions pasted on the exterior of the tank, she didn't have much trouble shutting off the heater, but the arcing stream of water kept spraying into the attic.

After picking her way back across the rafters as fast as she dared, she located a large red bucket in the garage and picked up a handful of rags, then hurried over to the leaking tank again. Bucket in place, she placed a rag over the leak but soon heard a loud *plop* as it became saturated and fell into the bucket.

So she tried the paper towel, her initial weapon of choice. It immediately became soaked but somehow stayed put, and miraculously the escaping water began to stream down the side of the tank and drip into the bucket.

Whew. She took a deep breath. As the water cooled, the pressure should subside and the water leak would stop.

But it didn't. The bucket began to fill, so she hurried to find another one. Returning with its green twin, she waited until the red one was half-full, then substituted the green one and carefully walked the rafters again.

Carrying the sloshing bucket, she felt like a tightrope artist. One misstep, and she and the bucket would crash through the Sheetrock attached to the bottom of the rafters and fall fourteen feet onto the concrete floor of her parents' living room. Not a pretty thought. She slowed her pace, dodging wires and climbing over air-conditioning ducts as if her life depended on it. Which it did, she finally realized.

After several trips, dripping sweat and her legs beginning to shake, she had to give in and call for help. Obviously she couldn't fix this problem.

Back downstairs, she picked up her cell phone. "Carolyn. Sorry to call so late, but the water heater's leaking. Do you know a plumber?"

Carolyn sounded groggy yet willing to help. "Have you turned off the water, honey?"

"No. The leak's in something called a pressure-relief tank. I thought turning off the heater would relieve the pressure, but it didn't."

"Go turn off the water, in front of the house. You know how to do that, right?"

Luckily, Bree had watched her father perform that task several times, so she grabbed a pair of pliers and an old plastic glass and ran out into the front yard. After she yanked the plastic cover off the hole in the ground, she bailed out the water that stood in it, reached down with the pliers, and turned the metal lever.

Back in the attic, she sighed as she saw that the water had finally stopped filling the bucket. She emptied the final bucketful, turned out the lights, and staggered back downstairs to find Carolyn, in her housecoat, waiting for her.

"You look a sight, all sweaty in your old T-shirt and underwear." Carolyn chuckled as she wiped a smudge of mud off Bree's face. "Come on. You can take a bath and sleep over at my place tonight. We'll call a plumber in the morning."

Bree nodded, her arms and legs shaky. Thank God for Carolyn.

Linda sat eating a bowl of cereal when the phone rang. She looked at her caller ID, then answered.

"You're up early. What's going on?" she asked Ann.

"I have to run to Walmart for a few last-minute things for my trip to Hawaii and thought I'd stop by for a minute, if you're decent."

"Of course. I'm up and dressed. I'm scheduled to visit a couple of patients in town, but I don't have to leave until nine thirty."

"I'm almost there. Have any coffee?"

"You know I always have a supply of Dark Magic, just for you."

"Bless you. See you in a few."

Linda stood rinsing her empty bowl and juice glass when Ann burst through the back door. "What's got you out and about so early?"

Ann threw her purse on the bar and walked directly to Linda's Keurig. "Coffee first, questions later. It's not easy for me to be up this early."

Linda laughed at her sister's dramatics. "Okay. How about a sweet roll?"

Ann assumed a martyred expression. "Oh, you know I shouldn't. Why do you even have these things here to tempt me? I thought you'd sworn off sugar and flour."

"I have. Check out this cereal bowl—Shredded Wheat."

"Ugh. And why do you keep hanging on to your mother's old Melmac dishes? You ought to toss them and buy yourself some nice new ones."

Linda stroked the edge of the bowl protectively. "No way. And I keep sweet rolls for hungry grandchildren and people like you."

Ann patted her teased bottle-blond hair and lit on a stool at the bar. "Like me? Whatever do you mean?"

Linda recognized her cue to heap praise on Ann. "People like you, who can eat whatever they want and never gain a pound."

Ann beamed. "Can I help it if I have a high metabolism rate?"

"No, but sometimes I wonder if we're even half sisters. I can just look at one of those rolls and gain five pounds."

Ann took the pecan-studded gooey bun that Linda handed her on a paper plate and bit into it. "Besides, I get a lot of physical exercise."

"I've never seen you working out." Linda selected a mug and fixed Ann's coffee, then placed it in front of her.

"No. I usually don't let people into my bedroom when I'm exercising." She grinned like a teenager.

"Oh, Ann. You're so bad."

"Well, I'm excited. I really think this new man in my life is the one."

"I hope so. You're leaving for Hawaii, what, tomorrow?" Linda returned her cereal box to the pantry.

"Yes. We're taking the puddle-jumper from Tyler to Dallas in the morning, then flying nonstop to Honolulu. It's just eight hours."

Linda wiped up a splash of milk. "You're sure you don't want to get married a little closer to home, so your family and friends can be there?"

"Oh, honey. Why bother? Weddings have become my vacations, and believe it or not, I've never been to Hawaii." Her Pacific-blue eyes sparkled.

"I don't want to be a downer, but Bree and I were discussing something last night—"

"You and Bree?" Ann pushed the remnants of her sweet roll away. "What were you two doing together?"

"I asked her to go to a women's dinner with me in Tyler. You know, the one I've invited you to but you've always told me you weren't interested in."

"You mean with all those lezzies? No way. You're determined to ruin your reputation by associating with those perverts, aren't you?"

"Perverts? What's your problem?" Linda turned on the dishwasher, which roared to life. "They're as normal as any of my friends here in town. I truly enjoy their company."

Ann pulled the rest of the sweet roll toward her again and pinched off a bite. "I suppose Bree felt right at home. Did she find somebody to flirt with?"

"Don't be silly. Most of the women there are couples." She finally sat down again, thinking about last night. "Though, now that you mention it, one of the few single women in the group seemed to be giving Bree the eye."

"I wouldn't doubt it." Ann's perfect complexion had become a bit ruddy. "She really has a way with the women."

"Well, if anyone knows, you should."

Ann drained her cup and jumped up. "Me? Why in the hell would you say something like that?" Now her face looked just a few shades lighter than her lipstick. "I hadn't seen her in a hundred years until she called me, Sunday. What was that all about?"

"How should I know?" Linda got up again, turned off the Keurig, and sprayed the bar with Countertop Magic. "I thought you two used to be close, so why shouldn't she call?"

Ann handed her empty plate to Linda. "*Used to be* are the key words there. Besides, she won't stay in town long enough for you to bother with. You better steer clear of her."

"Why?"

"She'll break your heart." Ann patted her on the shoulder and whirled around. "See you in a couple of weeks."

"Okay. Have a great honeymoon."

"I will, honey. You can bet your life on that." And then Ann was out the door and gone.

Linda slowly polished the smooth, cool bar. That was the second time in just three days she'd heard the words *broken heart* in connection with Bree Principal. First Sandy, and now Ann.

Maybe she should be more careful. But she'd been careful all her life, and where had it gotten her?

❖

In the hardware section of Walmart, someone nudged Bree with their shopping cart.

"Hi, stranger. Fancy meeting you here."

Bree turned around. "Oh—hi, Ann."

"Twice in one week is a record, after all this time."

Ann looked good enough to eat, but Bree restrained herself. "I'm buying some fresh batteries for my flashlight. Never know when you might need them."

"That makes sense"—Ann shrugged—"but I never bother with such things. I just call the nearest available man to come take care of whatever goes wrong." She looked smug.

"I'm sure you do, but I don't. I like to at least try to fix things myself before I call for help."

"I remember. But like I've always said, my way's faster and usually cheaper. Saves wear and tear on the body too." She gave

Bree an appraising look. "You're not getting any younger. You might consider it."

"Fat chance at this point in my life. The older I get, the more stubborn I am." Wearing her designer jeans and a beige suede jacket, Ann looked about twenty years younger than she actually was. Maybe getting others to do all your dirty work was the way to go, but Bree had always preferred to be independent. "So, what are you doing out and about this early? Shouldn't you be home getting your beauty sleep?"

"I don't need any more today, or didn't you notice?" Ann winked flirtatiously.

"You never stop, do you? I have to agree, though, that you do still look pretty good—"

"Stop right there. If you say *for your age*, I'll cram one of those batteries down your throat."

"You and whose troop of Girl Scouts? Besides, I wasn't planning to say anything."

Ann wet two fingers and smoothed an eyebrow. "No?"

"Cross my heart and hope to die. We women have the cards stacked against us when it comes to age, and I'd never do or say anything to make that situation worse than it already is."

Ann ran her tongue over her top teeth, drawing Bree's attention to her lips for a second. "Thanks. By the way, I just heard that Linda took you to Tyler last night to meet some of her new friends."

Bree nodded.

Ann stared at her. "Well, what did you think about them?"

She met Ann's gaze. "I enjoyed myself. They seem like the type of women I'd like to get to know better. You should meet them."

"Ha. Over my dead body."

Just then two well-dressed women walked by and glanced at them, then hurried away, whispering to each other.

Ann looked after the two women and frowned. "I've probably just been taken off the guest list for several parties in town because someone's already seen me talking to you. Associating with Linda's new friends would be social suicide." She tightened her hands on the blue handle of her shopping cart. "Wait a minute. You two have been spending more time together than I thought, haven't you? Did Linda send you to check up on me?"

Bree wasn't sure what to say. "She's concerned about you. Told me you'd had…a rough time awhile back. She confided in me because she knew how close we used to be. She thought maybe I could help."

"Help, my ass." Ann looked as if she might race away down some type of shopping-cart speedway. "The best thing you ever did for me was leave town and stay away as long as you have. You almost ruined my life, and I sure don't intend to let you do it again."

"Ruined your life? Are you crazy? Get ahold of yourself." Bree looked at her chocolate ice cream. She'd never make it home before it melted.

Ann took a deep breath, then another one. "You're right. I'm calmer now. Let's change the subject. What's done is done. If we're both going to live in this town, for a while at least, and keep running into each other, we might as well make the best of a bad situation. " She glanced around, obviously trying to come up with a safe topic of conversation. "Say, have you ever been to Hawaii?" she asked.

"A few times. Usually for a day or two on my way to somewhere in Asia to manage a transaction for the museum."

"So you haven't really seen it?" That realization seemed to soothe Ann. "Did Linda tell you that's where I'm going for my wedding and honeymoon? We're leaving tomorrow."

"No. She didn't mention it." Damn. That ice cream had to be beginning to melt by now.

"That's why I'm here—picking up some last-minute odds and ends for the trip."

"Congratulations. Who's the lucky guy this time?"

Ann tapped her shoulder in mock-anger. "Naughty, naughty. I could have done without you saying *this time*. Are you trying to get under my skin?"

"Under your skin? Why would I try to do that?"

"To see if you still can."

Bree frowned. "Don't flatter yourself. I'm here to buy batteries— and ice cream—not try to turn you on." She pointed to her basket.

"It's a good thing, because you don't have a whisper of a chance." Ann acted like she didn't realize ice cream might melt.

"Did I ever?" As if she didn't already know the answer to that question.

"That's for me to know and you to find out, if you ever want to."

"Hmm. I'll have to think about that." Maybe Ann did have a few feelings for her after all.

"Just let me know."

"I will, and have a wonderful honeymoon. I'll think about you while I'm eating my ice cream."

"Thanks. I will. Don't eat too much. It might upset your stomach."

Ann pulled her shopping cart away from Bree and turned in the direction of the beauty-and-health section. Then she paused. "Say, Bree. Do me a favor, okay?"

"Depends."

"Don't confuse my little sister any more than she already is. Associating with those people in Tyler isn't a good idea. She has to live here, and you don't."

Bree gritted her teeth but managed to grin. "Don't worry. I'll be as good as gold. See you around." How could anyone still irritate yet attract her as much as Ann did?

❖

Sarah Principal looked more animated than usual when Linda entered her room at Silverado.

"Carolyn called me first thing this morning," Sarah blurted out immediately. "You'll never believe what Bree did last night."

"Knowing Bree, I probably won't." Linda set down her bag of medical supplies and perched on the low stool she'd dragged over near Sarah's easy chair. "Tell me."

After Sarah described Bree's attempts to deal with the water-heater leak in the attic, Linda shook her head. "She's lucky she didn't break her neck. That was foolish, especially with no one else in the house. If she'd fallen through the ceiling…Has she always taken risks like that?"

Was Sarah as appalled as she was, or did she admire Bree's daring stunt?

Sarah settled back in her chair. "She's always been adventurous. Why, when they were young, she and Brett used to have contests to see who could climb a tree or swim across the lake the fastest. And after he died she seemed to become even more reckless."

"The other night at Sandy's," Linda said, "Bree told us all that Brett's death affected her more than anything she's ever experienced."

Sarah shook her head and slumped forward. "I'm sure that's true. It devastated all of us." She stared at Linda, grief and remorse clear in her eyes. "I hate to admit it, but I was so torn apart I wasn't able to pay much attention to her for a long time after it happened."

Linda stroked Sarah's veined hand. "You had to have been totally distraught. I don't know how you coped with losing him."

Sarah sat still, seeming to appreciate Linda's slow touches, then withdrew her hand and looked up. "I was devastated. But I should have spent more time with Bree, helped her through the aftermath more than I did." She straightened her spine. "Time flew, she left home before I knew it, and it was too late." Sarah turned and stared at her easel, which stood near a large sliding glass door. "I had my teaching and my painting, but she had to rely on her own resources. As a teenager, she must have had a hard time." She sighed as she stared out at the parklike grounds.

"I'm sure she did. We all did, but look how well she's turned out." Linda grasped Sarah's leg and propped it up on the stool next to her. "You must be proud of her."

Sarah beamed. "Of course I am. She's been a grand success in her profession. And sometimes I envy all the adventures she's had. Why, when she used to come visit us at our condo in Colorado, she always had tales to tell and the pictures to prove them. Siberia, Kenya, China—she was always going somewhere on business and doing things most people wouldn't dare."

Linda eased off the bloodstained netting that secured the bandage on Sarah's leg. "You make me almost wish I could have been with her on some of those trips."

"*Almost* is the key word. I worried about her when I didn't hear from her for weeks, especially when she was younger." Sarah's smile lit up her face. "But when she finally got in touch, she was always so excited about whatever she'd been up to, I didn't have the heart to dampen her high spirits." The smile turned wistful. "I just listened and encouraged her to keep on doing whatever seemed to make her happy."

Linda finished unwrapping the gauze bandage over the sterile pad on Sarah's leg and carefully lifted the bloody pad off the still-raw wound. "Your leg's looking better today," she said. Then she ventured a question she'd wanted to ask ever since she first saw Bree last week. "Did Bree ever bring anybody with her when she visited you and Mr. Principal in Colorado?"

"No. Never. And I wondered about that."

Linda wadded up the soiled bandaging and tossed it into a medical-waste bag, then cleaned the wound gently and applied a fresh coating of Bactroban.

"After Bree confided in us about her preference for women instead of men—she was in college then—I had a hard time resigning myself to never having any natural grandchildren. Especially having lost Brett not that many years earlier…"

Linda took out a fresh pad and positioned it over Sarah's wound. "That must have taken a while to come to terms with," she murmured.

"Yes. I never will." Sarah took a deep breath. "But I'm not the grandmotherly type, so I didn't fuss too much about Bree. When she never brought any women to visit us, I finally became concerned, though. I enjoyed being married to my husband so much that I wanted the same for Bree."

Linda took a long strip of gauze from her bag and began to wrap it around Sarah's leg, stabilizing the fresh pad.

"I didn't care if Bree wanted a woman," Sarah said. "I just wanted her to have a companion, someone to share her adventures…and her life. But it's her choice, and I don't have any right to interfere." She closed her eyes and seemed to drift off to sleep.

After Linda secured the gauze with a fresh piece of netting, she lowered Sarah's leg to the floor, stood, and gazed down at her. She looked so frail and vulnerable sitting there that Linda quickly kissed her forehead.

"Thank you, dear," Sarah murmured, and Linda swiped away a sudden tear as she picked up her bag and slipped out of the room.

CHAPTER ELEVEN

At one o'clock, after visiting her mother, Bree stopped by the local Whataburger for a burger and a free senior drink. She sat in a booth alone, pondering her recent conversation with Ann at Walmart and her encounter Sunday with Linda at the DQ.

She idly stirred her large cardboard container of Diet Coke with a plastic straw. How differently the two sisters affected her. Ann made her feel like lashing out at the people close to her. Linda made her want to understand and come to terms with whatever bothered her.

So Ann was getting married again. She needed to resolve these conflicting feelings once and for all, and maybe Linda could help.

Not that she'd just blurt out her dilemma. No, she'd merely hang out with Linda as much as possible, and surely they'd discuss Ann. She took out her cell phone and located Linda's number.

As she heard the now-familiar voice, her reaction surprised her. She was truly looking forward to spending more time with Linda.

Linda sat on a low stool in the flower bed that surrounded her saltwater pool. She hadn't wanted such an extravagant addition to their home, but Mike had insisted, saying it would keep the children occupied and provide a great place for entertaining their own friends and his clients.

He'd maintained it—backwashed it weekly and kept the salt and chemical levels properly balanced. And he'd taught their sons to gradually take over these routine tasks. But now Linda had to do that chore herself.

She'd always tended to the flower beds and loved the task. The windmill palms she'd planted at each end of the pool now shaded swimmers from the summer sun. Some parts of the large bed received lots of morning sun, though, and she usually filled those areas with pansies. She loved their various colors and cheerful little faces.

When she suddenly heard a passage from Handel's "Hallelujah Chorus," she pulled off a filthy glove and slid her phone from her pocket. "Hello."

"Sorry to bother you. Taking a nap?"

That voice—throaty, with a Northern accent covering the Southern twang lurking underneath it—made her inhale sharply. It was Bree.

"No. I'm out by the pool getting a little sun and exercise. What's up?" Her heart rate increased a bit. Carrying several flats of pansies probably hadn't caused the reaction. Or maybe it had.

It excited her to have a real live lesbian in town. Others might live here, but if so, they were hiding. And with her busy schedule she couldn't drive two hours to and from Tyler every time she wanted to talk to someone who felt the same way she did about women. Besides, almost all the lesbians she'd met in Tyler were coupled, whereas Bree surprisingly wasn't.

"Just grabbed a burger and wondered if you wanted some company."

"If you don't mind sitting out here and watching me work, I'd love some." Linda refused to let Bree take over her life, but she would enjoy spending more time with her. No telling how long she'd be in town.

"Are you sure?"

"Of course. All my grandkids are in school so it's pretty quiet for a change. I'd love to see you. Maybe you can give me some pointers on the care and feeding of water heaters." She chuckled.

Bree laughed good-naturedly. "I should have known Carolyn would blab to Sarah and she'd tell you about my experience. If I have to live in that old house for a while, I need to either get on a first-name basis with some of the local handymen or break out a few of my dad's old do-it-yourself books. He occasionally loved to tinker with our various electrical and mechanical problems, but most of the time he finally called an expert."

"You probably should tinker less and call more, but suit yourself." Linda enjoyed teasing Bree. Awed, she'd always stayed in the shadows and watched her and Ann banter. Finally joining the game made her realize how much fun she'd missed.

"If you're coming over here, you better get a move on," she told Bree.

"Why? Do you have plans for later?" Bree sounded like she might back off.

"No. Not right now. But I never know when I may have to go pick up someone from school or cart them to football practice or dance lessons. Having four grandchildren who can't drive puts me in rather high demand."

Bree made a grumbling sound. "Like getting an appointment with the president, eh? I didn't realize grandmothers were such a hot commodity."

Linda laughed. "You better believe it."

She paused, amazed. She'd just flirted with Bree Principal, and it felt damn good.

❖

Bree stretched out on an old-fashioned webbed recliner and absorbed the sight of the sparkling water and Linda digging in the dirt like a child in a sandbox. The sun warmed Bree's legs through her jeans, and her windbreaker kept the soft breeze from chilling her. It was a perfect November day.

The water hypnotized her, and the next thing she knew, someone was gently shaking her shoulder. "It's almost three thirty. You better wake up or you won't sleep tonight."

Linda stood over her, her soft white hair windblown and one freckled cheek streaked with dirt. The old white T-shirt she was wearing looked like she'd used it as a rag, and her faded jeans were crusty with mud and mulch.

"Did you finish whatever you were doing?" Bree wanted to fall back into the most peaceful sleep she could remember having in years.

"Yeah, no thanks to you." Linda put her hands on her hips, acting like she was exasperated.

But judging by the smile twinkling in Linda's eyes, she wasn't irritated. What color were those eyes exactly? Strange that she'd never noticed. She stared at them—as shining and clear and green as the reflection of the pine trees in the pool, the sun dancing off them as Linda gazed at her. How could she have never really seen them before right now?

"I warned you. I just learned I need to go pick up my granddaughter and take her to her dance lesson. Want to ride along?"

Bree wanted to kick herself for falling asleep instead of spending this amazing autumn afternoon with Linda. "I don't think I'm ready for that just yet. Can I have a rain check?"

"Oh, come on. What else do you have to do? It won't take long, and then I'll fix some of my famous spaghetti for supper. Interested?"

"Now you're talking. Let's go." Bree jumped up and walked with Linda to her CR-V.

Linda could make even a routine drive to pick up a kid sound like an adventure. Suddenly Bree was wide-awake and looking forward to something she'd never dreamed of doing.

The line of cars waiting at the elementary school stretched around the block. With a large placard bearing the name Riley Morton displayed prominently in the windshield of Linda's car, they inched closer to the front of the building. A group of youngsters was darting around like a bunch of minnows, a group of adults standing nearby, and Bree squirmed in the front passenger seat, tapping the armrest. This wasn't as enjoyable as she'd anticipated. In fact, the wait bored her silly.

"Do you have to do this very often?" she finally asked.

"Yes. Why do you think I bought this SUV?" Linda gestured toward the backseat. "Sometimes I have to pick up not only a grandchild but several of their friends."

Linda continued to inch forward, and when she finally reached the waiting children, a little girl sprinted toward them, carrying a backpack. The woman who seemed to be escorting her waved to Linda in acknowledgment.

"Hi, Granny," the girl called as she jerked open the back door. "Who's this?"

"This is Bree."

Bree unbuckled her seat belt, turned around in her seat, and stuck out her right hand. "Hi. And who are you?" She found herself face-to-face with a miniature Linda, only a few years younger than Linda had been when they first met.

Riley looked a little surprised, then said, "I'm Riley. Bree? That's a funny name. How old are you?"

"Uh, I'm sixty-nine. What about you?"

"I'm ten. Wow. You're really ancient, aren't you?"

"That's enough, Riley. Buckle your seat belt," Linda said as she threw the placard into the backseat. They reached the street and she began to accelerate.

"You too, Bree," Linda said.

Riley snickered as Bree clicked her seat belt into place again and said, "Yes, ma'am," with a grin. Actually talking to Riley was a lot more fun than waiting for her to show up had been.

"Did you learn much in school today, Riley?" Linda asked.

Just like her dad used to do, Bree thought and turned to look at Linda.

"Not really. We studied how to multiply our elevens and twelves, but I learned them last year." Riley stared at Bree. "Hey. Why's your hair two different colors?"

Bree glanced back at Riley. "Why's your hair red?"

Riley grinned. "That's just the way it grows."

"Well, this is just the way mine grows. It used to be all black, but then my bangs started turning silver so I just left them that way."

"Do you dye it? My aunt Ann dyes hers yellow."

Bree laughed, and Linda took a right, then a left onto a major highway. "You better not let your aunt Ann hear you say that, Riley."

"Why not? It's the truth. I saw her do it one day."

"Not all people like to hear the truth," Linda said. "Don't you remember how upset Aunt Ann got when you asked her how old she was?"

"Yes, ma'am. She told me she'd give me a whipping if I asked her anything else like that. She said it was none of my business. Why isn't it? She knows how old I am."

Just then Linda pulled up to a local dance studio. "Here we are, Riley. Your daddy will be by to pick you up when your class ends."

Riley grabbed her backpack and jumped out of the car. Then she walked over to the window next to Bree and knocked on it. After Bree lowered the window, Riley said, "I like you, Bree. But you better not hurt my granny's feelings like that other lady did." She blew Linda a kiss and ran away.

"Wow," Bree said as she raised the window. "What was that all about?"

Linda blushed. "I'll tell you over supper. Do you mind if we stop by Kroger for just a minute? I need to pick up a couple of things. No need for you to come in unless you want to."

As Bree sat in the car waiting for Linda, she couldn't stop chuckling. That little Riley reminded her of a small version of Linda with a big dose of attitude added. She liked her.

True to her word, Linda was soon back in the car, and they headed toward her house. "I don't want to rush you, but I have a board meeting at the church tonight and need to be there by seven. Is it all right if we eat a little early?"

"Fine with me. I'll take home cooking whatever time I can get it. I have only one requirement, though."

Linda glanced at her and raised a brow. "What's that?"

"You have to let me take you out to eat. I'm not a freeloader."

"I doubt anyone would ever accuse you of that. But it's a deal. The only problem is finding somewhere around here that serves good food. We have Italian, Asian, catfish, Southern, and Mexican, Mexican, Mexican."

Bree laughed. "We'll just have to try them all and see which one's the best. Finding a good place to eat out is a problem even in a big city like Chicago."

As they parked in Linda's driveway, Bree said, "Riley's quite a kid, isn't she? How many grandchildren did you say you have?"

Linda grabbed her small bag of groceries from the backseat. "Four. She's the youngest and the most outspoken."

Bree took the bag from her as they neared the house. "Whew. That's good to know. I'm not sure I could stand up to the grilling I'd get from three others like her."

Linda opened the back door and waved her in. "Believe it or not, the others are mild mannered and even a little shy around strangers, so you can take it easy. You've met the worst of the lot."

Bree looked around as they walked directly into a large kitchen. Shiny pots and pans hung from a pot rack over a large island, and light-colored cabinets lined the wall behind the sink. The kitchen opened into a large area filled with a dining table and chairs and a den-like area dotted with comfortable-looking sofas and chairs that focused on a large television set and a wood-burning stove.

"Just set that sack on the island. I need to put the spaghetti sauce on to cook first. Then I'll show you the rest of the house. Want something to drink?"

"I'd kill for a glass of water. Talking to Riley made me thirsty."

"Coming right up. Ice or not?"

"Ice, please. This is the South. Don't all drinks except hot coffee come with it?"

"Of course. I was just testing your memory of all things Southern."

Linda handed her a large red plastic glass full of ice water. "Go sit down and turn on the TV if you want. I won't be long."

"Can I help?"

"Nope. I've got it covered. Just relax."

Bree happily complied. She usually stayed as far away from a kitchen as she could manage, though now she wondered if Linda's presence might make it a more enjoyable place than she'd always found it.

❖

Linda loved the pungent smell of onions and garlic cooking. As she browned chopped onions and garlic along with the pound of ground sirloin she'd just bought, she glanced over at Bree, who sat engrossed in a magazine she'd picked up from the coffee table. She seemed completely at home in Mike's old large leather chair. How many times had Linda looked up from the stove to see him there?

She retrieved a jar of tomatoes and a can of tomato sauce from the pantry, opened them, and poured them into the steaming skillet. After adding water and seasoning, she placed a lid on the bubbling mixture and turned the heat to low.

Then she made a quick green salad and joined Bree. "What are you reading?"

Bree looked up as if she'd forgotten where she was and held up an old *National Geographic*. "Oh, just an article about what our Stone Age ancestors ate. That smells great."

Linda glanced around the room, which looked reasonably tidy. Thank goodness the cat hadn't made a deposit in her litter box in the corner. And the last grandchildren here hadn't left games strewn all over the place. She'd even brought in some wood for the stove in case it got chilly later.

"Nice room," Bree commented, looking around as if for the first time. She'd evidently zeroed in on the reading material when she first sat down.

"Yes. It's seen a lot of action over the years. I'm glad Mike felt guilty enough to leave me the house in the settlement."

Bree appeared as if she didn't know what to say, so Linda changed the subject. "You asked me earlier what Riley was talking about when she threatened you. Still want to know?"

Bree nodded. "I wasn't sure you wanted to discuss it. But yes, I am curious." Bree closed the magazine and tossed it back onto the coffee table.

Bree was right. Linda wasn't sure she wanted to talk about Riley's threat, but she didn't know anyone else who might understand as well as Bree might. Even Sandy had seemed a little mystified by the situation.

She took a deep breath. "After Mike told me he wanted a divorce, my world fell apart. It was odd. One day I knew exactly who I was and where I fit, and the next I felt like a stranger, to others and to myself." Bree's sympathetic look helped her continue. "Sandy and Carolyn blustered about what a jerk he was for running around on me, which did help salve my hurt feelings, but back then I didn't have the insight or the courage to admit my part in the divorce."

"Don't be too hard on yourself. You got married young and didn't have many role models. You did the best you could."

Linda shifted on the couch to face Bree more fully. "But you recognized your preference for women early on. Why couldn't I?"

"You must have wanted a family a lot more than I did." Bree shrugged. "How many women did you see having children and raising them as a married couple?"

"None."

"So how would you know that was even an option?"

Linda sighed in relief. Bree seemed to understand. "That's a good point."

Bree moved a little closer. "Tell me about the woman that upset Riley—if you want to."

"Oh. Where to begin?" The experience still embarrassed and puzzled her. "Mike had just moved out, and I had no idea how lonely I could be until that happened."

"When was that?"

"About five years ago. Riley had just turned five, and my oldest grandchild was ten, so I had plenty of company when I felt like babysitting. But my bed felt so big and empty with Mike gone."

"That's probably a normal reaction after sleeping with someone for, what, almost forty years?"

"You're right. But I sure didn't feel normal."

"I've heard divorce can really do a number on people. What happened?"

Linda took a deep breath. "Not long after the divorce was final, I had to go to a weeklong conference in New Orleans."

"And?"

If Bree hadn't listened so intently, Linda wouldn't have continued. "I met a woman there. She seemed strong and confident, and she didn't make any bones about being interested in me."

Bree grinned. "Attractive, I bet."

"Absolutely. And very sophisticated." Linda still remembered how much the woman had excited her. "We hit it off immediately, and after we had dinner together a few times, I drank a little too much

and ended up in her bed." She glanced at Bree, who acted like she'd
just confessed that she'd ordered raw oysters instead of saying she'd
slept with a woman for the first time.

"Did you enjoy it?"

Linda gulped, suddenly thirsty. "Yes. More than I ever thought
possible. Much more than I ever had with Mike."

"And you felt guilty."

"And thrilled and totally infatuated."

"Did she feel the same?"

"She definitely seemed excited."

"Go on."

Linda jumped up. "How about something to drink, Bree?"

"Sure. Water's fine."

"Great. Be right back." She grabbed Bree's empty glass.

Linda handed Bree a refill and downed half a bottle herself, then
sat down again.

"Okay. Back to my first lesbian affair." This time she confided
in Bree more easily. "The woman lived in Dallas, so we didn't have
much trouble seeing each other." Linda's earlobes felt hot. "In fact,
we even met at a motel in Tyler a few times. But mostly I drove to
Dallas when we had some free time, and we spent most of our time in
bed. Being with her was like a revelation, and I was over the moon."

"You didn't ask her to come visit you here?"

"No. Not for quite some time." Linda frowned. "I must have
sensed how she'd react."

Bree took her hand. "And how did she?"

"She hated being in a small town. Said it was boring and everyone
was narrow-minded. She obviously didn't like children very much
either, so that's why Riley said what she did."

"Not a very positive introduction to a new and different life, was
it?"

Linda shook her head. "We didn't see each other after that, and
I did miss the sex."

"So how did you find out about TAG?"

"That's a slightly different story, but I did have some help."

"What kind?"

Linda smiled with pleasure. "My daughter Maureen visited after living on her own for several years and came out to me. She said she'd wanted to for ages but was afraid I wouldn't understand."

"Perfect."

Linda nodded. "For both of us. I was obviously very accepting, and she told me about the PFLAG group in Tyler."

"Aha. That makes sense."

"Yes. I went to several meetings, and that's where I found out about TAG. It had just been organized."

"So now you're able to learn about the gay life at your own pace."

"You must think I'm extremely slow, but with all my other responsibilities and interests, I don't want to go overboard like I did at first. I've gotten used to sleeping alone, and knowing that other people similar to me live just an hour's drive away makes me feel a lot less lonely. Now that you're here…"

Bree patted her hand and pulled away slightly. "I'm glad you told me all this. I'm pretty up in the air right now, what with Mother's changed circumstances and being back in town after all this time."

"I hope you'll stay a long time, especially since I like to cook and you like to eat home cooking. Speaking of—I need to stir the sauce." She leaned over and pecked Bree on the cheek, then jumped up and hurried over to the stove, her lips throbbing and her cheeks burning. But now Bree knew what a loser she was—with women as well as men.

"Yum. Delicious. What's your secret?" Bree asked after she tasted the spaghetti Linda had heaped on her plate. Poor Linda. Bree couldn't imagine how hard it would be to have her first lesbian affair with such an insensitive woman. It had been difficult to have Ann break her heart when she was eighteen, but at sixty? That took a kind of strength Bree wasn't sure she had.

"My secret's probably the homegrown tomatoes in the sauce. I grow a couple of rows of them every summer and can the ones we don't eat fresh."

Bree refocused on their meal and broke off a small bit of the piece of crusty French bread. "I didn't know anyone did that anymore."

"We don't have gardens like our parents used to, but a lot of people still have small ones." Linda sipped her glass of ice water.

"Really?" Bree hadn't paid much attention to that sort of thing when she was younger. She'd been too busy with school activities and her social life.

Linda put down her fork. "Really. You should see the garden centers of our local Lowe's, Home Depot, and Walmart. As soon as all the decorations and trees are cleared out after Christmas, those areas start filling up with fertilizer, mulch, garden soil, and bedding plants. People start planting in February or March to beat the heat."

Bree watched Linda butter her bread. "Do you have cows and make your own butter too?"

"No, silly." Linda wrinkled her nose. "But my grandmother did when she lived out on the farm. When the family moved closer to town in the 1930s, they didn't bring anything except some chickens." Linda chewed a bit of bread. Wiping away a few crumbs, she said, "All I remember are the small gardens, though people still plant enough to share with their neighbors."

Bree forked a tomato from her salad. When had she last eaten a tomato fresh from the vine? "Doesn't a garden take a lot of work?"

"Yes. You have to get the ground ready, plant, fertilize, kill insects, and water the plants. But it's fun to watch them grow."

"It makes my back ache just to think about it." Bree groaned and pretended to rub her own back.

Linda mock-frowned at her. "You also have to pick whatever you've grown and either cook it, can it, or give it away—usually all three."

"And you do this why? Going to Kroger is enough work for me."

"Everything tastes better, it's great exercise, and it makes me feel like I've accomplished something." Linda turned serious. "But most of all, I enjoy being part of nature. Remember? That's fundamental to the way of Wicca."

Bree lowered her fork as she chewed another bite of spaghetti. "I'm glad you brought up that subject. I understand gardening, but I never expected to find a coven in this part of the country. And for you to act like it's no big deal amazes me."

Linda shook her head as if Bree's statement didn't surprise her. "When you understand the basics of Wiccan beliefs, it's *not* a big deal. But outsiders have so many misconceptions, we keep our little group very secret."

"So enlighten me more, please." Bree took another bite of the tangy sauce heaped on angel-hair spaghetti. "Before you do, though, what makes this sauce smell so spicy?"

"The green peppers. Every summer I grow several plants, and when I have extra, I just rinse the peppers, cut them into chunks, and freeze them in a Ziploc bag. Simple. Even the onions are from my garden."

Bree raised an eyebrow. "Wow. This is a true gourmet meal. My parents never had the gardening gene, and in Chicago it's probably extinct by now, so all this is a revelation."

"It's actually very enjoyable and, like I just said, makes me a lot more aware of the cycle of life."

"That Wiccan thing you just brought up, eh?"

Linda took another drink of water. "Yes. As Sandy mentioned at Samhain last weekend, this time of year is a period of contemplation, when we enjoy what we've accomplished during the fertile period we've just been through."

"So by eating these vegetables you've grown, we're celebrating your success as a gardener?" Bree had never considered that a meal could have so much meaning.

"Something like that. It's also a time to think about the final phase of the life cycle."

"The final phase? What do you mean?"

Linda spoke slowly, as if emphasizing a very important point. "This time of the year we let ourselves rest and reflect on what we've done. It's like letting the earth lie fallow."

Bree nodded. "That makes sense, especially if you think of Samhain as a kind of New Year's. But I've been wanting to ask you something."

"What?"

"How do you reconcile going to church with Wicca? I can just imagine the expressions of the women in your Sunday-school class if you announced that you're, gasp, a witch."

Linda laughed and pushed back her empty plate. "Yeah. They'd probably think we were all running around naked in the woods having orgies with warlocks and with each other."

"You're not? Shoot. Count me out." Bree laughed. "Though I have to admit that was one of my first images on Halloween night when Carolyn told me what was happening at Sandy's."

"Really?" Linda laughed even louder. "Orgies?"

Linda laughed with her but finally said, "Seriously, Christianity and Wicca share many of the same gods and goddesses, holidays, and beliefs. Halloween isn't a Christian holiday, but All Saints' Day is important in the Catholic faith. If you study Wicca enough you'll see a lot of common roots."

"Hmm. That might make for some interesting reading. Can you loan me some books?" Bree had been looking for something to occupy herself until her mother adjusted to her new situation, when she'd feel better about heading back to Chicago.

"Sure. I can give you an armful," Linda said. "But there's one thing I especially like about Wicca."

"What's that?"

"Its lack of organization."

Bree scraped her plate clean, wishing she wasn't too full to ask for seconds. "Okay. I'll bite. How does Wicca lack organization?"

"I could be a solitary witch, if I decided to, and perform whatever ceremonies I want." Linda wiped her mouth on her napkin.

"So a coven's not necessary?"

"That's right. But if I want to celebrate with a group, we can make up our own rituals honoring whatever deity we choose, if any."

"Hmm."

"The books I loan you will give you plenty of examples of what I'm talking about." Linda glanced at the kitchen clock and began to clear the table.

Bree got up too. She'd forgotten Linda had a meeting. "So, how did you get involved in this?"

Linda rinsed the plates and silverware as Bree handed them to her, talking as she worked. "Oh, Sandy influenced me. She learned a lot on the West Coast."

Bree nodded.

"When she found out I was interested in that sort of thing, she started teaching me."

Linda picked up her sweater from the sofa, where she'd tossed it earlier. "Sorry we don't have time for dessert, but I need to leave. I'll bring you some books about Wicca next time I see you."

Bree pulled on her jacket. "Sure. Thanks a million for the great meal. Next time's on me, at whatever restaurant you recommend. I'm looking forward to it."

And as Bree walked through Linda's back door, she realized she'd meant what she'd just said. A fresh breeze seemed to have just swept through her life, bringing a hint of spring with it.

CHAPTER TWELVE

Linda couldn't get Bree out of her mind during the board meeting and woke up the next day thinking of how easy it had been to spend time with her. She wanted more, so after she finished dressing she reached for her cell phone. "Hi, Bree. What are you doing today?"

"The usual. Visiting Sarah and worrying about what I'm going to eat." She laughed. "Just kidding. I can take care of myself in that department. What about you? By the way, thanks again for yesterday. That was fun."

"It was. I need to visit a couple of patients, but then I'm free for the rest of the day. Doing anything later?"

"Not after eleven. Have something in mind?"

Linda picked up her keys and headed out to the garage. "Since you've spent so much time working at a museum, want to go to Kilgore and see one there?"

"The oil museum? I've been meaning to visit it since it opened. I've heard it's well done but wouldn't mind seeing for myself. Have you been?"

Linda started the car. "A long time ago, but I'd love to visit it with an expert. What do you think?"

"Good idea." Bree sounded more energetic than she had yesterday. "Are you sure you don't have anything better to do than babysit me?"

"Positive." Linda began to back out of the driveway. "Look. I need to run. How about I pick you up about eleven fifteen? We can grab some lunch in Kilgore."

"Sounds great. Casual clothes?"

"Absolutely. Let's just relax."

"Looking forward to it, and thanks, Linda. You don't have to be my tour guide, but I appreciate it. I'll do the same if you ever come to Chicago."

"Sure thing, Bree. See you later." She backed into the street and headed toward Silverado.

Linda didn't like the idea of Bree going back to the big city, but evidently that's where she wanted to be. Linda steeled herself to make the best of what time they still had together.

❖

Bree sat across the booth from Linda at The Back Porch in Kilgore. "How's your burger?" Linda asked.

"Not bad. And these hush puppies are good. Haven't had any in years." Bree examined the patty of the burger she'd enjoyed a bite of. "The meat's great. But in Texas, I wouldn't expect anything less."

Linda waved a hand, her mouth full.

"And in case you want to know," Bree sprinkled a little salt on her fries, "I did just thank the young steer who sacrificed himself for my burger."

Linda grinned. "So you actually remember some of what I've told you about Wicca?"

Bree nodded, but she didn't want to tell Linda that, compared to a Chicago burger, this one was rather unimaginative. Where were the tomato jam, the Hook's cheddar cheese or double cream Gouda, the pickled onions, and the brioche bun she'd become accustomed to in the Windy City? No, this food was good yet basic, and she suddenly felt homesick for Chicago and its variety.

She dipped a crispy fry in some plain ketchup. "You know, I really have wanted to visit the oil museum, but the only times I've been home have been for Father's funeral last year and an occasional Christmas. I never stayed long enough to do anything except visit my parents."

Linda took a bite of her beans. "Yes. I didn't realize you'd even been in town, except when your dad died. You had so many people around you at the visitation and the funeral, I didn't want to intrude."

"That's all a blur. Even if I'd had time to visit with anyone, I doubt if I'd remember now. But we're making up for lost time now, aren't we?" She finished her burger and wiped her hands on her paper napkin.

She hadn't noticed Linda at the funeral, but Ann hadn't been there, which made the day even more painful. As a teenager, Ann had spent so much time at their house, and her father had always tried to make her feel special. In fact, if she hadn't known how much in love her parents had always been, she might have been angry when Ann flirted with him. But he'd always rebuffed her with a joke and a laugh, which annoyed Bree only because Ann had paid attention to someone except her.

Linda finished her glass of water and reached for the check the waitress had just left, but Bree grabbed it. "Oh no, you don't. Remember our arrangement? This is my treat."

"You don't have to, Bree. I had to cook for myself last night anyway. I'd have had leftovers and probably ended up throwing them away."

"Ha. You saved me from either eating out, begging Carolyn to feed me, or trying to rustle up something for myself. No, I like our agreement just fine, though it's too bad you're getting the short end of the stick."

Linda stood up. "Okay. If you're happy, I'm happy. Ready to go see the museum?"

"Sure. Where is it?"

"Not far." Outside, Linda looked up at the clear sky. "In fact, why don't we walk?"

"Good idea. I don't usually eat this much back in Chicago, so a little exercise might help me keep my girlish figure."

Linda looked at her appraisingly. "I'd say you've done a good job of that."

From anyone else, especially another lesbian, the comment would have sounded flirtatious. But Bree didn't detect anything other than a sincere compliment. How refreshing.

"Thank you. I'm blessed with good genes, and believe it or not, I don't think about food unless I'm really hungry."

"Really? I can't imagine. I love to eat."

"You know how a lot of people eat when they're stressed?"

"Do I ever!"

Bree shrugged. "I'm just the opposite. I forget to."

"Must be nice."

As they strolled down a sidewalk past a series of white brick structures, Linda pointed out the college auditorium and central administration building. "Remember the Kilgore Rangerettes?" she asked.

"Sure. They put Kilgore Junior College on the map back in the early '40s, didn't they?"

"Yep. The dean wanted to attract young women to the school and keep rowdy fans in their seats. They were drinking too much and getting into fights under the grandstands during halftime."

"How funny." Bree laughed. "I do know that the contemporary art museum in Houston honored the woman who founded the Rangerettes for creating a living form of art."

"Score one for the women. Come to think of it, they have a small museum here. After we visit the oil museum, we might take a peek."

"Suits me. The more museums the merrier, I always say, even if I am mangling a cliché." What a relief to casually visit such a place instead of oversee it. Bree took a deep breath. Maybe life was more than a job after all.

❖

The big-band music engulfing them made Bree feel like dancing as they entered Boomtown, the oil museum's major attraction. She and Linda glanced around at the full-size replica of a typical East Texas oil town during the '30s.

"Hey, listen to that swing tune," Bree said. "It's called 'Sing, Sing, Sing.' My folks used to play it when Brett and I were kids."

"Before my time." Linda smiled.

Bree ignored Linda's joke. "I'll never forget my dad running in for lunch one day and putting a new record on. It'd just been released." Bree suddenly felt like dancing. "He and my mom acted like it was a major event they'd been looking forward to forever."

Linda seemed to catch fire from Bree's memory. "Yeah. Dad used to tell us all about going dancing at the Cooper Club."

"My folks talked about that club too. According to my mom, everybody in town looked forward to the big bands that played there. Even Duke Ellington and his band performed in the club."

Bree looked into a formal-wear store. "Check out that satin evening gown. My mom said everybody dressed up to go to the club, but she was too young. By the time she turned eighteen the war had started and it'd gone out of business."

Linda walked into an old newspaper office and scanned the clippings thumbtacked to a bulletin board. "This area must have really prospered during the oil boom to attract so many big bands."

Bree pointed to an article. "Yeah. According to this, the bands could make more money hitting a lot of small places than staying in the cities, where the Great Depression hit so hard."

As they left the newspaper office, Linda touched Bree's shoulder. "Hey, want to go to the drugstore? We could have a Coke float or a lemonade."

"Sure. Those fries made me thirsty." In the drugstore, Bree headed for the jukebox. "Check out these song titles—'I've Got You Under My Skin,' 'The Way You Look Tonight,' 'It's De-Lovely.' Weren't the lyrics romantic back then?"

"Yeah. A lot more than the ones in the '60s." Linda sighed and read some more titles. "I'd love to return to those old June-moon-spoon songs and have someone treat me so special. In fact, Bob Dylan's new album earlier this year features ten hits Sinatra sang."

"I have that album and have almost worn it out, especially 'Autumn Leaves' and 'Some Enchanted Evening.'"

Suddenly Bree saw past the shy, gangly teenager Linda had once been. She'd like to become more intimate with the woman she'd just glimpsed.

But then Linda's expression changed. "Our generation lost all the romance our parents enjoyed and valued."

Bree opened her mouth to disagree but nodded instead. "I remember hearing 'Annie Had a Baby' in the third grade."

Linda laughed. "Definitely before my time, but I remember the Beatles singing 'Why Don't We Do It In The Road?' Not very romantic for sure."

Bree selected a sentimental song from the '30s, and Linda asked, "Did you know my dad met his first wife at the Cooper Club dancing to that kind of mushy music?"

"Really?"

"Yep. In the stag line. He saw her dance by with another man and cut in. After that, he made sure they danced in a corner of the room, as far away from the stag line as he could get."

"She must have been attractive to catch his eye that way."

"You bet. I've seen her picture, and it's eerie how much Ann looks like her."

"Hmm. Guess that's why he wouldn't want another guy to horn in." Bree shook her head. "What happened to Ann's mother? I don't remember anyone ever talking about that."

Linda sat down at a small, round table. "I'm not sure. I just know she died rather quickly and left Dad with three children to raise."

Bree stood across from her. "I think I will have something to drink. How about lemonade?"

Linda agreed, and Bree brought them two glasses from the soda fountain. "So he married your mother not long after his first wife died?"

"Yes, in 1949, I think, because I was born in 1950." Linda stirred her lemonade with her straw, then took a sip. "Ann was about three when they got married, so she was really young when she lost her mother."

Bree drank her lemonade straight from the glass. "That's so sad. Makes me realize how lucky I am to still have mine."

Restless, she strolled back over to the jukebox and flipped to another group of songs. "Hey. Look at this. It says Ella Fitzgerald performed at the Cooper Club. Wow."

Linda took a last sip of her lemonade and joined her at the jukebox, their shoulders touching as Bree bent to look more closely at the song list. "Being here helps me understand better why you enjoy your profession. Preserving the story of people's lives must be gratifying."

Linda's statement jolted Bree inside, like their brief contact just had. It felt good to have someone realize why she'd always loved her work so much.

"They've done a great job re-creating how rutted the roads of the time were, haven't they? It's one of my favorite parts of this place," Linda said as they wandered past a barbershop and a gas station. "It's hard to imagine life without paved roads, but this sure helps make the point."

Bree studied the exhibit from her perspective as a professional curator. "I'm impressed. Boomtown's a creative way to let people experience what life then must have been like."

"Glad you like it. Want to go to the movies now?".

"Sure. My feet could use a little rest."

The movie showed actual footage of the '30s boom and how an oil well was drilled. As they sat side by side in the darkened room, Bree noticed each time Linda's arm accidentally brushed hers, especially when Linda squeezed her forearm to emphasize something they were viewing on the screen.

But the sensation that swept over Bree wasn't lust or excitement. She was too well acquainted with those responses. It was more like the refreshing pleasure of a cool breeze on a hot summer afternoon or the welcome taste of cold water when she was thirsty.

"How about it?" Linda asked as they left the building. "Are you up for another museum, or have you had enough?"

"Enough museums? Are you kidding? I'm a pro. Let's go visit the Rangerettes."

Bree hadn't enjoyed herself this much in a long time.

From the oil museum, Bree followed Linda back toward where they'd parked to eat lunch. Linda stopped and pointed across the street at an imposing building. "That's the Van Cliburn Auditorium, named, of course, for one of Kilgore's most famous gay residents."

"I forgot Van Cliburn grew up here. My piano teacher took private lessons from his mother, who taught him to play. When Sarah and I drove my teacher to a concert in Dallas years later, we briefly met him and his mother," Bree said. "That was probably as exciting for me as people at the Cooper Club getting to hear such celebrities as Duke Ellington and Ella Fitzgerald."

They strolled through a campus block lined with large two-story white brick buildings. "There's the Rangerette Showcase Museum." Linda pointed across the street. "It's more straightforward than the oil museum. It has models, costumes, photos, and newspapers, plus videos of their performances."

Inside, they saw several models of Rangerettes. "The red, white, and blue costume hasn't changed much over the years," Bree said.

"Yes. Ann used to say she liked how that big belt felt cinched around her waist. Said it made her feel secure."

"Ann! When did she ever try on a Rangerette outfit?" Just the mention of Ann's name made Bree lose some of her connection to Linda.

Linda stared at her. "She was part of the group for two years. I thought you knew that."

"How would I? That summer after high school when she told me she never wanted to see me again, I went to Colorado with my parents. Then I rushed back home, packed, and moved into the dorm in Austin. Ann never tried to get in touch."

Linda wrinkled her brow. "Why, that's when she tried out for the Rangerettes. She was really nervous but thought she had a good chance. She'd taken dance lessons forever and had a fantastic high kick."

"I know." Bree had felt like Ann had kicked her right in the gut that summer. "Perfect qualifications for a precision drill team."

"Tryouts were rigorous, she said, but being part of the team was harder. She seemed to enjoy it a lot, though." Linda sounded like she envied Ann, or at least had wished she were more like her in some ways. "Of course, that doubled or tripled the number of boys who asked her out and hung around the house, hoping she'd pay them some attention."

Bree began to understand why her mother had referred to Linda as a type of Cinderella the other day. How must it have felt to grow up in the shadow of someone like Ann?

She stared at a 1963 issue of *The Saturday Evening Post* displayed in a case. "Hey, there Ann is. Right in the middle of the drill-team line." She looked closer. "Check out that white Western hat tipped over one eye and her right knee up at exactly the same angle as the other girls'." Though she felt sorry for Linda, she'd liked to have seen Ann dressed like that. "Those white boots, belts, and hats really set off her red blouse and blue skirt. Simple but classy."

Linda took a long look. "I remember when that magazine came out. Ann was so excited she must have bought ten copies, and everybody in town talked about it."

A heavy sense of loss broadsided Bree. "And I never even knew. I wish I could have shared that with her." Bree realized she was being insensitive, but it was too late to retract her reaction.

"I don't know if she'd have had any time to spend with you." And instead of acting hurt, Linda spoke in a sympathetic tone. "She had to keep her grades up and practice practically every day, be at every Ranger football game, and travel to out-of-town events." She pointed at several other photos in the case. "Look up there. As part of the Rangerettes, she performed at the Cotton Bowl in Dallas and participated in the Macy's Thanksgiving Day Parade in New York City."

Bree sighed. "And I thought she was just being stubborn and ignoring me. She knew what she wanted out of life and went for it, didn't she?" How could she have acted so crass? And now she'd pushed Linda into second place again behind Ann.

Linda patted her arm. "Don't feel bad. She made quite a splash, but after those two glory years, she didn't seem to know what to do with herself."

Bree reveled in Linda's kindness. "What do you mean?"

"After she graduated from Kilgore Junior College and couldn't be a Rangerette any longer, she decided not to go on to a university."

"Why not? My education got me out of here."

"Can you picture yourself doing precision high kicks and holding an audience's attention as successfully as a bunch of football players could?"

Bree winced. "Absolutely not. That's not my thing."

"Look." Linda pointed at a shot of a slender, beautiful woman, who seemed totally at ease in front of a group of girls staring at her in awe.

"Wow. She could make even me want to do a high kick."

"Yes. That's Gussie Nell Davis, founder of the Rangerettes. She wanted to help girls be self-confident, disciplined, and cooperative, as well as skilled dancers, like this news clipping says."

"That's great. So why didn't Ann find a way to keep going in the direction this Miss Davis pointed her?"

Linda frowned. "That's the fly in the ointment."

"What do you mean?"

"Well, in this article she says she wanted to prepare young women to be marriage material."

"Oh. I see. Ann did what Miss Davis said instead of what she did."

"Exactly like I did," Linda said, "though I didn't receive such direct advice. It was apparently in the water around here. Get married, have kids, go to church. Or maybe in the air. We all absorbed these commandments from somewhere. Only a few women, like you and Gussie Nell Davis, escaped."

Bree sighed. "So Ann did what?"

"She gave up her own ambitions and married the football player she'd flirted with since just after high school. After that she lived through his accomplishments instead of achieving her own."

"That's sad. Come to think of it, Carolyn mentioned him and said she wasn't too impressed."

They walked around the rest of the museum, talking mostly about Gussie Nell Davis, who'd led the group for almost forty years. But soon Bree said, "I've seen enough. Ready to leave?"

It had clouded over during their brief stay in the small museum. Thunder rumbled in the distance, and wind began to whip the tree limbs. Bree felt sad for Ann but torn between her old feelings for Ann and her new ones for Linda.

On the drive home, Bree didn't say much for a long time. But finally she seemed to shake off her stormy mood. "When we were coming back from Tyler the other night, you promised to tell me Lou Anne and Kay's story. Remember?"

"Oh. Thanks for reminding me."

"I'm waiting."

Bree was probably still thinking about whatever Ann had done all those years ago to upset her, but maybe this story would distract her. "Lou Anne was married for almost forty years and raised four children with her husband. He was a successful educator and made a good salary."

"So?" Bree seemed determined to hang on to her foul mood.

"When she was about sixty, she finally realized she wasn't happy and asked him for a divorce."

Bree glanced at her. "Okay. I'll bite. Why wasn't she happy?"

"She had a crush on a woman in her Sunday-school class."

Bree gave a short laugh. "I guess that's as good a place as any to find a woman you like."

"I suppose so." Linda shrugged. She was getting a little tired of Bree's drama about whatever had happened with Ann so long ago. "Anyway, after a lot of soul-searching, Lou Anne finally acknowledged that she was a lesbian. She even told her husband that's why she wanted out of their marriage."

"That took guts."

"Yes, and that's not all. She was a very active member of a big Baptist church in Tyler and one of their best Sunday-school teachers for adults. She was also involved in a lot of church and community activities."

"So? Did she tell any other church members except her ex-husband?"

"A few, but she met Kay at a PFLAG meeting a year or so later and eventually started living with her and taking her to church with her. Then everyone knew."

"And how did they react?" Bree looked out the window.

"They immediately asked her to resign from teaching her class, insisting she and Kay couldn't have any type of leadership role in the church."

"Ha. Guess they thought she'd set a bad example."

"I suppose so."

"Did things calm down after that?" Bree turned toward her.

Linda shook her head. "No. Several months later, she and Kay signed up to take part in a weekend camping trip at a nearby lake sponsored by the church."

Bree shrugged. "Not my cup of tea, but I guess they enjoy that sort of thing."

"Yes. Especially Kay. They had their small travel trailer all packed and ready for the trip. But at the last minute, they got a letter from the associate pastor."

"And?"

"He said the members didn't think it appropriate for Lou Anne and Kay to be part of a family outing. He also returned their deposit."

"That's awful." Bree frowned. "How did they respond?"

"Lou Anne went to see him."

"Good for her. What did she say?"

"That she was angry and considered his actions unchristian."

"He certainly deserved that visit, but he probably weaseled his way out of it."

Linda scoffed. "Yeah. But he left a scar. Lou Anne confided in me that he made her feel like the epitome of evil. Most of us have advised her and Kay to leave the church and find a more accepting one."

"I sense a *but* coming."

"They insist they've always been Baptists and have a right to be part of whatever church they choose."

Bree clenched a fist. "So they've taken on the most powerful denomination in the South?"

"Yes. And now Lou Anne's published a book detailing her experience."

"That's great."

Linda smiled. "And she's not finished. Kay's setting up venues for her all over the South and the Southwest. She's speaking mainly to PFLAG groups and any churches that are interested. It's not an easy fight, but they're apparently in it to stay."

"How old is she?" Bree had been sitting on the edge of her seat, but now she relaxed back into it.

"Seventy-five, though she's as active as any fifty-year-old."

"Good for her. I'm not into the church, but I admire anyone who fights for what she believes in. Next time we see her, remind me to buy a copy of her book. She and Kay deserve all the support they can get."

"That'll please them." Linda relaxed her tight grip on the steering wheel, relieved to have diverted Bree from dwelling on the past and on Ann. People like Bree, and Lou Anne and Kay, had enough battles to fight in the here and now. No sense wasting energy on old ones.

CHAPTER THIRTEEN

Bree dumped a jigsaw puzzle onto a small lounge table at Silverado, and she and her mother began to turn the pieces over.

"Let's group them by color, okay?" Sarah said.

"That's fine, but I'd rather do the border first."

Sarah reached for a small blue piece. "Tell you what. I'll focus on the colors, and you deal with the outside part."

They worked in silence, and then Sarah asked about Bree's recent excursion to Kilgore.

Bree snapped a piece covered with wildflowers into two others. "The oil museum's innovative and brings the boom years to life. After Linda and I visited it, we toured the Rangerette museum too."

Sarah finished picking out all the blue and white pieces. "Never been there. How was it?"

"All the memorabilia interested me, probably because I heard so much about the Rangerettes and Gussie Nell Davis when I was growing up. Did you know her?"

Rummaging through the pile, Sarah found two silver pieces. "No. But I heard she was well educated and beautiful."

"Yeah. We saw a picture of her when she was young. Fantastic figure, with a lot of style."

"Ambitious too. Supposedly wanted the Rangerettes to outdo the Rockettes by kicking higher and using more of a variety of routines." Sarah picked up another silver piece. "I did see the group perform at halftime several times. Their flying splits and rapid-fire high kicks were absolutely perfect. Didn't miss a beat. And they used unusual props."

"Like what?" Bree finished a long stretch of the left border, where green trees met wildflowers.

"Lassos and scrubbing boards. Umbrellas and huge Mexican straw hats bigger than the umbrellas. You never knew what they'd come up with. That was part of the fun of watching them."

Bree spotted some parts of the border that looked like purple and gold clouds and started trying to fit them together. "When did you see them?"

"The early '50s. Carolyn babysat you and Brett." Her voice cracked at the memory, even after all these years. "The men stayed glued to their seats the entire halftime. They seemed more interested in the drill team than the football game, if you can imagine that." Sarah unearthed several more silver pieces and added them to her pile.

"And how did the women react?"

Sarah paused and gazed at her. "Some of them were probably jealous because they thought their husbands wished they looked like the girls on the field." She finished picking out the silver pieces and started on the bright-orange flowers that dominated the puzzle.

"And the women were probably wishing they still looked that good too."

"Yes. Those girls were the ideal shape that most of us believed we needed to be." Sarah looked thoughtful as she sifted through the blue and white pieces she'd gathered. "When I was young I'd look at myself in the mirror and think how ugly I was because I was so skinny and had curly hair and so many freckles. None of the stars I saw on the screen looked like me, and I'd never heard of airbrushing a photo. The Rangerettes set up those types of unrealistic expectations for girls, I'm afraid."

"That's what I'm thinking. I even Googled Gussie Nell Davis last night and found an interview. She bragged about being a perfectionist. Said that's why the Rangerettes succeeded and why she never married. If she had, she'd have devoted herself a hundred percent to her husband, and she preferred to spend all her time and energy on her career."

"Hmm. Sounds like someone I know and love." Her mother glanced up from their puzzle and briefly touched Bree's arm.

Bree had to will herself not to flinch. Her mother touched her so rarely she didn't know how to respond. She usually froze, but this time she tried to savor the rare gesture. "You may be right. I never wanted to marry a man, and I've certainly enjoyed my career. But if I'd openly married a woman, I'd probably never have become a curator."

Sarah gave her an appraising look, then returned to the reddish-brown pieces she'd begun to sort. "I know why you couldn't marry a woman when you were younger, but why can't you now?"

Bree had just finished putting together a short strip of bright-yellow pieces, and she stopped and stared. "I can't believe you just said that."

"Why not? Women received the right to vote just five years before I was born. It's not too late for you. You're only as old as you let yourself think you are."

Bree kept staring. "Did you ever regret giving up your dreams of moving to New York and becoming a famous painter?"

Sarah idly sorted through the reddish-brown pieces she'd grouped together. "I can barely imagine it now. I'd probably have enjoyed it, but the war was in full swing when I graduated from high school. And then I met your father." She sighed. "I fell in love and put my ambitions on hold. At least I graduated from junior college before you and Brett came along, then finished my four-year degree."

"And that satisfied you? You could have been in New York with Jackson Pollack and his cronies and participated in all the excitement of the abstract expressionist movement." Bree joined a long section of green to one of purple sky.

Sarah's eyes gleamed as she picked up a couple of hunter-green and dark-brown pieces. "My life here gave me more than enough. Oh, it was hectic with your father, and you two, and school, but I loved everything I did and was. I don't regret my choices, and I don't want you to ever regret not doing what you care for."

Bree swallowed the lump in her throat that her mother's uncharacteristically personal words caused. "So you aren't sorry you weren't a Rangerette?"

Sarah laughed. "No. I finally accepted my imperfections. I've always managed to have everything I wanted, with all the heartbreak that went along with it. Now I truly want the same for you." She reached over and squeezed Bree's hand as she moved a long strip of wildflowers into place. "Find a woman who'll make you as contented as your father and you have made me, and I'll die happy."

Bree quickly brushed away a tear with her other hand. "There. The border's done. Now let's fill in the pieces you've sorted so well, and I promise to think about what you've said."

❖

Linda pushed through Sarah's door after knocking. "Hello. Anybody home?" she called.

Sarah stood at her easel painting a bright autumn scene, filled with green leaves on one side and blazing oranges, yellows, and reds in the center.

"Sorry I'm so late today. Looks like you've been busy," Linda said as she enjoyed the energy and warmth radiating from the painting and from Sarah. "Who's in the center of your painting?" She pointed to the figure of a woman wearing a red coat and black boots and standing in the middle of the deep woods she seemed to be entering.

"Someone about to find her bliss, though she hasn't recognized it yet. I'm just trying to help her visualize it."

Linda set down her bag, puzzled by Sarah's cryptic words. "It's beautiful, and I hope it achieves what you want. Now how about letting me look at your leg?"

As Sarah sat down and pulled up her pants leg, she said, "Bree stopped by earlier."

Linda's heart stuttered. "Did she mention our little expedition?"

"She certainly did. She seems to have enjoyed herself quite a bit."

"I'm glad." Linda slowly removed Sarah's bandage. "Oh, your wound looks so much better. You must have been thinking a lot of healing thoughts since I saw you last."

Sarah smiled. "As a matter of fact, I have. And Bree brought me a puzzle featuring the four main characters in *The Wizard of Oz*. We spent several hours working on it together, and it's cheered me up."

"Puzzle-healing—that's a new technique I'll have to recommend to my other patients."

"Might be a good idea." Sarah nodded. "But tell them to work with someone they care a lot about. That seems to be the key."

Linda picked up her bag. Sarah Principal didn't seem like her usual self today, but Linda liked the new, happier version of the woman who'd recently seemed so melancholy. Bree's presence was obviously making a difference, which delighted Linda.

CHAPTER FOURTEEN

"Great day for a festival, don't you think?" Bree held a jar of old-fashioned syrup she'd picked up in one of the booths lining the main streets downtown.

"Sure is," Carolyn said. She looked around at the crowd, which seemed to be growing by the minute. "Had more than thirty thousand people here last year."

"Wow. I had no idea this one was so popular."

"Yeah. I was a little worried earlier. The wind and rain made it as cold as a witch's tit—pardon the old expression. Thank goodness the weather cleared off."

Bree paid for the syrup and slipped the glass bottle into her large purse. "Speaking of witches, weren't we supposed to meet some of the other coven members here?"

Carolyn took Bree's arm and pulled her away from the booth to a less crowded spot. "Yes, but keep your voice down. We never use the words witch and coven in public. We call ourselves Greenies."

"Greenies?"

"Yeah. Almost all of us are green about witchcraft. Sandy knows quite a bit, but the rest of us are just learning."

Bree glanced around. The people strolling from booth to booth seemed set on nothing but having a good time, but you never could tell. "Got it. I suppose a lot of people still think of witches as devil worshippers who cast evil spells and perhaps even sacrifice an animal or two."

"Exactly. A lot of area preachers wouldn't hesitate to rail against us as immoral and indecent if they even suspected we exist." Carolyn frowned, an uncharacteristic expression for her.

"Greenies. That's an interesting choice. Reminds me of Brownies—little Girl Scouts."

Carolyn's frown turned into a smile. "Yes. But we chose the name mainly because we're interested in green witchcraft."

"I've never heard of that." Bree spotted a booth selling earrings and began to nudge Carolyn toward it.

"It's all about the natural rhythm of the seasons. Also, the importance of goddesses as well as gods. And it relies more on a personal approach instead of being part of a group."

"I'm confused. I thought you were a group." Bree fingered a pair of silver dangling earrings set with green stones. They'd look pretty on Linda—match her eyes.

"Yes. But we're mainly a group of friends who get together when we feel like it. We don't have a lot of fancy rituals or even believe in some of the same things. We simply like the basics of green witchcraft and want to know more about them and how to apply them to everyday life."

Bree impulsively handed the vendor some cash for the earrings and dropped them into her purse. Then she glanced down the street. "Let's go look at those antique cars."

They strolled past a cluster of booths offering brochures from various hospitals and service organizations in the area, but she didn't see any familiar faces. "Where are Sandy and the others we're supposed to meet?"

"Down by the old train depot. Surely you knew it was transformed into a museum years ago. It's the center of cultural activity." She waved a hand. "Downtown's the commercial part of the festival."

They examined some of the antique cars parked near the courthouse. Then Carolyn pointed to a long flatbed trailer filled with square bales of hay to sit on. "Let's catch a ride on one of those wagons. It's not far to the depot, but I'd rather save my legs for walking around there."

The brief trip was bumpy, but the smell of the hay and the rain-cooled air soothed Bree as they headed through the familiar shady streets. The leaves had begun to change color and reminded Bree of her mother's most recent painting. She'd seen it when she'd visited earlier and had felt pulled in, almost as if she were the woman in red about to enter the glorious autumn forest.

"We're here," Carolyn called, and they both accepted a hand down from the wagon.

Something smelled good—sweet, yet salty. Kettle corn, popping in a huge black vat. "I haven't had anything to eat since breakfast. Hungry, Carolyn?"

"You better believe it." She waved at someone and then looked around. "Sandy's supposed to save us a table."

"Wonder where she is."

"Over there," Carolyn said, after they pushed their way through the crowd. "And Linda's with her. Come on."

Bree noticed Tornado Taters, links, hamburgers, barbecue, and some of the best-looking Mexican food she'd ever seen as they hurried past various stands. By the time they reached Sandy and Linda, she'd decided what she wanted to eat.

"Hey. Good to see you again." Sandy pulled her into a big hug, and Linda touched her arm with a shy smile.

"We're famished," Carolyn announced. "What do you want, Bree? You sit here with these little piggies while I go get something for us."

"We got tired of waiting for you two," Sandy said, then took a bite of her barbecue sandwich, while Linda sipped a large drink. "See anything interesting downtown?"

"The old cars. And I bought some ribbon-cane syrup."

Carolyn took Bree's order and hurried away toward the food stalls.

"So what's going on here?" Bree asked as she sat down in a folding chair next to Linda and across from Sandy.

"Obviously this is the food area," Linda said. "And that building over there's part of the museum. It has a lot of exhibits demonstrating how people used to make things."

"Such as?" Bree asked.

"Oh, quilts, lace, soap. You'd probably enjoy it."

Sandy finished eating her sandwich and wiped a spot of sauce from her cheek with a napkin. "The main part of the festival is in that fenced-off section behind the old depot. Over there." She pointed at the long red building that had stood beside active railroad tracks when Bree was a child.

Bree raised a brow. "Remember what we used to call the only train that ever came here?"

Sandy laughed. "Sure do. The *H* and *O B* and *F*."

"That must have been before my time. What on earth?" Linda asked.

"We all called it the Henderson and Overton Back and Forth," Sandy and Bree said at the same time, and laughed.

Carolyn walked up, her hands full. "What are y'all cackling about?" She handed Bree her food and sat down next to Sandy. "You might know I'd miss something good."

"The *H* and *O B* and *F*. Linda never even heard of it."

"Why did they call it that?" Linda asked in a little-girl voice and put on a pouty expression.

Sandy finally explained. "The train went from Henderson to Overton once a day, and when it reached Overton, it didn't have room to turn around, so it just backed up from Overton to Henderson."

"That's not funny. That's sad," Linda said.

"Why sad?" Bree asked.

"Well, the townspeople must have expected great things when the railroad company went to all the trouble to build the tracks and such a huge depot. But the train later just became a joke for all the kids to laugh about. That's why."

"I remember when they used to ship cotton and tomatoes on the train," Carolyn said.

"And they must have shipped canned goods too, because a big warehouse full of them burned down in the early '50s," Sandy said.

"But you're right, Linda," Bree said. "It is sad."

"Thank you." Linda gave Bree a smile.

"Actually, a lot of history's sad," Bree said. "It makes us realize we're getting older and how things change and we can't do a thing about it."

Sandy slammed a hand down onto the table. "But we're still alive and kicking. So after you and Carolyn finish feeding your faces,

Bree, let's go enjoy the rest of the syrup festival and celebrate still being here and able to enjoy such a beautiful day."

❖

After they paid their admission fee, Linda and the others strolled through the old depot and looked at the various exhibits depicting the history of the county and its still-flourishing folk arts. She always liked to study the quilts on display. Judging by all their tiny stitches, a quilt-maker must have spent hundreds of hours to produce just one. How patient the women were who decided on a design, found just the right fabric to use, cut it into squares, and then sewed them together, even if they used a sewing machine instead of their fingers.

A tune popped into her head, something about handmade quilts and handmade love. After a few minutes, Linda found herself humming.

"I've heard that one," Bree whispered to her, and winked. Linda blushed.

"I'm tired of standing around. I want some action," Sandy said. "Let's go watch the mule make syrup."

As they walked down the ramp from the old depot to the area behind it, Linda stopped to survey the scene. It spread out in front of them like a Bruegel painting, full of people bustling around and engaged in so many different activities it was hard to process them all.

Huge oak trees provided plenty of shade, and people clustered under them selling homemade jams and jellies, soap, herbs, and brooms. Children darted in and out, and adults strolled over to inspect the tractor exhibits and ate kettle corn from huge bags.

"Let's go over there," Sandy said. "I need a new broom."

"Is your Dyson on the blink?" Carolyn asked, deadpan, and Sandy gave her a knowing glance.

"No, silly. You know why I want a new one."

Linda and Bree lagged behind, and Bree asked, "What's going on with them?"

"She uses a broom to sweep our ritual area before every ceremony. You know, for the Greenies."

"Oh. Not to ride?" Bree chuckled, and Linda elbowed her with a grin.

"Don't even joke about it," Linda whispered. "Somebody might take you seriously. Hey, I need some herbs. Let's go over to that table."

While Linda examined the plants, Bree wandered over to watch the syrup-making. Linda joined her eventually, carrying a brown paper bag with some plants sticking out the top of it.

"So is this what the festival's supposed to be about?" Bree asked. "Exactly what are they doing here?"

"Making syrup from sugarcane. It's fairly simple. See the machine in the center of that area?" Linda pointed to a large fenced-off section. "It has three steel rollers inside. And you can see how the mule's hitched to the long pole attached to the machine."

Bree nodded.

"Watch. As the mule walks, he makes the rollers turn."

"Wonder how he feels," Bree murmured. "Poor old thing.'"

Warmed by Bree's concern for the mule, Linda took her hand and led her closer to the fenced-off area. "The guys wearing overalls and baseball caps are feeding ribbon cane into one side of the machine and pulling the crushed canes out on the other side," she explained. "Then they collect the juice in buckets and cook it in big vats until it produces the kind of syrup you bought."

Carolyn and Sandy emerged from the crowd and stood beside them, watching the mule plod around and around. Finally Carolyn broke their trance. "Want to go listen to the sacred-harp singing?"

The eerie music had always appealed to Linda, and as she stood at the edge of the crowd listening to the songs her ancestors had sung, she felt pulled back into another time. People had been connected more strongly to the changing seasons and to their surroundings back then. That was one reason witchcraft attracted her. Also, the magic had disappeared from her life, and she wanted to find some way to regain it.

Bree murmured, "Let's go sit down. I'd like to enjoy the music awhile."

Maybe Bree had a similar thought.

They found two empty seats near the merry-go-round, and the almost-discordant music evoked a type of peace Linda hadn't felt for a long time. She blew out a deep breath and watched the children ride the carousel. It seemed like she and Bree existed inside a bubble as they sat there side by side. She grew philosophical. Was everyone riding in a circle until the music stopped and they wandered to a new destination?

Linda glanced at Bree. What did she think of all this? What did she think of her? Every time she was near Bree, she wanted to know the answer to these questions even more.

Bree tried to make sense of the magic whirling around her. Oak trees, eerie music, brooms, herbs—what had Linda, Carolyn, and Sandy stumbled into? Ever since she'd attended their Samhain celebration two weeks ago, she'd begun to look at the world differently. Oh, the change was subtle. She was seeing the same objects she'd always seen, but some of them had an underlayer she'd never noticed.

Even the puzzle she and her mother had begun to put together yesterday seemed to hint at a deeper meaning. To begin with, why had she even chosen it from the huge assortment she'd found at Walmart? Was she Dorothy, traveling down the yellow brick road through a field of wildflowers with her three companions, headed toward a yellowish-purple sky? Being back here in her hometown reminded her of being in Oz. Everything was familiar, yet everything had changed. Or was only she changing?

Suddenly, someone shook her. "Hey, Bree. Snap out of it." Sandy had her hand on her shoulder. "We want you to see the old doctor's office and the three-hole outhouse our local historical society has preserved here on the grounds. Somebody with your background in museums should appreciate them."

Bree followed her friends, though her Oz-like feelings still tickled her.

A chill breeze had begun to overshadow the sun's warmth when Carolyn looked at her watch. "This has been so much fun. Why don't we keep it going at my house? I've got several pounds of peeled frozen shrimp. What do you say to some creole?"

"I'd forgotten how much people down here like to eat," Bree said. "But count me in. I'll even make dessert."

"I wouldn't want to miss that," Linda said. "How about I go home and grab some veggies and a loaf of French bread, Carolyn? You can start making the roux, and I'll help cook when I get there."

Sandy jumped up from her folding chair. They'd wandered back over to listen to the last music performance of the day. "I don't want to be left out. I'll go home and whip up a green salad and see you over at Carolyn's as soon as I can."

At her home, Linda rushed inside and gathered the ingredients she'd promised. Then she foil-wrapped the bread she'd bought this morning and drove to Carolyn's.

Soon they stood side by side in her kitchen. Linda minced garlic and chopped two onions while Carolyn stood at the stove, stirring the roux. After it turned a dark brown, Linda dumped the pungent vegetables into the hot iron skillet.

A gust of steam smacked her in the face when the vegetables sizzled. "Love that smell," she said as she watched Carolyn caramelize the onions and garlic in the roux. Linda then opened two quart jars of tomatoes and a bag of frozen green peppers.

"Nothing like that aroma, is there?" Carolyn said.

"Nope. Where'd you learn to make a roux like that?"

"In the Beaumont area. I had a lot of Cajun friends who'd moved there from Louisiana, and they taught me to appreciate their French culture. It's a whole different world down there."

"Different how?"

"More relaxed. You know. *Laissez les bons temps rouler.*"

"Yes. I haven't spent any time in Southeast Texas, but I have been to Razzoo's restaurant in Tyler. They definitely let the good times roll there, especially if you buy one of their oversized drinks. All four of us could get drunk on just one."

"Speaking of alcohol, will you grab a couple of bottles of white wine from the rack over there and stick 'em in the fridge? Just enough to chill them."

"Sure. What kind of dessert do you think Bree's going to bring? I didn't think she cooked at all."

Carolyn dumped the tomatoes into the roux mixture, then chopped the peppers and added them. After pouring in a little water and letting the mixture boil, she covered the skillet and turned the fire to low. "No telling what Bree'll come up with. She's probably at Walmart or Kroger right now, standing in their frozen section and trying to decide."

Linda located the wine and put it in to chill as Carolyn washed their cooking utensils. "The shrimp are thawing. We can add them after Sandy and Bree get here."

Linda stuck the loaf of bread she'd brought into the oven. They could warm it later.

"Let's go rest." Carolyn wiped her hands on a dish towel. "Do you want something to drink now, or would you rather wait for the others?"

"I better wait. I'm not a big drinker, and it'll be more fun with all four of us here. Like an impromptu ceremony or ritual."

"Agreed."

They settled down in Carolyn's den. "I've been dying to ask you something, Linda. Are you and Bree seeing each other?"

"Seeing each other? What do you mean?" Linda positioned a cushion behind her back as she found a comfortable spot on Carolyn's oversized couch.

"Like in dating? Sarah mentioned that you two drove to Tyler to some kind of dinner with some other women and to Kilgore to see some museums."

Linda laughed. "So because we're both lesbians, we must be sleeping together. Is that what you mean?"

Carolyn looked like she'd been caught shoplifting at Walmart. "Why, no."

"I hate to disappoint you, but we're just friends. Lesbians don't have sex on their mind all the time. And they don't fall into bed with each other at the drop of a hat, even if that's what most straight people think."

Carolyn squirmed in her easy chair. "I didn't think that. But you know how people talk."

"At our age? We're just getting to know each other. We were never really friends. If Bree and Ann were spending this much time together, though, people might have something to talk about."

Carolyn raised a brow. "What do you mean? Ann's had five husbands and is due to come home any day now with number six. She's straighter than a stick."

Linda squirmed, and her face felt unusually hot. "I just meant… oh, I don't know why I even said that. I meant, they were so close once." Someone rang the doorbell. "Just forget what I said. But remember—Bree and I are just friends."

"I sure will," Carolyn said as she got up and headed toward the door. "I'm coming," she called.

Linda just sat there. Why on earth would Carolyn, or anyone, think anything special was going on between her and Bree? Why, Bree was as sophisticated as Linda was country. She'd never be interested in her. Besides, she was apparently still hung up on Ann, which depressed Linda more than it should.

As Bree walked in behind Sandy, Carolyn said, "It's about time you two got here. Take a load off."

Bree carried a big bag that contained their dessert into the kitchen, and when she reentered the den, Carolyn handed her a glass of wine. "This okay for you?"

"Perfect."

They all looked at her expectantly, and Linda said, "Okay. We already have a bet going. I say you actually made the dessert you brought, and these other two said you bought it."

Bree sat on the couch next to Linda and took a sip of wine. "You're all right. I made some baked apples and brought some store-bought Blue Bell ice cream to go on them. They're hot from baking, so I put them in Carolyn's oven. When she heats the bread they can finish cooking and still be warm after we finish our creole."

"Oh, shit." Carolyn jumped up. "I forgot to fix some rice. Is instant okay with everybody?"

Sandy cradled her wineglass in her hands and gazed into it as if it were a crystal ball. "I see gummy, gooey white rice instead of the flaky, long-grained brown rice I'd envisioned slathering my creole over."

Carolyn laughed and swatted Sandy's arm with the evening paper she'd picked up on her way in. "All right. I'll fix brown. But it'll take a lot longer than instant."

Sandy held up her glass. "How many bottles of this did you chill?"

"Two. And I have more in the wine rack."

"I vote for brown rice," Linda said.

Bree nodded. "And I support the majority decision."

Carolyn hurried back into the kitchen, singing out, "I won't be but a minute. Don't talk about me while I'm gone."

Bree looked around at the others. "While we wait, I want to know more about this type of witchcraft you've become involved in. All kinds of weird stereotypes of hags in black dresses riding broomsticks are flying around in my head."

Sandy grinned. "I felt the same way when my friends in California introduced me to it. But it's actually a lot simpler than you'd think."

"Okay. I really would like to hear more."

"Let me try to explain," Linda said. "When you were a kid, were you ever impatient for something to happen or for someone you really liked to come visit you?"

Bree thought for a minute. "Yes. I'm going back a long way, but I remember playing in our sandbox and wondering when two of my dad's cousins would drive in from West Texas. He was looking forward to seeing them so much, his excitement must have rubbed off on me."

"And how did you handle the situation?" Linda asked.

"I recall thinking for a long while that I'd explode if they didn't get there. Then, finally, I got so caught up in making some kind of sand project, I lost track of time. Before I knew it they were pulling into the driveway. It was like magic."

"Exactly. That's the kind of magic green witchcraft deals with."

Sandy had scooted forward on the couch and seemed to want to say more. "I slip into that magic place when I'm driving cross-country or staring into a flame."

"For me, soaking in a warm bath filled with good-smelling herbs will do it every time," Linda said. "I slow down and let go of whatever's trying to make me anxious, and not only does time disappear, but I begin to feel more centered."

"And that's all there is to it?" Bree asked. It was such a simple concept she wasn't sure it even deserved a name, especially such a loaded one as witchcraft.

Carolyn, who'd come back and was standing in the doorway listening to their conversation, said, "One of the things I like best about our brand of witchcraft is visualizing both a goddess and a god."

"Why's that? I don't relate well to deities, regardless of their gender."

Sandy jumped into the discussion. "I have a Catholic background, so the concept of revering both a female and a male deity isn't so foreign to me as it would be to a Protestant. It helps keep me balanced spiritually and emotionally."

"If I haven't been involved in any type of religion in forever, would it work for me to visualize a strong butch and a strong femme figure?" Bree was half serious and half joking.

Linda sat still for a minute. "I don't see why not. I've told you we're not a formal group. We meet when we feel like it, but we never try to impose our beliefs and practices on each other. We're kind of a spiritual support group."

Bree looked at her friends. They were apparently serious, and their premise intrigued her. "So how do you join?"

Carolyn smiled. "You have to undergo a rigorous background check."

"And have references from several influential members of the group," Sandy added.

"Don't forget the grueling initiation." Linda's eyes twinkled. "What do you think, girls? Does she qualify?"

Sandy and Carolyn looked at Linda, who inclined her head a fraction, then stared at her for a long minute.

"Will you be true to yourself and try to be the best and most authentic person you can be?" Sandy said in a deep, solemn voice.

Bree's throat tightened unexpectedly as she considered Sandy's question. "I'll do my best."

Bree's friends exchanged glances and then each nodded. "I'm happy to say you're now a novice green witch. Welcome to the Greenies. If you have any questions, just ask one of us and we'll do our best to answer them. And if we can't, we'll make something up." Sandy grinned.

Carolyn held up her wineglass. "To Bree. Welcome home."

"It's great to be back," Bree said. And she meant it. She finally was beginning to feel like she belonged somewhere.

"The homegrown vegetables in the creole make a world of difference." Bree took another fork full and examined the mixture. "Canned can't rival these tomatoes."

"Bree's right. This creole's the best I've ever eaten, Carolyn," Linda said as she spread a ladle full of it over some rice for a second time.

Bree stirred her fork through the salad in her bowl. "And your salad's so full of interesting things, Sandy. Did you stick some magic herbs in it?"

"You'd think the poor woman never got anything to eat after she left home." Carolyn winked at her.

Bree chewed, content as the familiar flavors flooded her. "You know, I've eaten exotic food all over the world, from Peking duck in Beijing to fūl in Egypt, plus a lot of things whose names I can't even remember. But I never found anything I preferred to my mother's cooking. Until now."

"I'm truly flattered. That's quite an endorsement," Carolyn said. "Next time I visit Sarah I'll make a list of everything she used to cook for you. That way, maybe we can entice you to stick around. Why go back to Chicago when you can have food and friends like us down here?"

Bree hesitated. "I left this town because I was a misfit. Don't you really think I'd fit in even less after all this time?" She wanted to be wrong, but now that she thought about it, she wasn't sure small towns had changed all that much, even in the fifty years she'd been away.

Sandy shook her head. "Just look at me. I'm like a triangle stuck in a circle here, but I do touch the circle at a few points. I love living on my acreage with Zoe and Cowboy and getting together with my friends like this. Nothing fancy, nothing exciting, just everyday life with a little magic thrown in to keep me content. I don't have to prove anything to myself or anybody else, so I can just relax and enjoy whatever comes along. "

Bree put down her fork and scratched her cheek. "Yes, but you're so much older than the rest of us, Sandy."

Sandy tossed a crust of bread at Bree, which hit her on the arm.

"Now, girls," Carolyn intervened, "Sandy's just six years older than you, Bree. Don't forget I'm almost eighty, and I can still cut the mustard. The older you get, the more life speeds up, if you let it. You need to start looking around and realizing what's most precious to you and how you want to spend what time you have left."

Linda jumped up. "That's enough talk about getting old. What I want to know right now is how well Bree can actually cook. Didn't we say those baked apples are part of our decision about whether to let her into the Greenies?"

"You said nothing of the sort. You've already let me in." Bree put on a panicked expression.

"Rules can change, if the majority agrees. Can't they, girls?" Linda looked around at Carolyn and Sandy.

"Absolutely. Especially if the candidate makes disparaging remarks about a member's age," Sandy said.

Carolyn nodded. "I concur. Bring out the baked apples."

Bree slowly rose from the table and cleared the others' plates from it, then trudged into the kitchen as if she were about to present her doctoral dissertation to a committee of demanding professors.

Linda came in carrying the dirty bowls and silverware and whispered, "Want some help?"

Bree sighed like a martyr. "I better do this all by myself. Don't want to be disqualified."

She removed the apples from the warm oven and carefully spooned one into each of the four brightly colored bowls Carolyn had set out. Then she scooped a large dip of vanilla ice cream onto each apple and carried two of the bowls into the dining room.

"For the seniors," she said as she defiantly set the bowls in front of Carolyn and Sandy. When she returned with the other two desserts, she served Linda first and then herself.

"You better start eating before your ice cream melts, Bree," Sandy said.

Carolyn took a big bite of apple. "Hmm. Soft yet still a bit of crunch. Though maybe a little too much cinnamon."

"Not too much brown sugar and butter," Linda added.

"And exactly the right flavor of ice cream to complement the apple." Sandy scraped her empty bowl. "What do you girls think? Shall we admit Bree unconditionally?"

Linda wiped her mouth with her napkin. "I vote yes."

"But she didn't call you old," Sandy said. "What do you think, Carolyn? After all, you said she added too much spice."

Carolyn wiped the side of her mouth with her finger. "I can do with a little more spice in my life. I've known Bree all her life and think highly of her mother, so I'll have to go along with Linda's endorsement."

"I guess it's up to me then," Sandy said and assumed a stern expression. "We can't let just anyone into the Greenies."

"Hey, what about majority rules?" Bree asked.

"Sorry, but this isn't a democracy." Sandy looked even sterner, then broke into a big smile. "And I declare this one of the best baked apples I've ever eaten. If you can put up with our teasing, we'd love for you to be part of our group."

Bree puffed out a big breath. "You actually had me worried there for a minute. I can't promise how long I'll be in town, but as long as I am, it looks like I'll enjoy myself." She gazed around at her friends and wondered again why she'd always avoided visiting home.

CHAPTER FIFTEEN

Hey, good-looking," a woman's voice said over the telephone. Bree sat in the back-porch swing, enjoying the cloudless sky.

"Hey, yourself. Who's this?" Bree couldn't quite place her.

"Who'd you expect? Linda?"

The tinge of jealousy clued Bree in. "Ann. Are you calling from Hawaii?"

"No, silly. I decided to come home early so I could see you."

Yes, this was definitely Ann in her jealous-flirtatious mode. How could Bree ever forget it? The few times she'd tried to break it off with Ann in high school, her possessiveness had surfaced immediately and pulled Bree back in every time.

"I thought you'd be happily married by now and have decided to stay even longer." Bree tried not to sound bitter but couldn't stop herself.

"No. Things didn't work out the way I expected. Can you imagine being bored in Hawaii?"

"No." Bree watched a large leaf float to the ground.

"Well, imagine it. Same old beach every day. Same old food. Same old man. I decided if he bored me in Hawaii, I'd never enjoy being married to him, especially living in this dull town."

"At least you had that revelation before you tied the knot, again." Bree sniffed and finally recognized a familiar acrid odor. She hadn't just sat and enjoyed the smell of burning leaves in forever. Retirement might not be such a bad idea.

"Live and learn. Though I probably sacrificed a healthy divorce settlement." Bree could picture Ann's shrug. "But even that couldn't entice me. Enough about me though—what have you and Linda been up to?" Her seductive tone was impossible to miss.

"Linda and I? Let's see. We went to a couple of museums in Kilgore and to the syrup festival here. And we've bumped into each other several times at Silverado, the retirement home." Now that Bree thought about it, those experiences had been the highlight of her visit so far.

"Sounds like a laugh a minute. So admit it. Aren't you glad I'm back?" Ann shifted into full flirtation mode, her husky voice promising illusions she'd too rarely fulfilled. "Maybe you and I can have some real fun before you desert us for Chicago again."

"Just what do you mean by real fun?" Bree couldn't believe she was still attracted to Ann, but she felt a familiar quicksilver streak dart up her inner thighs, followed by the crazy idea that maybe Ann would finally publicly admit her desire for her. To make things worse, after only a few minutes, Bree was already flirting back.

Ann gave a soft laugh. "Oh, you know. Just hanging out. I have this entire house to myself now." She sounded like a secret agent delivering confidential information. "We don't have to worry about anybody overhearing us, especially a sneaky little sister like Linda." Bree couldn't believe she was listening to this stuff. "What do you say? Want to come over tomorrow night, after I've unpacked and recovered from my jet lag?"

Bree struggled to ignore her soaring imagination and throbbing clit. "Where's Mr. Right going to be? Or did you give him his final walking papers?"

"Oh, he's tired from the trip." Ann blew out an impatient breath. "He won't be able to function for several days. In Hawaii he couldn't keep up with me."

Bree tried to keep the sudden disenchantment out of her voice. "So I'm a temporary distraction. Is that it?"

"Oh, honey. You're the best distraction I've ever come across." Ann practically purred. "If you weren't a woman, you'd be a permanent fixture in my life. In fact, if you intend to stick around here, maybe we could make that happen." Bree pictured Ann's smug expression. "I bet Carl wouldn't mind an arrangement like that. It'd give him an occasional breather."

How blatant. As a teenager Ann had been so subtle Bree had never been sure what she'd wanted from her. Had she become desperate or so used to getting her way she'd lost any type of guile?

Bree took a deep breath. "I have plans for tomorrow afternoon, Ann, and they might extend into the evening."

Ann drew in a sharp breath. "Plans you can't break or postpone? What? A bingo game at Silverado?"

"It's really none of your business, but Linda's invited me to go to tea in Tyler tomorrow."

"Tea?" Her laugh sounded more like a cackle. "Does she plan to introduce you to some Junior Leaguers over there?"

"Hardly." Leave it to Ann to think of a high-society event. "It's a weekly gathering of some freethinkers in the area. They discuss politics and religion and anything else that interests them."

"Sounds as boring as a sermon. Well, try to enjoy yourself with my little sister. But if you decide to indulge in some real fun, you know where to find me."

Bree wanted this conversation to end. "I'll keep that in mind, but I wouldn't hold my breath. Too much water's flowed under that bridge for me to want to get wet again."

"Ah, honey." Ann's wheedling tone resurfaced. "And to think I came home from a paradise like Hawaii just to be with you."

"Are you kidding me?"

"Not at all." Ann actually sounded serious. "I started worrying you might have already left town, but when I called Linda on Sunday, she said you and she and Sandy had been to a party at Carolyn's." She paused and took a deep breath. "That's how I knew you were still around. She seemed to have had a great time, and for a minute I wondered if you and she had—you know—gotten together after the party."

Did Ann really care who she spent time with?

Ann kept talking. "So I decided I better come stake my claim before she raised her hopes too high." Staking a claim? How objectifying could Ann get? "You wouldn't want to hurt her too badly, would you?"

Bree couldn't believe how little Ann thought of Linda…and of her. "What do you think I am, a gold mine?"

"Oh yes. The richest vein I've ever discovered. And I certainly don't intend to let anyone else put a shaft in you, especially my dear little sister."

Was she finally beginning to see behind the screen Ann had always used to project herself as a great and mighty Oz? "Good talking to you, Ann," Bree said, forcing herself to be civil. "Look, I promised my mother I'd help her finish something we started last week and need to go. See you around."

"But—"

Bree hung up before Ann exposed her unattractive side more fully. Even Bree liked to have a few illusions. If she didn't, she'd probably have to give up on people altogether and hibernate for the rest of her life.

❖

"You haven't worked much on our puzzle, have you, Sarah?" Bree asked as they sat at the small folding table in the lounge area at Silverado where they'd left their puzzle spread out, half finished.

"Actually, I've been too busy. Remember that old 1918 telephone book we donated to the Houston Historical Society?"

"Yeah. I was glad we found a home for it."

"The members wrote a big article featuring it and asked me to pose for a picture to accompany it. That was yesterday's adventure."

"So that's why you asked me to buy you a new silk blouse and had your hair done."

Sarah smiled like the cat that got the cream.

"Why didn't you tell me?"

"I'm sorry for being greedy, but I wanted to keep it all to myself awhile. It's not everyday I'm involved in something like this anymore."

"You certainly kept your secret well."

"I'm not sure how. I couldn't eat or sleep after they told me about it. And posing for that picture yesterday almost wore me out. But I had a good night's sleep, and now I'm ready to settle down with our puzzle."

"I'm proud of you. You've always been important, not only to me but to everyone who knows you."

Sarah reddened and reached for a puzzle piece. "Thank you. That means a lot." She finally met Bree's gaze. "I know I've been silly, getting so excited over something that must seem trivial to you." She sighed with what sounded like contentment. "But it's nice to still feel a part of the mainstream, if you know what I mean. Out here, it's too easy to feel shuffled to one side, like we don't have anything left to contribute to anybody."

They sat in silence, Bree absorbing Sarah's uncharacteristically intimate confession.

"Guess who came home early?" Bree finally said.

"Came home from where?"

"From her vacation."

"I don't know anyone who's been on vacation."

"Okay, from her honeymoon. I just gave away my surprise."

"You mean Ann?" Sarah looked up with a glint in her eyes.

"Yes."

"So, what's her last name now? I can't keep up."

"The same as when she left town last week."

"You mean she didn't go through with it? What happened? And how did you find out?"

"She just called me not an hour ago, complaining of being bored with Hawaii and with Carl. That's his name, I just found out."

"Bored in Hawaii?" Sarah lifted a brow. "She ought to try living out here. We have to struggle to keep our life interesting."

Bree glanced around the small open area, furnished with various sizes of tables and chairs. Residents often gathered here to work jigsaw puzzles. After a lost-looking man had slowly pushed his walker past them and disappeared down the hall, Sarah said, "Ann always expected everyone else to entertain her, didn't she? Frankly, I never understood why you were so crazy about her. Still are, aren't you?" She seemed to look right through Bree.

"I can't believe you just said that."

Sarah shrugged. "I'm finally learning that sometimes it's best to just state what you think and not worry about the fallout."

So that's why Sarah had acted so different lately. Bree decided to see how open she'd be. "Since we're on the subject, what do you know about the relationship between Ann and Linda?"

"Why do you ask?" Sarah assumed her old evasive expression. Their unfiltered conversation certainly hadn't lasted long.

Bree brushed her bangs back and hoped she appeared nonchalant. "After spending so much time with Linda, I'm beginning to see her side of things. I've always thought of her as just Ann's annoying little sister."

Sarah frowned. "So Ann considered her annoying? Hmm." She didn't speak for several seconds. "That doesn't surprise me." She paused again. "And her dad probably had a hand in that too."

"Her dad?" Where had that come from? What was her mother talking about? "Why would he take Ann's side and not Linda's? I thought parents usually spoiled the youngest child."

"Not always. Not when she's not…"

"Not what? What do you mean?"

Sarah pressed her hand over her mouth, a cautious expression shuttering her eyes. But Bree held her gaze and slowly pulled the hand away. "You can tell me. You've kept whatever secret you've held back long enough, don't you think?"

Sarah grasped one of her own hands with the other and massaged the base of her fingers. Finally, she blew out a long breath. "You're right. I don't want to die knowing something that might make a difference to others—especially someone as sweet and caring as Linda."

"You're talking in riddles. You're not going to die anytime soon. But won't you tell me what you know now?"

Sarah sighed and sat back in her chair. "I hope Linda's mother, God rest her soul, will forgive me." She took another deep breath. "But I need to get this off my chest. And you and Linda need to know what I'm about to say." She glanced around the area as if she saw strangers lurking behind the potted plants. "Let's go back to my room so we can have some privacy."

As Bree walked slowly down the hall beside Sarah and her red walker, she glanced at the woman who'd once seemed so aloof and independent.

"Here we go," Bree said as she pushed the door open and waited for Sarah to sit down in her recliner. Bree perched on the only other chair in the small living area. Did Sarah really know something about Linda's mother, or was she fabricating it to keep herself from being bored?

Sarah stared at her as if she could read her mind. "I know what you're thinking, Breanna Principal. I can see it on your face. But what I'm about to tell you is as true and as real as that television set or that microwave over there."

"Okay. I'm listening. And no one can overhear us in here."

"You won't tell anyone what I've said unless you truly believe it'd help them have a better life?" Sarah fixed her with a glare she recalled from childhood.

"No. I'll be as careful and considerate as you've been all these years." Bree had no idea what she was agreeing to, but she wanted to find out what Sarah had to say.

"I met two women at an art exhibit in Dallas during the war. They'd moved to France just after World War I, and their son Patrick still lived there. Brett and I stayed with him and his French wife and son when I studied painting in Paris during the summer of 1948."

"I remember. I was just three, but I'll never forget how you and he stayed gone what seemed like forever. I don't know which of you I missed most."

"I missed you too and swore I'd never leave you again for that long."

Bree felt a stab of pain. "Why did you take Brett and not me?"

Her mother looked apologetic yet firm. "He always needed me more than you did, and your father and Carolyn's parents took good care of you." She rubbed her cheek. "I couldn't leave two babies with him though."

"I always envied Brett. Sometimes I think that's why I chose a profession that involved so much travel."

"Perhaps. I'm sorry."

"Me too, though now I'm glad you could do something you loved so much." Bree paused. "But what does your summer in Paris have to do with Linda?"

"I know you think I'm rambling, but you need a little background so you can understand what I'm about to tell you."

Bree let out a huge sigh. What had she done to deserve a mother who considered genealogy as important as the three *R*s?

"The next year, Patrick came to Dallas to visit his mother Molly and her partner Jaq. He stayed with us several weeks too."

"Now I remember him." Bree got up and opened a Diet Coke, then poured it into a glass of ice. "Tall, red hair getting a little gray by then. And so nice." She took a sip. "Funny. I'd forgotten all about him being here."

"He wanted to see an old farm down at New Hope, where he lived as a boy, so we all drove out there one day." Sarah gazed over at the sliding glass door and into the courtyard. "We visited his grandmother's grave in the community cemetery, and his dad's too. He seemed quite emotional."

Bree began to calm down and enjoy Sarah's reminiscences. But what was her point?

"Patrick was delightful—well educated and the perfect guest." She looked wistful.

"Did he enjoy his visit? I don't remember much about it."

Sarah smiled. "Evidently, he did. I had no idea how he occupied himself when he wasn't at the house with us, but a few months after he left, I found out."

Someone knocked on the door, and a woman who lived down the hall came in. "Ready, Sarah?"

Her mother glanced up at the clock. "Gracious. The time's flown." She lowered the leg rest on her recliner. "Be ready in a minute." Sarah jumped up as fast as she could manage. "I need to go, or I'll miss supper. Come back in the morning and I'll finish my story."

"Are you serious? Aren't you almost through?"

"I've waited this long and kept this secret so close, I need to hold it another day. See you tomorrow."

Bree got up, disappointed, and waited until Sarah disappeared down the long corridor toward the dining room.

As she meandered out to her car, her mind whirled with the events of the day—her feelings for Ann and Linda, and now her mother's strange behavior. What was Sarah being so mysterious about, and why?

Chapter Sixteen

Linda crouched in her backyard, digging up some amaryllis whose green, swordlike tops had begun to turn yellowish-brown. She'd wanted to divide them and plant them in another flower bed for several years now, but she always got too busy or forgot to dig them up at the right time.

She'd just stuck her trowel deep into the rich soil to dig a trench, when her cell phone rang. She should have left the noisy thing inside, but she never knew when a grandchild might need a ride somewhere or she might have to babysit.

She jerked off her filthy glove and picked up her phone. Her grandbabies would be grown before she knew it, and she wanted to enjoy every minute of their childhood. "Hello."

"Hey, Linda. Guess what? I'm home early."

"What's going on, Ann?" Linda sat on the ground, its damp coolness immediately seeping through her overalls.

"Oh, I decided to postpone getting married and didn't see much point in staying any longer."

Linda reached for a nearby bottle of water and took a sip. "I'm sorry it didn't work out. Like I told you Sunday, everything's been fine here and at your place."

"Yeah, well, thanks for looking after things. What have you been up to, besides going to that silly old syrup festival?"

Linda struggled up from the wet ground and walked over to a chair near the pool. "Nothing different." She sat and sighed with relief. "Though I am taking Bree to meet some people in Tyler tomorrow afternoon. She doesn't have much to do except visit her mother every day. She'd lost touch with everybody but Carolyn, so it's almost like she's new in town."

"You're just being a Good Samaritan, eh?" Ann's tone was a little more acid than usual, probably because her plans hadn't worked out in Hawaii.

"Oh, I like Bree, a lot. But I don't have that much to offer her. She's used to a lot more excitement."

Ann's laugh sounded rather brittle. "Well, you're in luck. Don't go out of your way to entertain her anymore. I'll take over." Her tone had turned demanding. "After all, she was always *my* friend, not yours."

Linda stood and brushed off the back of her overalls. "Thanks for your concern, but I don't intend to cancel our plans." Sometimes Ann tried to push her just a little too far. "Surely Bree has time for both of us."

"We'll see." Ann sounded surprised yet determined. "Well, I don't want to keep you any longer. I'm sure you have lots of exciting things to do. 'Bye now."

Linda clicked off her phone and stared at it. What had all that been about? She shrugged and stretched her back, then walked over to her flower bed and picked up her trowel again. She wished Ann were still in Hawaii, happily married.

Linda had managed to dig up all her amaryllis and now sat on the concrete pool deck with the bulbs spread out in front of her. Her phone rang again.

"Hello." She answered more brusquely than usual. Her conversation with Ann had left a sour taste in her mouth, like biting into a plum that had gone bad.

"Hi, Granny. What's wrong?" It was Riley.

The sour taste in Linda's mouth turned sweet. "Oh, baby. Sorry I sounded grouchy. I'm a little tired. What's going on?"

"I just got home from school and wanted to say hi. Can I come over?"

"Of course. You mean right now? Is anything wrong?"

"No, not really." Riley sounded upset. "I've been missing you."

"I'll be right there. In fact, I need you to help me with something. I'm glad you called. Be sure to wear some old clothes."

"Good. See you soon. Love you."

"Love you too." Linda clicked off her phone, jumped up, and walked into the house to grab her car keys. Riley was just the person she needed to see.

❖

Wearing a faded pair of jeans and an orange-checked flannel shirt, Riley sat on a low plastic stool and held out an amaryllis bulb. "What are we supposed to do with this, Granny?"

Linda handed her the water hose and turned it on slightly. "We'll rinse off all the dirt first. And be sure not to pull any roots off."

Riley sprayed the water carefully on the bulb. "Okay. It's clean. Now what?"

"Turn it upside down and look at the bottom." When Riley did as asked, Linda pointed. "See those little bulbs growing around there in a circle?"

"Yeah. Look at all of them." Riley grinned.

"Those are all babies that grew from their momma."

"Wow. That's a lot. What do we do with them?"

"If we don't take them off her, she'll stop blooming." Linda could relate, but she'd always tried to keep her work and family responsibilities light enough that she could enjoy them instead of feeling overburdened. She wanted to teach Riley how to do the same with her life. "I want you to be really careful and break each one of them off. You can put them in a pile right over here."

"Won't that hurt them?"

She chuckled to herself. Riley had always been softhearted. "I'm not sure how much plants feel." She kept her tone firm. "But even if it does hurt a little, in the long run the babies will have a chance to grow and be beautiful flowers just like their momma."

"Or their granny?" Riley carefully snapped a small bulb from the root plate.

"Thanks, sweetheart." Most of Linda's pique at Ann slipped away. "We call the little bulbs clones. They'll look exactly like their momma, who looked exactly like her momma, so you're right. They'll be identical to their grandmother."

Riley smiled proudly. "Oh, goody. I want to be just like you when I grow up."

Linda swelled like a wilted leaf on a hydrangea bush just watered after a drought. "You will, Riley. And I hope you'll be even better than I am."

After they separated the amaryllis bulbs, Linda said, "Now we need to settle these into their new homes so they can start growing." Riley was one of the best results of her marriage.

"Where should we put them, Granny?"

"See that flower bed?" She pointed. "It gets sun most of the morning but is in the shade all afternoon. That way the hottest sun of the day won't scorch the flowers. You can help me carry them over there."

She hoped Riley never got scorched the way she had—by a divorce and a beautiful sister who always got what she wanted. Linda's earlier bitterness began to return.

As they started to dig holes in the rich, damp soil, Riley asked, "Won't the babies be lonesome all by themselves?"

Again, Linda chuckled to herself. "Maybe at first, but they'll get used to it." Linda recalled her lonely months after her divorce when she'd thought her life had ended. "And then they'll grow up and have beautiful flowers every year. They'll hold their heads high." Linda wished she could feel that way about herself right now. Why had Ann always made her feel so inadequate?

Riley eased a bulb into one of the holes they'd just dug. "Is this right?"

Linda spent some time inspecting it. "Don't plant it too deep. Just let the top of its head peek out." She made a minor adjustment, then smiled at Riley. "That's perfect, sweetheart. Good job."

Riley beamed and patted the dirt firmly around the bulb.

"After we finish," Linda said, "we'll spread some mulch over the bulbs, like a blanket. It'll keep them warm all winter. And in the spring, around Easter or Mother's Day, they'll shoot right up and bloom as pretty as can be. Do you know what a lot of people call them?"

Riley screwed up her mouth as she concentrated on planting the next bulb just right. "No, Granny. What?"

"Tulips of the South."

"I've seen pictures of tulips in one of our books at school. Don't they grow best in Holland?"

"Yes. They like the cool weather there."

"And amaryllises like it hot, I guess."

Linda almost laughed aloud. Riley had no idea of the double meaning of her words. "Yes, they like it hot, like we do."

They'd almost finished planting the bulbs when Riley said, "Granny, when you were little, you had lots of friends, right?"

So that's why Riley had sounded upset on the phone earlier. "Yes."

"Did any of them like somebody else better than they did you?"

Ah. That had to be the crux of the problem. Linda sighed. "They sure did. They always seemed to have a favorite, but they'd change their minds a lot. I felt great when I had a best friend, but then we'd have a fight or something and wouldn't like each other best anymore."

"Oh. Did that happen to you and Gramps?" This seemed to be a new realization for Riley.

"Yes. It's just the same. In some ways people get smarter as they get older, but in others they feel and act like they did when they were kids."

"Well, I don't like it when somebody likes another girl better than they like me." Riley stuck out her lower lip.

Linda imitated her expression and patted her arm. "Neither do I, Riley. Neither do I." Thank the Goddess for children, she thought.

On her way back from taking Riley home, Linda swung by Bree's house on a whim. Her little Mustang was sitting in the driveway so Linda pulled up behind it.

"Linda. What a surprise. Come on in. I was just burning some bacon. Want to eat a BLT with me?"

Linda sniffed the tangy air. "Sure. If you'll let me fry my own meat." She grinned.

"Gladly. How am I going to get this horrible odor out of the house?"

"Just use a little Febreze."

"What's that?"

"Honestly, Bree. Haven't you ever been in a kitchen? How have you made it on your own all these years?" Linda tossed the black strips of what used to be bacon into a garbage bag and washed out the frying pan. "Febreze is an air freshener. Just buy some at Kroger."

Bree stuck out her lower lip in a way that reminded Linda of Riley. "It's not my fault. Mother never let me in the kitchen because she wanted some peace and quiet when she got home from teaching school." Then Bree grinned and transformed into the woman Linda was beginning to treasure. "Besides, I was usually outside or involved in some project. So as an adult I've always stuck to the very basics or ate out or hired someone to come in and cook for me once a week."

Linda laid four strips of bacon side by side in the skillet and clicked on the gas, then lowered the blue flames to a medium height. "Poor thing. I bet Riley can cook better than you." She smiled. "But I can teach you the basics, if you want." She set the skillet on the fire.

"Would you? I always wanted to learn. Cooking seems as mysterious to me as overhauling the engine of my Mustang. What do I do first?"

Linda looked at the copper-bottom pans and skillets hanging from the nearby pot rack. "Timing's important when you prepare a meal, and making a BLT's a good place to start." She pointed to the refrigerator. "Get a tomato and a head of lettuce out of the refrigerator." Bree didn't move, and Linda pretended to be impatient. "You do have some, don't you?"

"I can shop for groceries, if that's what you're asking. I even have fresh bread," Bree said as she opened the refrigerator door.

"And grab the mustard and mayonnaise." Linda was beginning to enjoy her unfamiliar role as Bree's instructor.

"All I have is mustard. Okay?"

"It'll have to do. And don't forget pickles, preferably dill chips."

"Got it." Bree lined the items up on the white tile counter. "Now what?"

"You better turn the bacon over so it'll brown evenly on both sides."

Bree held the long black plastic fork awkwardly but managed to do as Linda directed. "Ouch. Some hot grease popped on my hand."

"What a sissy." Linda laughed. "Who'd ever suspect? And I used to think you could do everything you tried perfectly."

Bree pretended to be offended. "I can do almost everything perfectly. But why should I learn to cook when I can get someone to do it for me?" She put her hand over her mouth. "I sound like Ann, don't I?"

Linda pulled a paring knife from a knife block and waved it at her. "A little. Now, turn down the fire so the grease won't pop so much, and then I'll check some more of your skills." She handed Bree the knife. "Let me see you peel this tomato."

"Peel it?" Bree looked like she'd asked her to perform brain surgery. "I never peel tomatoes."

"Did you read the label?" Linda shook her head.

"No. Why should I?"

"To find out where the fresh produce you buy was grown."

Bree squinted at the small print on the tomato's white label. "It says product of Mexico."

"That's why you should peel it." Linda put her hands on her hips. "Haven't you ever heard of salmonella?"

"Of course I have."

"And you still feel safe eating an unpeeled tomato from Mexico?" Linda raised an eyebrow.

"Well, now that you mention it...Hey, you sound like my mother."

"And that's a good thing. Now peel the little sucker." Linda was really getting into the role but warned herself not to overdo it.

Bree hacked her way around the vegetable, wasting at least a third of it. "There." She held the massacred tomato up like it was a trophy. "How's that?"

"It'll have to do." Linda handed her a paper plate from the stack she'd found in the pantry. "Okay, slice it onto this plate and then go turn the bacon again."

"What a slave driver," Bree muttered as she stood at the stove. "No wonder I never learned to cook. It's more complicated than I realized." But she grinned. "What next?"

Linda held out a head of iceberg. "You need to core and wash this lettuce."

"Oh, that's easy." Bree immediately grabbed a knife and began to plunge it into the bottom of the head.

"Whoa. That'll work, but let me show you a better, faster way."

"Jeez." Bree laid her knife down. "I'm going into information overload."

Linda laughed. "I promise it's not complicated. Just hold the lettuce in two hands, the core side on the bottom."

"Like this?" Bree gazed at the iceberg as if it were an alien artifact.

"That's perfect. Now, slam it down onto the counter as hard as you can."

"Slam it? Really? Won't that hurt it?"

"I've never had one complain. Come on. You can do it."

"All right, but I just hope I'm not arrested for lettuce abuse."

Linda laughed. "I know a good lawyer in Tyler who can get you off if you are."

Bree took a deep breath. "Here goes." She winced as the head of lettuce hit the counter, then turned the head over and stared at it. "Now what?"

"Just pull the core out, wash the lettuce, and it's ready for our BLT."

"Hey, it worked." Bree acted like she'd just won a tricky hand of bridge.

"Yeah. Here's a couple of pieces of paper towel for you to put it on after you wash it."

Bree looked around the kitchen after she finished that chore. "Now what?"

"Bacon?"

"Oh, right." She rushed over to the stove and turned the pieces, brown and beginning to crisp. "Does it look almost done to you?" she asked as she peered into the skillet.

"Almost. I don't like mine very crunchy. What about you?"

"I like mine almost burned, but not as much as my first try."

"Then take mine out and drain it on some paper towel. By then, yours should be about right."

Bree toasted her wheat bread while Linda spread mustard on hers straight from the loaf. Then they loaded their two pieces with the ingredients they'd assembled and carried them to the square kitchen table.

Bree tossed several bags of chips onto the table. "What would you like to drink?"

"Milk, please."

"Two glasses of milk coming up. I can handle this part of a meal. Sarah always made me set the table and get the drinks."

"Great job." Linda bit into her sandwich. "Hmm. Delicious. I didn't have any idea of what to eat tonight. I'm glad I stopped by."

Bree sat down and tried her sandwich. "Yeah. Best BLT ever. I'll remember your lessons. How did you learn to cook?"

Linda chomped on a large Frito. "I always helped Mom in the kitchen, from about Riley's age. Maybe even younger. We thought of it as our special time together, by ourselves."

"Didn't Ann help?"

Linda shrugged. "Oh, she always had a date or did something else. She never liked to cook or clean."

"But you did?"

"I really did. Mom and I were close, I suppose because she was my real mom and just the stepmother of Ann and our brothers. She must have felt sorry for Ann, like I did, because her real mom had died, so she let her do what she wanted to."

Bree suddenly looked up from her sandwich and wiped a spot of mustard from the side of her mouth. "Hey, I guess you heard Ann decided not to get married and came home from Hawaii instead."

Linda took a drink of milk. "Yeah. She called me today. In fact, that's the main reason I stopped by. She acted weird, said I wasn't your friend. She also told me to stay away from you."

"Yeah. I kinda got that message too." Bree ate several potato chips, then stuck her hand back into the bag.

"Do you still want to go to tea with me tomorrow?"

Bree drained her glass of milk. "I wouldn't miss it for anything, or anyone. Ann's a grown woman, and she needs to act like one, at least most of the time."

Linda wasn't sure why, but Bree's words thrilled her so much she almost hugged her.

Chapter Seventeen

"Y ou're here bright and early." Bree's mother put down her paintbrush and limped the short distance to her recliner.

"Yes. I have plans this afternoon, but I wanted to hear the end of your story."

"Don't be in such a rush." Sarah pointed to a straight-backed chair. "Sit down and try to make yourself at home. I need to ask someone to bring me a softer chair. I chose that one to discourage visitors, but I'm beginning to enjoy having company."

Bree fit herself into the chair like a cat curling up in a small box. "My rear end would really appreciate it."

"Good. Now tell me about your plans for today."

"I thought I'd mentioned them, but Linda's taking me to Tyler to visit Tea at Troy's. It's a support and discussion group for nonconformists."

"Ah. A bunch of subversives. Sounds intriguing."

Bree had never considered her mother a nonconformist, but her love for painting and her summer in Paris had probably broadened her horizons more than Bree realized.

"Yes, it does. One of the hosts, Tom, used to teach English at several universities." Her mother nodded. "And the other one, Troy, got kicked out of the air force under Don't Ask, Don't Tell, back in the '90s. The first person that ever happened to."

"Wish I could go hear his story."

"Me too, but the doctor says you shouldn't walk any more than you have to. When you get better, maybe we can take you."

"I'll hold you to that. By *we*, I assume you mean you and Linda?"

"Yes, we've become friends. Last night she dropped by and taught me to make a decent BLT."

"I'm impressed. I always thought of her as talented, but I didn't realize she could work magic." She grinned. "No offense, darling, but your skills in the kitchen aren't top-notch."

Bree winced. "Don't I know it."

"Don't worry about it. I never did."

"You were a great cook."

"But I didn't worry about it. I just enjoyed myself."

"That's good to know, but why the big delay with your story?" Bree studied her. "That's suspicious."

Sarah blew out a long breath. "And deliberate. I can't decide if I should tell you the rest."

"You can't let me down now. You can trust me."

"But Linda's mother trusted me, and I don't want to betray her."

"Okay." Bree nodded. "I respect that. At least tell me about whatever you're painting now."

Sarah glanced over at her canvas. "It's based on a strange dream I had last night, about you trying on a long, Renaissance-looking dress and holding a homemade lute with twine strings. You sat in a movie theater, and suddenly a woman several seats away from you began to play an instrument similar to yours. Her beautiful song enchanted and awed us, especially when she hopped on a broomstick and zoomed up into the sky. I'm trying to paint her playing her lute."

"Wow. That's…different. It should be beautiful."

"I hope so. And now I think I'll finish my story."

"You'll never stop amazing me." Bree settled down even more, happy, yet puzzled over the meaning of her mother's dream.

"Several months after Patrick left, Linda's mother, Helen, stopped by to visit. She seemed frantic. She told me she was pregnant."

"When did you say that happened?"

"I didn't, but it was September," Sarah said.

"And Linda was born in early 1950. When did Helen get married?"

"She and Mr. White told everyone they ran away to Oklahoma in June of '49, but…"

"But they didn't?"

"No. It was actually later that very September. Being pregnant without being married back then would ruin a girl's life."

Bree nodded. "And it still could in the '60s. Remember how girls had to drop out of school, and most of us nice girls wouldn't associate with them?"

"That's exactly right."

Bree suddenly screwed up her face, thinking about Linda's mother. "Don't tell me. Patrick was the father and already married, so Helen was stuck."

"Yes. She confided in Mr. White, a close friend of the family who was recently widowed, and he offered to save her reputation. Oh, did I mention that Helen was gorgeous, and he had three young children who needed a mother?"

"That figures." Bree shook her head.

"He was also fifteen years older than her, and she was underage. Even her own mother told her not to do it."

"And Helen didn't love him. She loved Patrick. Right?"

"Uh-huh."

"So why did she discuss it with you?"

"She wanted to talk to someone besides her mother and knew I could keep a secret." Sarah shrugged. "She and Mr. White planned to get married the next day, and she had second thoughts."

"What did you advise her?"

"To make the best of a bad situation." Sarah rubbed her hands up and down her thighs as if trying to warm them. "I've regretted those words a lot. I wish I'd encouraged her to go somewhere far away and have her baby and try to find someone she loved."

Bree sighed. What a heavy burden to live with. "I'm sure you did the best you could. And she made her decision, not you."

"I realize that." Sarah blew out a deep breath. "But after that, I tried not to get involved in people's personal lives."

"I can understand, but finding out about Patrick's going to turn Linda's world upside down. She's considered Mr. White her father all these years."

"Exactly. Should we tell her the truth and upset her life completely, or should we just keep it to ourselves?"

Bree rested her head on one hand. "That's a hard decision. But I'm glad you told me. Maybe it'll help me understand what's going on between Linda and Ann."

❖

Bree and Linda chatted as they drove to Tyler, and Bree kept stealing glances at her. For sixty-five years Linda had lived with a lie about her father and her half sister. Did Ann know the truth? How much difference would it make to either her or to Linda if they found out?

She'd poke around a little before she said anything she might regret.

"How's Ann? Heard from her today?"

Linda seemed uneasy. "Why do you ask? Has she called you?"

"Nope. Not a peep. Just thought you two might talk to each other every day." How unsubtle could you get? Knowing about Linda's father somehow changed everything.

Linda sighed as she gazed at the road unwinding in front of them, the sun high in the sky. In contrast to the brown pastures and green pines, the rest of the trees had begun to blaze with red, orange, and yellow. "No. I've wished we were closer, but most of the time it's like we didn't even grow up in the same house, with the same parents. You'd think we'd have more in common."

She obviously didn't have a clue about what had really happened. "What's it like to have a sister? Do you recommend it?"

"Honestly, Mom seemed more like a sister than Ann did. And Ann seemed more like a mother."

"What do you mean?" Neither Linda nor Ann had ever said this before.

Linda gazed into the distance, like she was seeing far beyond the road, into the past. "I can't put my finger on it, but Mom and I were always like best friends." She glanced at Bree.

"That's nice. Best friends how?"

Linda smiled, evidently recalling fond memories. "I've already told you how we had the kitchen all to ourselves because Ann wasn't interested in cooking."

"Yes. Several times. You've convinced me you learned plenty about the subject." Bree laughed. "And can act like a drill sergeant in the kitchen."

"Wait till I get you out in the yard." Linda shook a warning finger. "You'll think of last night as a picnic."

Bree pretended to shudder.

Linda's voice took on a faraway tone again. "Mom loved the outdoors. She always had an herb garden and grew vegetables. She taught me all about herbs and how to use them, but Ann stayed a mile away."

"I wonder why."

"At times she acted like she didn't think she fit in. Strange," Linda said.

Not so strange, Bree thought, but sad. Apparently neither Linda nor Ann knew the truth.

"Which herbs did your mom grow?"

"Rosemary, basil, mint, dill, thyme, lavender, parsley, and sage. That's all I can recall."

"Sounds like an old Simon and Garfunkel song."

Linda laughed. "You're right. Mom and I used to love one in particular, uh…'Scarborough Fair'?"

"That's the name. You cooked with the herbs?"

Linda nodded. "Yep. At harvest time, we'd go out in the garden on a dry day, each of us with a basket on our arm, and gather them."

"What fun."

"It was. Mom taught me to tell each plant why I took a piece of it and ask its permission." Her face reddened a little, as if she was worried about Bree's reaction.

Bree laughed. "Did any of them refuse?" She enjoyed teasing Linda.

"No. They were very kind, agreeable plants." She also enjoyed having Linda tease her right back. But then Linda's expression grew serious. "However, Mom taught me to always be kind to everything and everyone, especially when asking for something."

"That makes sense."

"Does it?"

"Of course. Isn't Wicca's lone rule *Do no harm*?"

Linda's smile was radiant. "You're exactly right. She'd be proud of you for learning so quickly."

"And of you for teaching me."

Linda blushed again, as if brushing off the compliment.

"What did you do with the herbs?"

"Tied some of them into little bundles and hung them to dry in a small greenhouse where Mom stored her gardening tools." She took a deep breath, as if visualizing the little house. "I put the loose flowers and leaves in cloth bags, and then we hung them from nails, along with the bundles."

Bree wished she'd explored their property more fully, but Ann had never encouraged her to. "Bet that smelled good. What did she do with the herbs?"

"Used them in cooking, candles, and oil. Oh, and rosemary sachets."

"Did your mom ever mention the herbs to Ann?"

"Once."

"What happened?"

"Mom hung a rosemary sachet in Ann's closet and told her it symbolized love."

"How nice."

Linda frowned. "Yeah, but Ann threw it on the floor and stomped it. She said she didn't have any problem finding love on her own, called Mom silly and superstitious."

That didn't surprise Bree. Nothing but expensive French perfume would impress Ann. "What did your dad say?"

"He agreed with Ann, though in a lot more diplomatic way. He said Mom's herbs wouldn't hurt anybody and to just ignore them—they weren't worth getting upset about."

"Sounds like a little stepmother-stepdaughter thing." Bree was surprised she hadn't sensed it, but she'd focused mainly on Ann and her dad back then.

Linda sighed. "Yes. I tried to ignore it, but it wasn't easy. Dad got caught in the middle of a lot of their disagreements. He tried to smooth them over, but it seemed like he sided with Ann most of the time." Linda stopped at the red light near the Dairy Queen and turned on her blinker, then turned left.

Poor Linda, Bree thought, as they passed several churches and the UT Tyler campus, headed for the loop. And her poor mother, Helen. She was evidently more into pagan beliefs than her husband ever suspected. She probably revealed them only to Linda, and indirectly even then. But Ann wouldn't have anything to do with them and saw them only as a threat to her normal way of life and to the memory of her mother.

Telling Linda and Ann about Linda's real father would certainly open a big can of worms, as the locals would say, but they deserved to know the truth about who Linda was. Having this information would help level the playing field between the two sisters. But was it her secret to tell?

Linda drove around the loop until she hit Broadway, then turned left at a major intersection. The Christmas shoppers were already doing their thing at Dillard's, JCPenney, and Sears in the old enclosed mall she and Bree were passing now, the traffic in stop-and-go mode even on this early Thursday afternoon.

In two weeks, when Black Friday hit with all its craziness, the number of people in town would triple with shoppers from the outlying towns and communities, and she'd try to avoid Broadway altogether. At least the new mall would divert a lot of the holiday commercial traffic south of town, but it was located on Broadway too, so the entire street might become a giant parking lot similar to a Dallas freeway at rush hour.

"Started your Christmas shopping?" she asked Bree as they inched forward. They'd already sat through the traffic light twice, and she was beginning to be afraid they'd be late to tea.

"What Christmas shopping? The only people on my list are Sarah and Carolyn. I always give my mother some art supplies, but if you can think of anything else she might want or enjoy, how about letting me know. And does Carolyn need any witch supplies?" She chuckled. "I just can't get used to the idea of a coven existing right in the middle of a small East Texas town."

She smiled. "Correction. The First Baptist Church is right in the middle of town." She finally made it through the first traffic light. "Our coven's definitely on the outskirts of town, in more ways than one."

Bree settled back in her seat and adjusted her seat belt. "At least you're there, exercising the freedom-of-religion clause of the First Amendment. I say hooray for you."

They finally made it through four more traffic lights, necessary because of the endless stream of big-box behemoths, and reached the new mall on their left.

"I guess you knew about this addition to Tyler," Linda said, pointing to the shopping area that resembled a small city.

Bree stared at the recent development, then frowned. "No. All this was totally wooded the last time I drove by. What a shame."

Linda tried to sell it to Bree just to see what she'd say. "This mall has a hundred stores. And this new toll loop we're driving under right now should make this area boom, especially when it's finished all the way east to I-20."

"That's exactly what we need. New places to buy more stuff and a more direct route to get there." Bree looked like she'd bit into a lemon. "I've always thought of East Texas as a natural paradise, but it's beginning to look more like Chicago every day."

Linda shrugged. "It's not all bad. People from out of state are moving in all the time, and a lot of them are bringing new ideas and open minds."

"It just hurts me to think of those huge old trees giving their lives so I can have yet another place to buy a new brand of dog food or a set of tires."

"I know what you mean." Linda slowed down. "We're almost to Troy's," she said as she took a right onto a country road.

"This is more like it," Bree said as they passed huge heavily wooded tracts of land dotted by small businesses and residences. She pointed at a large sign identifying an attractively landscaped area that sprawled to her left. "South Campus. What's that? Another part of UT Tyler?"

Linda shook her head. "Afraid not. The largest Baptist church in town runs this campus. We've heard they teach teenagers how sinful homosexuality is and hold workshops here about how to deal with gays."

Bree frowned. "Do I want to know more about that subject?"

Linda didn't want to disillusion Bree so thoroughly that she'd catch the next plane back to Chicago, but she refused to lie. "No. It's not a pleasant one, but it's definitely a reality of life in this area."

"Almost makes me want to go pack my bags, but I'm not a quitter. In a way, it makes me want to stay and fight such insanity."

Linda straightened up with relief. "Well, those are some of the issues we discuss every week at tea, so you should feel right at home."

After they passed a large horse farm on their left, Linda turned right, then left.

"This is a beautiful neighborhood," Bree said as they passed brick houses lined up on comfortable-sized lots with tasteful landscaping. "I love the way they've left so many of the large trees."

"Yes. Tall Timbers is an appropriate name, isn't it?" They passed several more houses, each one featuring a tall brick mailbox built near the street.

Linda pulled up and parked behind a white Cadillac SRX. It and several other cars sat in front of a one-story brick home, its lawn neatly mowed and a pecan tree in the yard. She killed the engine and turned in her seat to face Bree, who was looking around curiously. "Here we are. Welcome to Tea at Troy's."

Hopefully, Bree would bond with this group of liberal Democrats who were trying to survive in an area dominated by conservative Republicans. It might even help her decide to stay in East Texas a bit longer than she'd planned.

Linda wasn't sure why she wanted Bree to stay. But she did.

Standing on the small covered front porch, Bree gazed at a bronze-colored plaque of a man's face. "It's the Green Man," Linda whispered. "Tom, Troy's housemate, loves Celtic folklore."

Just then, the door opened, and a tall, well-built middle-aged man wearing rainbow-dyed jeans and a purple paisley shirt wrapped his arms around Linda in an enthusiastic hug. "Troy, this is my friend Bree," Linda said when she recovered her breath. "Bree, this is Troy."

Bree received the same treatment. The man obviously liked to hug. "Thanks for letting me visit, Troy."

"No problem. Come on in and meet the group."

The living room looked out through three large windows and a multipaned door onto a grassy backyard, protected by a privacy fence. But the outdoors didn't interest Bree because the room was overflowing with art objects. After Linda made the rounds and greeted several other people seated in a square around a large coffee table loaded with food, she began to introduce Bree to them.

"This is Tom, Bree," Linda said. "He's Scottish and the one responsible for the Green Man out front."

From the couch, Tom pulled her down into a hug so fierce she almost fell into his arms. Apparently in his late seventies, Tom wore an olive-green T-shirt that featured the Green Man, as well as a small gold medallion with the same image around his neck and a rainbow bracelet on one wrist. Sweats and sandals completed the look, and with his short white beard and hair, he reminded her of a laid-back Santa.

"How wonderful to meet you, Bree," he said, helping her regain her balance and squeezing her hand. "Welcome to our weekly gathering, and be sure to come back."

"I will, Tom. Thanks." She noticed the tall grandfather clock that stood behind the brown soft-fabric couch where Tom sat. He seemed as regular and dependable as the timepiece.

"Hi, Bree," came two voices from across the room. "You remember us, don't you? From the women's dinner last week." She turned and waved to Lou Anne and Kay, the Baptist couple determined to stay in the denomination they grew up in.

"Of course. It's good to see you again." They sat side by side in an oversized brown leather chair. "I'm glad to have a chance to get to know you better."

Behind Lou Anne and Kay stood an old windup Victrola, and on the top shelf of a nearby bookcase, Bree spotted an ancient camera. With its removable lens cover instead of a shutter and a dark cape to cover the photographer's head and shoulders, it was a prize any museum would love to display.

She turned to Tom and Troy. "You have some amazing pieces. Seeing them is a treat."

As Troy carried in several large glass containers and set them on a serving cart, Tom said, "I understand you've been a museum curator in Chicago. How wonderful. Sometime we'd love to show you all our little treasures."

Linda had just placed a dish on the low table in the center of the room and was removing foil wrap from it. Bree hadn't even noticed it earlier. "What's that?" she asked.

"Oh, we usually bring something to nibble on. I woke up hungry for deviled eggs this morning, so I fixed some."

Bree's stomach growled. "That's good. I didn't eat lunch."

Troy stopped juggling teacups long enough to point at the spread of food. "Help yourself. We always have plenty of cheese and crackers for absentminded professors and museum curators."

Everyone laughed. "Don't mind him," Tom said. "Troy's the resident comedian. If he can't make everybody laugh, he thinks he's had a bad afternoon. Just ignore him, if you can."

"Don't worry," Bree said. "I think I'm going to enjoy myself even more than I anticipated." The warm welcomes and variety of art objects and participants had already impressed her.

A very slim, youngish man, wearing tight jeans and a tailored turquoise shirt, had already hugged Linda. "Bree, this is Don. He usually hosts game night for our group once a month."

Don's bright-blue eyes gleamed as he sat down again in the multicolored, striped cushioned chair he'd jumped up from. "I hope you'll be there. We have a great time and always have loads of food. Be sure not to eat before you come."

"And make sure you don't break any of the crystal and china Don uses," Troy said as he handed Lou Anne a cup of tea in a sturdy mug.

Don mock-scowled at Troy. "I serve my guests on only the best."

"As do I. Only my best is less expensive than yours." Troy shot back at Don without missing a beat.

"Okay, you two," Lou Anne said. "Let Linda finish introducing our group members to Bree."

Linda led her over to Joe, a man with large ears and receding gray hair who braced himself on a cane made from an old oak limb, the Texas flag painted on it. "Sorry I can't get up, but my legs aren't so good," he said in a resonant voice. He sat in a straight chair in front of a large-screen TV flanked by tall shelves crammed with vintage record albums. "It's too bad my wife isn't here to meet you, but she's not feeling well these days. It's a wonder I'm even here, since I'm blind in one eye." He pointed to the foggy left lens of his glasses.

"If you see an old man in a blue Honda Accord on the road, you better watch out," Troy said as he handed Don a cup of tea.

"You..." Joe waved his cane at Troy, and Bree half expected him to call Troy a young whippersnapper. Joe's voice boomed like the sound Bree expected would come from the four-foot-tall African drum standing to his right.

"I'm not afraid of you," Troy said, his eyes twinkling. "Anyone who used to star on *Romper Room* and play piano in Dallas lounges can't be too scary."

"But I fought in World War II, young man, so you better watch out."

"Well, I went to the United States Air Force Academy," Troy said. "Just because they kicked me out of the service for being gay doesn't make me any less fierce."

Kay chimed in. "Calm down, guys. You're upsetting the dogs."

A small white poodle that apparently belonged to Tom had started barking and racing around the room, and a large beige mutt had stopped cadging for treats from a woman with short dark hair who sat across the room from Joe in front of the hearth, holding a plastic bag full of small dog biscuits.

"Bree, this is Connie, canine-lover extraordinaire."

"Glad to meet you, Bree." Connie looked down at the two dogs, who kept their eyes fixed on her. "And this is Rennie, who belongs to Tom"—she pointed to the poodle—"and Penny, Troy's dog. We're all happy to meet you." She slid some treats into the openings in a dog toy and handed it to Penny. "Sorry my partner isn't here to meet you today, but she had to finish editing a novel and couldn't make it."

"Maybe another time," Bree said. As she looked up above the mantel, she spotted several bronze statues and a print by a Texas impressionist artist named G. Harvey. "What's this painting called?" she asked Troy.

"*Immigrants in a New Land*, I believe. Harvey's one of my favorite painters."

"He's a native Texan, right?" she asked.

Joe looked up, and Bree wondered how well he could actually see the painting. "Well, I'll be a monkey's uncle. I didn't know that. I've looked at that painting every week for a long time now. No wonder I like it so much."

Linda sat down in the straight-back chair next to Joe and began to chat with him, and Bree chose a similar chair directly across the room from her, with Tom to her left and Connie to her right. "I hear you're an academic," she told Tom, and they quickly discovered several mutual acquaintances at the University of Chicago.

Across the room, Linda was inspecting what looked like a recent cut on Joe's right arm and listening to his account of his wife's poor health. She recalled Linda mentioning earlier that his wife, in her early nineties, had once worked as a reviewer for *The Dallas Morning News* and had a keen interest in politics and women's issues. Bree was disappointed she couldn't meet her.

She nibbled on one of the deviled eggs Linda had brought, as well as several pieces of cheese and crackers and assorted sandwiches and chips and dips while she continued to alternately chat with Tom and participate in the group discussion as a whole. It centered on Lou Anne and Kay's six-week trip throughout New Mexico and Arizona to visit PFLAG meetings and several church groups, where Lou Anne spoke about her book and coming out as a senior citizen. She'd also just been invited to be part of a panel at the First Baptist Church in Austin, which was thinking of openly accepting and supporting the gay community.

"So, is anyone interested in a piece of the Italian cream cake I made for today?" Lou Anne finally asked them, and everyone immediately smiled.

"Me, me!" Joe spoke for the rest of them as they simply nodded.

As Lou Anne handed out pieces of cake and Troy refilled his guests' teacups, Bree pondered why Linda seemed to be so close to Joe. Then it hit her. He probably reminded her of her own father because of his down-home simplicity, though his varied life experiences lent him a sophistication Linda's dad had lacked. How would Linda's biological father, Patrick, with his European life and lesbian mothers, have measured up?

Just then, the tall, good-looking woman who'd arrived late to the women's dinner breezed in. "Sorry I'm running behind, everybody," she announced. "Just got out of court and thought I'd stop by for a few minutes." She placed a container of decadent-looking chocolate cookies on the coffee table.

Then she claimed an empty chair next to Linda and began whispering to her, though the rest of the group didn't seem to mind. Tonda, that was her name. Bree had asked Linda about her after the dinner but never heard anything about her. Were she and Linda involved?

The group discussion didn't stay entirely serious. Every time the conversation threatened to bog down, Troy and Don jumped in with a quip or a jibe or a joke, no matter how silly, and made them all laugh and move to a new topic.

Before Bree knew it, the grandfather clock behind Tom struck four, and everyone immediately jumped up and began to gather their cups and plates, as well as whatever remained of the food they'd brought to share. What an enchanting afternoon.

"Thank you so much," she told Tom and Troy and the others as she hugged them good-bye. "I enjoyed meeting you."

"Be sure to come back next week," they called as she and Linda closed the front door behind them.

❖

"So Tom and Troy started the Tyler Area Gays organization?" Bree asked on the drive back.

She glanced over and noticed Linda's straight nose and how her chin rounded in a pleasant way. Nice.

"Yes. They organized it six or seven years ago and led it for several years."

"Has Troy always lived here?"

"No. He grew up in Kansas, I think, and after the air force, he ran a bar in North Carolina before he got sick and came home. He met Tom and Lou Anne and Kay at a local PFLAG meeting, and they eventually decided to establish TAG."

"So Tea at Troy's has been going on quite some time."

"Once a week since then, with a few month-long breaks when Tom and Troy travel to Scotland to visit Tom's friends and colleagues there. He's a rather prominent scholar in his field. Wrote the definitive book on some famous eighteenth-century British author."

"You'd never know it if you saw him in the grocery store, would you?" Bree glanced out the window at the long line of five o'clock traffic stopped in front of them as they drove back up Broadway.

Linda shook her head. "No, especially in the summer when he's wearing shorts and sandals."

"And Troy? What's the story there?"

"It's long and sad." Linda sighed. "In fact, he's published a book detailing his situation. He contracted HIV after sleeping with some man he barely knew, and when he developed AIDS, he lost his career in the military. His stepfather and brother drove to North Carolina and brought him home, almost dead."

"That's so sad. Is that why he likes to joke around so much?"

"I suppose so. In fact, in his book, he stresses how much he values humor."

"Well, their eclectic collection of art objects completely impressed and fascinated me."

Linda glanced over at her and grinned. "Wow. What a mouthful. You sound exactly like what I'd expect of a big-city museum curator."

Bree laughed at herself. "It took me a long time and a lot of hard work to lose my politically incorrect Texas accent and vocabulary. Did you ever get kidded for saying *fixing to*?"

"Can't say that I have." Linda kept her eyes on the road.

"You didn't run in the same circles I did. Academics can be terrible snobs, which I learned years ago, the first time I attended a major scholarly convention out of state. Everything seemed okay until I opened my mouth." Bree frowned. "When the highly educated people I mingled with heard my Texas drawl, they turned into piranhas. I, in turn, felt like a pariah and immediately signed up for a speech course to correct my accent, which apparently identified me as an undereducated Southern bigot."

Linda glanced at her in spite of the heavy traffic. "Wow. I'm glad I worked in the nursing field and stayed here in East Texas most of my life, at least professionally. Though I did run into that reaction a few times when I lived in the DC area." She smiled sympathetically, then shrugged. "Luckily my husband had a lot of money and a rather powerful position as a lobbyist, which somehow made my Southern accent sound quaint and charming."

Bree chuckled. "I'd almost have married a man to have that kind of immunity. But I did it the hard way, and it's not that easy to slide back into my native way of expressing myself."

"I bet. But it's probably like the proverbial bicycle. Hang around this part of the world long enough, and pretty soon you'll be saying *y'all* and *fixin' to* like you'd never left home."

Bree and Linda laughed and chatted idly the rest of the way back. Finding another potential circle of like-minded companions delighted Bree. She just might stick around here longer than she'd intended.

CHAPTER EIGHTEEN

As they neared home, Bree's cell phone rang. Who in the world? She jerked it from her pants pocket. "Hello."

"Bree Principal?" The voice sounded strained, worried, rushed. Bree thought she recognized it.

"Yes?"

"This is the administrator at Silverado. I've just called an ambulance to pick up your mother. We believe she's had a stroke, and we're taking her to the local hospital. Can you meet us there?"

"Of course. We can be there in"—she glanced at Linda, who'd already sped up—"twenty minutes. Thanks for calling."

"It's Sarah." Bree clicked off her phone and stared at it. When she looked at Linda, everything seemed to move in slow motion. "Can you drive me to the hospital in town? She's had a stroke. Please hurry."

Linda took her right hand off the wheel and let it rest on Bree's leg. "Of course. I'll get you there as fast as I can."

Bree stared out the window as the world flew by. The tears crowding her eyes blurred the kaleidoscope of falling leaves deserting every tree they passed. They lay in large drifts along the road, piled under the foliage arching over the road, blowing in the wind that seemed to pick up speed and grow colder as the sun hid behind the dark-gray rain clouds gathered ahead of them.

"…everything will be okay, Bree." Had Linda been talking all this time?

Bree forced herself to focus on the warmth of Linda's hand on her leg, the slight pressure making her realize she hadn't actually turned to stone. She could still feel. Her own heart still beat; her own brain functioned normally, unlike her mother's.

She turned to Linda. "What exactly is a stroke?"

As Linda explained in a calm, even tone, the leaves seemed to quit whirling quite so fast, and the sun peeked out again.

Finally, they reached the hospital, and Bree pushed open the car door as soon as Linda pulled up to the entrance. "You go on in, and I'll park. Wait for me in the lobby."

"Thanks. I appreciate it." Bree rushed into the hospital, not sure where to go, but Linda would know. She slowed, relieved not to have to face the situation alone.

❖

"Your mother's going to be fine," Linda said as she sat beside Bree in the hospital cafeteria. She rested her hand on Bree's for a final minute, then picked up her fork.

Being unlinked from Bree made Linda feel nude. She'd held Bree's hand practically all evening while the flurry of hospital staff had rushed around them, tending to Sarah. She and Bree had even held hands after they finally left the hospital room and walked here to the cafeteria.

"Are you sure?"

"Of course. She'll probably outlive us all."

Bree seemed so lost, so ill at ease, as if she were in the jungles of New Guinea instead of a hospital. No, she would probably have felt more at home in New Guinea or some equally exotic place. "I hope so. How old was your mother when she died?" Bree looked as if she'd never even considered the possibility that her own mother wouldn't live forever.

"Only seventy-two. We buried her ten years ago in March."

Bree toyed with her green salad. "I'm sorry. Are you okay talking about it?"

"Sure. I still miss her, a lot, but I can always talk about Mom." Linda's throat tightened, and she took a drink of water.

"She was really special, wasn't she? And what a great cook. I don't know how she did it. Feeding a husband and four kids every day, plus assorted overnight visitors like me, must have taken a lot of time."

"Yes." Linda stared at the piece of fried chicken she'd just forked and shuddered. How could something nearly burned still ooze blood? She thought about her mom's golden, crispy chicken, fresh from the skillet and served with cream gravy. "She could do just about anything we needed around the house." She finally took a bite of the meat and almost spit it out. "Yuck."

Bree pushed a piece of wilted lettuce aside. "But she didn't stay at home all the time, did she?"

"Oh no. She had all kinds of hobbies, especially gardening. But most of all, she loved to dance. In fact, after I left home and got married, she persuaded my dad to join a square-dance club with her. She ended up teaching dance classes all over East Texas, and he always helped her."

"I had no idea. What did she die of?" Bree picked up a chunk of tomato from her salad, then dropped it and tried a square of red Jell-O.

"Alzheimer's." She still hurt when she said the word.

"How horrible." Bree lowered her fork, gray eyes full of compassion, and touched Linda's arm.

"Yes. The disease robbed us of her before it took her body. Seeing someone so vivacious disappear a little at a time like she did…" Linda felt as lifeless as the soggy green beans she tried and then shoved aside.

"I'm so sorry."

Linda's throat ached now. "Her death devastated Dad. They'd been married fifty-five years, and after she got sick, he spent practically all his time with her."

Bree kept her hand on Linda's arm and lightly squeezed.

"Just a few hours before she died, he crawled up into bed with her and kissed her at least ten times with these big, sloppy kisses. *I love you, Helen,* he said, over and over. *I'll always love you.*" Linda swallowed her sadness and tried her mashed potatoes, lumpy yet tolerable.

"How romantic," Bree said.

"Yes. Mom hadn't spoken in weeks, but when Dad said that, she made sounds deep in her throat that sounded like she was trying to say *I love you too*."

A tear rolled down Bree's cheek, and Linda fought hard to keep talking. "We'd all known she didn't have much longer, but Dad couldn't grieve. After that, though, he went home and cried for hours, he said later. She died during the night, and when we went to tell him the next morning, he didn't seem surprised. He passed away a month after she did."

"Fifty-five years together," Bree murmured. "I can't imagine."

"Neither can I." The knot in Linda's throat loosened as she gazed at Bree and wiped her eyes dry with a scratchy paper napkin. "Neither can I."

❖

Bree heard the telephone ringing as she unlocked her back door, waved good-bye to Linda, and then turned off the porch light. She didn't run to pick up the phone. If whoever was calling wanted to talk to her bad enough, they'd try again.

She hung her keys on a hook near the door, then pulled her wallet and cell phone from her pocket and deposited them in a drawer. But what if the hospital had been the ones calling? The house phone rang again, and she rushed over to pick it up.

"Hello."

"Where the hell have you been? I thought we had a date tonight, and it's ten o'clock."

"Who's this?"

"Ann. Who'd you think?"

"The hospital." Bree walked over to the refrigerator and poured herself a glass of milk. Her empty stomach burned.

"The hospital? Why on earth—"

"I've been there all evening, and I'm beat." She flopped down in an easy chair and took a sip from her glass. If only Ann's voice could soothe her like the milk did.

"What's wrong? Did you hurt yourself?"

"No. I'm fine. It's Sarah, my mother. She had a stroke."

"Is she okay?"

"Yes. I think she's more scared than anything. She's not used to having anything wrong with her, and now all of a sudden—"

"That's good. But why didn't you answer your cell? I've been trying to locate you since six."

Bree blew out a long breath. "The battery died right after the hospital phoned me about Sarah. I probably need a new one."

"Poor baby." Ann's voice lost its shrill edge and turned seductive. "This hasn't been your day, has it? Should I come take care of you?"

"No." Bree stood and began to unbutton her blouse. "Linda was with me when I got the news and—"

"Linda! I might have known. Is she there now?"

Bree kicked off her shoes. "No. She just dropped me off."

"What kind of woman would leave you to spend the night alone after going through something like that?"

One that realizes I'm dog-tired and not interested in anything but getting some sleep, Bree wanted to say. But she didn't. She didn't want to wind Ann up any tighter. "An exhausted one probably. Like me."

"Oh, baby. I'm sure you're wiped out."

There it was again, that sultry, sexy voice Bree could never resist. But just then she looked down at her hand and recalled how safe she'd felt when Linda held it earlier.

"Thanks for calling, Ann," she said in the firm yet dismissive tone she'd perfected when dealing with difficult employees and patrons at the museum. "Maybe we can get together after Sarah's settled back at Silverado. Keep in touch." She hung up, finished undressing, and fell into bed.

❖

As soon as Linda got home she phoned Bree to check on her but got a busy signal. Curious, she called Ann, who usually stayed up late watching television. Her phone beeped busy too. Damn.

Linda lit a parsley-scented candle in her bathroom, and as its fresh, crisp scent began to soothe her, she undressed and stepped into the shower. She hadn't realized how tired she was until she stood there unmoving, the hot water beating down on her back. She rolled her tight neck and let the pounding water engulf her.

Had Bree called Ann, or had Ann started pursuing Bree? And whatever happened between them—was it any of her business? She was Bree's friend, but Bree and Ann had obviously had strong feelings for each other in the past. Did feelings like those ever change or die? Ann usually got what she wanted, and Bree had once tried to give it to her, until apparently Ann had made it clear she didn't think Bree could provide it.

Linda wet her washrag, then squeezed on some new rosemary bodywash she'd recently concocted. The warm water enhanced its tangy lemon aroma.

Had Ann finally realized she preferred women to men, like Linda had? Or was Ann merely jealous that Linda seemed to be getting some of the attention Bree had always lavished on her? If so, she'd try to regain control of Bree.

Linda slid her washcloth over her arms carefully, slowly, paying special attention to her hands. She felt like a teenager, reluctant to bathe away any lingering residue of Bree.

Relaxing into the aroma of rosemary and parsley that mingled together, she picked up a bottle of shampoo scented with thyme. Her mother had taught her how to add herbs to nonscented bath and beauty products, and Linda enjoyed playing with these skills.

She wet her hair, then squirted a dollop of shampoo into her palm. Its strong herbaceous, woody smell assaulted her for a minute, then blended with the odors of rosemary and parsley she'd already released. As she soaped and rinsed her hair, she felt stronger.

Ann had had so many chances with Bree and had blown each one of them because she apparently didn't think Bree would ever measure up to what a man could offer her. Linda stepped out of the shower. It was her turn now, and she wouldn't back away.

She toweled her body and her hair vigorously, then sat in front of her bathroom mirror applying lotion to her feet and calves and humming the old Simon and Garfunkel song that had kept running through her mind since Bree had mentioned it. The earthy, natural smell of the sage in her lotion grounded her as she thought about her mother teaching her the meaning of the various herbs mentioned in the song.

Parsley is for comfort, her mother had said, taking Linda's hand and holding it. *It can also purify and protect you and those you love.*

Linda glanced at the light-green candle still burning near her bathroom sink and inhaled deeply, thinking of how comfortable she'd felt holding Bree's hand.

As she rubbed sage-scented lotion on her thighs, she could almost hear her mother say, *Sage is for strength, also protection, wisdom, and health. Use your strength wisely, and cherish your health and that of others.*

Linda gazed at herself in the mirror and at a photo of her mother that sat nearby. "I promise I won't harm Ann in any way, but I'll keep on caring for Bree and her mother as long as they need me," she whispered, then blew a kiss toward the picture.

Rosemary is for love. It was almost as if the photo were speaking to her now. She could feel her mother near and thought she heard her say, *It keeps negativity away and brings health, protection, and blessing.*

The faint tangy aroma of the rosemary from Linda's bodywash still lingered on her arms. "I won't think bad thoughts about Ann," she murmured to her mother. "I'll try to protect and bless her as much as I do Bree and her mother."

She sighed as she covered her stomach and her breasts with the sage-infused lotion, then slowly massaged it in. *Hopefully I can keep that promise.* She winked at herself in the mirror.

And thyme is for courage. Linda could definitely hear her mother's voice now—rich, soothing, strong, and full of love. Immediately the pungent aroma of the thyme in her recently shampooed hair caught her attention.

She'd heard her mother refer to thyme's ability to teach courage so many times, but the lesson had never sunk in like it did now.

She'd also never felt fear like she did when she thought of standing up for herself against Ann. Ann was more beautiful and more articulate than she was, wittier and shrewder, her dad's favorite child. Ann seemed invincible, and even Linda was almost as devoted to her as she was to her mother.

But Linda's mother had loved her best, and with her mother's help, Linda might have a tiny chance to convince Bree that she could care for her in ways Ann couldn't. She didn't want to alienate Ann though.

Linda rubbed lotion into her arms and hands, then applied her nightly face cream, brushed her teeth, and fell into bed thinking about Bree.

CHAPTER NINETEEN

B ree was sitting in the magazine section of the public library browsing through yesterday's *Chicago Tribune* when someone tapped her arm. Frowning, she glanced up.

"Why, Linda." Relief washed through her. She couldn't face anyone except Linda right now. In fact, she wished she'd run into her several days ago. "What are you doing here?"

Linda grinned. "I needed to pick up some milk and bread."

"I know"—Bree lowered her newspaper—"that was a silly question. How's it going? I've missed seeing you lately."

Linda dropped into the worn leather chair next to her, smiling yet appearing concerned. "I'm fine. What about you? I've stopped by the hospital to see your mom every morning, but you're never there. I thought you might have left town."

Bree shook her head and whispered, "Don't I wish?" She glanced around but didn't see anyone else. A librarian stood behind the checkout counter on the other side of the room, and an older man browsed the stacks at the back of the library. "Sarah's a little difficult to deal with right now, and when I haven't been with her, I've tried to get some sleep."

Bree described how her mother couldn't stand to be left alone at night and had insisted she stay with her, and as she talked, she began to feel better. Why hadn't she called Linda to share this? "Sarah's supposed to go back to Silverado today, so I'm here unwinding before I pick her up. I've always loved the peace and quiet of the library."

Linda started to stand up. "Don't let me bother you any longer then. I—"

"No. Don't go." She caught Linda's arm and gently pulled her back down. "I've wanted to talk to you ever since last week when we went to tea in Tyler. I really enjoyed that. But I haven't had much free time lately."

"I can certainly understand that," Linda said as she leaned back in the cushioned chair. "What's on your mind?"

Bree took a deep breath and sat up a little straighter. "I don't know how to say this, so I'll just get right to the point." How did you gently turn someone's life upside down? She'd planned to have this conversation in a private place, but not too many people were visiting the public library this time of day.

Linda nodded, appearing apprehensive. "Okay, I'm listening."

"Sarah and I had a talk the morning before she had her stroke, and she told me quite a story."

"About me?"

"Yes, though it's more about your mother…and your father."

Linda shifted in her well-used chair. "What about them?"

"It seems they didn't tell the whole truth about when they actually got married."

Linda smiled. "So they got carried away and didn't want to admit they'd been fooling around, eh?" She chuckled fondly. "That's interesting. It makes them seem more human."

"I wish it were that simple." Bree blew out a long breath. She could do this. Now she understood why her mother had always avoided becoming involved in people's personal affairs. It wasn't a picnic.

Linda looked mystified. "What else could it be?"

Bree lowered her voice. "Your mother was pregnant by another man."

Linda seemed to droop into the chair cushions and sat there, speechless. Bree powered on.

"A friend of my mother, a fellow named Patrick. Charming and redheaded. According to her, he spent his early childhood on a farm near here but went to France with his mothers when he was about ten."

"Mothers?"

"Your real grandmother was apparently a lesbian," Bree said.

Linda shook her head, as if having a hard time digesting that piece of information. "At least that makes me feel a lot better about myself." Then she frowned. "But France? Who was this man? How did he get here, and why didn't he want me?"

Bree told Linda what she knew.

"Mom tried to tell me about him not long before she died, but I didn't believe her." She stared into space. "I even saw a picture of him with a woman I suppose was Mother, for God's sake, though that was just a few weeks ago."

Linda put her head in her hands as if trying to hide the sudden tears that glistened in her eyes. "Why didn't I question her more about him? Now I'll never know the rest of her story."

Bree leaned forward and placed one hand on Linda's white, springy curls. They felt so soft as she stroked Linda's head. Finally Linda looked up, and Bree pulled her hand away.

"Thanks. I'm sorry for falling apart and for involving you in my family drama." Linda screwed up her face. "I could kick myself. If I'd just listened, you wouldn't have had to spring this news on me. It can't have been pleasant for you, especially since you're having to deal with your own mother right now."

"Don't worry. She's doing well. I just hope I was right to tell you all this."

Linda slowly straightened up and clasped Bree's hand. "I'm glad you did. Though it might take me a while to digest it, I prefer to know the truth." She glanced at her wristwatch. "But we both have things to do, so we better get going. Thanks for being such a good friend."

Bree stood and tugged Linda to her feet. "You're more than welcome. See you soon?"

"Absolutely." Linda headed for the front door of the library.

Bree stared at Linda as she hurried away, looking stiff and awkward. She would give Linda some time to mull over the news about her parents, but after everything settled down, she wanted them to pick up where they'd left off. Being around Linda made her feel at peace with herself in a way she'd never experienced.

❖

Linda's head spun during her drive home. *The blood of some stranger runs through my veins. I've always called the wrong man Dad! Why did Bree's mom confide in Bree instead of me? Can I trust anyone after being lied to all these years?*

Then it hit her. *Ann and I aren't even half sisters.* Did Ann and her brothers know what really happened? Surely not.

But everyone had always said how much she resembled her mom yet not her dad. As a young man, he'd had blond hair, like Ann, and her mom's had been dark. A few people had even teased her that her real dad was probably the milkman. Well, they hadn't been far from the truth. At least now she knew where her hair color came from.

If only Sarah would tell her the whole story. That should help her understand all the details. But Sarah didn't need any added stress right now. Linda would have to muddle through this revelation alone, because Bree had her hands full too.

As Linda pulled into her driveway, her cell phone rang. She hurriedly parked. "Hello."

"Hi, Linda. This is Tonda."

"What's up?"

"I thought you might want to finally come over and let me take you out to eat at Bernard's, like I've been asking for the past two months."

Linda opened the car door and stepped out into the chill mid-November air. "As a matter of fact, I would. When and what time?"

"How about Friday around seven?"

"Give me your address and I'll put it in my GPS. Better yet, why don't I just meet you at the restaurant?"

"Sure thing. I'm looking forward to us finally getting together."

"Me too."

As they said their good-byes, Linda let herself into her house, sank onto her couch, and stared at the blank TV screen. A distraction. That's just what she needed. She might have more in common with Tonda than she thought. And a night out with no emotional baggage would be a relief.

She grabbed a throw pillow and squeezed it to her chest. Oh, if only things hadn't changed so abruptly and she were going out with Bree instead.

CHAPTER TWENTY

F riday night, Bree called Linda. She hadn't seen her at Silverado for the past couple of days, though she thought Linda was still checking on her mother's leg wound occasionally. An aide was rebandaging it daily now.

Linda's phone rang several times before the answering machine clicked on. As Bree left a brief message, she considered calling Linda's cell. But what if she was out on a date? Bree didn't have any more claim on Linda's time than Ann did on hers. And Bree only wanted to say hello.

Less than five minutes later, the phone rang. Oh, good, she thought as she picked up and blurted out, "You must have been too busy to talk earlier."

"Who do you think this is?"

"Uh, uh, nobody." She was stammering.

"Liar. You expected Linda, didn't you?"

"Well, yes. I've gotten used to spending time with her."

Bitterness tinged Ann's laugh. "You better get out of the habit. Linda has a date tonight, with a criminal-defense attorney in Tyler to go to a posh restaurant."

"Really? Is her name Tonda?"

"How did you know?"

"I've met her a couple of times."

"What did you think?"

"She's younger, attractive, a sharp dresser, and available."

"Ha. Good for Linda. I never thought I'd say this, but if she's determined to choose this alternative lifestyle, at least she has enough class to associate with desirable women."

"Yes. I'm happy for her too. But she didn't choose her sexual orientation."

Ann scoffed. "Whatever. I've heard all those tired old arguments. Believe me, when it comes right down to it, it's a choice."

Bree sighed. Why waste energy arguing with Ann? "To each her own. So, what's on your mind? Where's your precious Carl?"

"Down at his hunting camp near Jasper, for the weekend. It's a tradition for a lot of local guys. Gives them a chance to act like boys again, I suppose."

An icy finger seemed to touch Bree's heart. She shivered and moaned softly.

"Oh, baby. I forgot. I'm so sorry. Tomorrow morning is when…"

Bree took a breath so deep she felt as if she'd inhaled all the air in the room. "Yes. Tomorrow morning Brett will have been dead fifty-seven years. I'd love to forget this anniversary, but I can't."

"I'm so sorry. You don't need to be alone. I'll be right over."

Bree blew out her breath like a gust of wind. "No. You don't need—"

The dial tone buzzed in Bree's ear. Ann was on her way. Damn. Bree hoped she could control her feelings. They were usually all over the place this time of year.

Linda spotted Tonda sitting in the crowded reception area of Bernard's, one leg crossed over the other and swinging up and down, as if waiting annoyed her. She wore her black dress jacket, obviously expensive, with the air of someone who never asked what anything cost. Damn. Why had she said yes to this date?

She'd convinced herself she was looking forward to this. But she'd actually rather be sitting in front of her own fireplace, babysitting Riley, or even better, enjoying a quiet evening with Bree.

Tonda's restless sophistication attracted yet frightened Linda. Her eyes seemed to bore right through Linda, as if searching for hidden flaws and secrets. Linda didn't have any secrets that she was aware of, but she certainly had flaws. Come to think of it, though, she had a huge secret—her real dad was a philanderer who hadn't wanted anything to do with her.

"Hi. Sorry I'm a little late." She stood in front of Tonda. "The traffic seems to get worse every day."

Tonda jumped up and gave her a brief one-armed hug. "Glad you could make it." She stepped back and took in Linda's new white cashmere sweater, her eyes lingering on Linda's breasts. "You look almost good enough to eat." Her laugh was low and sensuous. "Speaking of which, I'm famished."

Just then the hostess approached and led them into a dimly lit room to the right, its decor making her think she'd been teleported to Italy. After the woman seated them at a secluded table near the back, Tonda slipped her a bill along with a sly look.

"I'm glad I finally persuaded you to go out with me." Tonda's expression reminded Linda of the one she'd always imagined on Little Red Riding Hood's wolf.

Their waiter bustled in and placed a bottle of red wine on their table. Tonda immediately picked it up and fondled it. "I think you'll like this cab. It's a very good year and tastes of black cherry and vanilla." Tonda sipped the sample the waiter poured for her and nodded. After their glasses were filled, Tonda handed her one.

She accepted it hesitantly. "Thanks. I enjoy wine, but I have a long drive home, so I need to be careful."

Tonda gazed over the top of her tulip-shaped glass, her eyes burning. "Don't worry about that. You can always spend the night with me."

Linda inadvertently rocked back in her chair, then took a drink. "Hmm. The black cherry certainly dominates the vanilla, doesn't it?" she murmured. Would Tonda catch her innuendo?

"Yes, it certainly does. That's one reason I ordered it." Tonda ritually sniffed, swirled, chewed, and finally drank. "Ah. Just what the doctor ordered after a busy week."

After a few minutes of small talk, Tonda glanced at her menu, then dropped it. The waiter hurried over, and Tonda said, "We'll start with the baked brie and the salmon appetizers, followed by a bowl each of your French onion soup and the palm-and-artichoke salad. And for the main course, bring us each your nine-ounce Filet Franscati. We'll decide on dessert later." She glanced at Linda. "Oh, is all that okay with you?"

Stunned, Linda merely nodded. She'd never had a date, female or male, who didn't consult her before they ordered.

"And we may need a second bottle of wine later," Tonda added. "So be on your toes."

The waiter bobbed his head and darted away.

Tonda took a long drink of her wine and lowered her glass, her smile smug. "I've learned the hard way to deal firmly with servers. If you don't, they tend to become lax."

Linda murmured something inane. She would limit herself to one glass while she ate and then develop a debilitating migraine.

Before Bree had time to change from her sweats into something more presentable, the front doorbell rang. Carolyn always came to the back, so Ann must have set a new speed record getting here.

Bree strode to the rarely used front door. She'd talk to Ann briefly, then make up an excuse to get her to leave. She didn't want any company, especially today. She usually concentrated on Brett during these few days of the year, replaying all their good times as kids and wondering how her life would have differed if he'd lived. Maybe she'd have had a grand-niece like Riley and—

Ann pushed her way in as soon as Bree unlocked the door. "What do you mean, hiding in here? You should have called me. It's not good for you to be by yourself right now." Ann looked and sounded genuinely concerned.

"Thanks, but I'm used to it. It doesn't feel right to just go about my regular routine."

"You should at least visit your mother." Ann followed Bree back into the den, where she'd been sitting in the near-dark room. "For God's sake. It's like a tomb in here. Why don't you turn on some more lights? And what about some heat? It's freezing."

The overhead light fixture almost blinded Bree when Ann flicked it on. Immediately turning it off, she clicked on a couple of other lamps in the room.

"Sorry." Ann seemed to mean it. "I don't want to intrude on your grief. I just thought that after all these years you'd reconciled yourself to Brett's death."

Bree sat on the old blue velvet couch, where she'd huddled under a blanket, and patted the cushion next to her. "I'll never do that."

Ann opened her mouth to speak, but Bree gently put her hand over it. "Let me talk."

"Okay, baby." Ann simply sat still and waited.

She took a deep breath. "I've learned to live with what happened to him and made a tolerable life for myself." She gazed down at her lap. "But I've never quit wishing I'd died instead of him."

Ann placed her hands on one of Bree's and squeezed.

When Bree finally looked back up, tears shone in Ann's eyes. "How can you say that, Bree?"

Bree curled up under her fleece blanket again. "Because it's true."

Ann snaked a hand under the blanket and clasped her arm. "How can you even think that?"

Bree didn't pull away. "My father would have had the son he wanted to follow him as president of the bank." Ann's hand didn't move. "And my mother would have had her favorite child living here. He would have given her not only grandchildren, but probably great-grandchildren by now."

"Oh, Bree. You can't be sure of any of that."

Bree took a deep breath. "Maybe not. But I'm sure Mother got left with an oddball not even capable of forming a lasting relationship with a suitable partner."

Ann moved her hand to Bree's thigh. "How absurd. You know I'm right. I don't even have to explain why."

The words hung in the cold air between them. Bree wanted to reach out and grab them, pull them inside herself and let them warm the freezing places she'd protected for so long. Could she?

Ann stroked her leg. "Your parents have always taken pride in you. You've broadened their world."

Could this possibly be true? Ann wasn't exactly a reliable source.

Ann didn't pull away. "Life happens. And death happens."

That made sense.

"We don't have a choice in the event itself." Ann slowly pulled Bree's blanket from one side of her and covered herself with it too. "We can only choose how we respond to it."

Bree relaxed against Ann's warm body, puzzled. Ann had always been shallow and self-centered. But she'd evidently changed...or hidden this side of herself.

"You may be right." Their combined body heat relaxed her more fully.

Ann laughed. "You bet. I'm not always the airhead everybody considers me." She took Bree's hand and gazed into her eyes. "That's just an act. And you know what?"

"What?"

"Carl's finally made me realize it's okay to be normal."

Carl? Bree struggled not to jerk her hand away. "Normal. What do you mean?"

"You know." Ann pulled away a little fraction of an inch. "I can like guys, want to get married and live happily ever after, want a nice house and yard, enjoy shopping and buying pretty things." Her words came out in a rush. Now she appeared defiant. "For me, that's normal. Around him, I can even give up my dumb-blonde act."

Bree felt like Ann had just punched her in the gut. "You've got to be kidding."

"Nope. You always impressed me so much, I thought something was wrong with me because I didn't feel about you the way you felt about me."

Bree almost doubled over. Chilled again, she wanted to pull the blanket away from Ann, cover only herself with it. "That's insane."

"Yes. Exactly my sentiments."

Bree wished she could climb inside Ann's head so she could understand. "Let me get this right. You always thought you were weird because you didn't love girls, and I thought I was abnormal because I did."

Ann looked relieved that Bree seemed to understand. "That about sums it up."

Something loosened inside Bree, as if a hawk had been released from a cage Bree had carried around inside herself forever. "Quite a couple, weren't we? No wonder we never made a go of it." The hawk seemed to circle the room, testing its wings after being cramped in a small, tight space for so long.

"Yeah. We'd have probably made each other more miserable together than we would have staying apart like we've done."

Gradually, as they huddled together under the blanket, for the first time since Brett died, Bree felt free. She could choose her life, be exactly who she wanted to be without worrying what others thought about her. She had a few good years left, maybe many more than a few, and suddenly she didn't want to waste any more of them mourning the past and what might have been.

She and Ann talked until they both began to yawn. "This is Friday night, isn't it?" Ann asked.

"Sure is. Think we ought to drive out to your house so I can spend the night with you, like we used to?"

Ann laughed. "Forget it. That's too far. If you have an extra toothbrush and T-shirt, I'll stay here. It's about time to climb out of our old rut."

"Suits me. But you better sleep in the guest bedroom. I snore, and you probably do too. Okay with you?"

"Sure is. Getting a good night's sleep can outweigh getting off," Ann said. "Though you never heard me say that. It'd ruin my reputation."

"I agree, though it'd ruin mine too. I just need a hug at this point."

"I can do that."

"Thanks for understanding, Ann."

"Anytime, Bree. Anytime."

Bree wrapped her arms around Ann and felt only the comfort of familiarity, like slipping on a pair of worn jeans. She couldn't wait to tell Linda about her change of heart. Or rather the sensation of discovering she actually had a heart.

Linda gripped the steering wheel as she sped home from Tyler. Though it was almost ten o'clock, she swung by Sandy's dome home and spotted a light on in her bedroom. Good, she was awake.

Linda stood at her door, her breath turning to fog as she shivered. A cold front had recently blasted their summerlike weather into winter with hardly a bow to the temperate climate autumn was supposed to supply. She pushed the doorbell again.

Dogs barked, and then a light blinked on overhead. "Who the hell is it?" Sandy called.

"It's Linda. Who do you think it is? Or do women usually beat on your door in the middle of the night? Open up. I'm freezing."

Linda had to laugh when she saw Sandy holding a shotgun in one hand and trying to keep Zoe and Cowboy back with the other. She wore a heavy purple robe over red flannel sweats.

"What in the world are you doing out so late?" Sandy laid down the gun and tried to hush the dogs, who kept jumping around like they hadn't seen Linda in years.

"It's a long story. Can I stay, or would you rather I come back tomorrow?"

"Of course you can stay. Come on in the bedroom. It's the only warm room in the place. My central heat's on the blink, and I let the living-room fire die down a couple of hours ago and went to bed to read." She led Linda to the bedroom and pointed to the bed. "Take off your coat and shoes and climb in. Zoe and Cowboy won't mind you lying in their place. How about a cup of decaf tea to take the chill off?"

Linda snuggled into the cozy spot Zoe and Cowboy had left. "I'd love one, if it's not too much trouble."

"Are you kidding? Be right back. But don't go to sleep. I want to know what the heck you've been up to."

Snuggled in next to Sandy, comforted by the steaming mug, Linda didn't feel quite as angry as she had earlier.

Sandy lay down on her side and stared at her with a grin. "So, what's going on?"

Linda described her evening in detail, including the food and the atmosphere.

"Well. I've never even eaten at Bernard's, so right off the bat, I'm jealous. Your meal sounds great."

"It was. But that's not what upset me." Linda felt a little silly now. Some people would put up with just about anything to be treated to dinner there.

"I understand. It sounds like your date tried to treat you like a piece of the filet you two ate."

Linda nodded. "Exactly. And I let her. That's what makes me the most angry."

"Yes. I'd probably have told her off and made a big scene, then regretted it. Granted, you took the path of least resistance, but I bet you made your point by leaving as soon as you gracefully could. Of course, some people never read between the lines."

"She's an intelligent woman, so I imagine she got my message." Linda took a sip of tea. "Maybe she came on so strong because she was nervous and wanted to impress me with her knowledge of the menu there."

"And maybe you're being too nice. Women can be jerks just like men can. You probably read her correctly and ended what could have become an unpleasant situation in the easiest way for both of you. No harm, no foul. If she asks you out again, you can just turn her down a couple of times. Even the most inflated egos deflate eventually."

Linda stared into her mug. "Why do you think I'm so drawn to dominant women?"

"Well, I never hung up my shingle, but I did take a lot of psych courses while I lived in California." Sandy rested her head on her hand, supported by a bent elbow, and gazed at her with mock seriousness.

Linda assumed her most innocent expression. "So, Dr. Porter. What's your learned opinion?"

"Something to do with your dad, I'm sure."

"An Electra complex maybe? I wanted to kill my mother and marry my father?"

"Not exactly. Actually, I'd say you have a bad case of sibling rivalry."

"Sibling rivalry? You mean with Ann? For my dad's attention?"

"That's what I mean. And for his love."

"Why do you think that?"

"Oh, a thousand little clues. I'm not just another pretty face, you know. I watch people. And based on what I've seen, you never stood a chance with those two."

Linda's heart dropped like a stone into a creek. No one had ever been this honest with her. When she recovered enough to speak, she said, "What do you mean?"

"Exactly what I just said. At least that's my theory."

"Spit it out then. Don't hold back on my account."

"No. I've wanted to mention this for a long time, but now I think you're finally ready to hear it."

Linda finished her tea and rolled over to set the mug on a side table. Besides, she didn't want Sandy to see the moisture glazing her sight. She considered telling Sandy about her real father, but for some reason, she wasn't ready to yet.

Sandy's callused hand gently rolled her over again, so they lay facing each other. "None of this is your fault. It's just the way things are. For what it's worth, I think your dad always favored Ann because she reminded him so much of his first wife. They looked almost identical."

"You know, I never even saw a picture of her, so that never occurred to me. Silly, eh? I should have thought of that."

"You were a baby, a little girl, a teenager. You just knew, or felt, that your dad smiled a little wider when Ann told him a story, laughed a little louder when she did something cute, and expressed his appreciation for the Christmas presents she gave him a little more enthusiastically. Right?"

Linda closed her lids, and the moisture turned into drops crowding the corners of her eyes. She took a gigantic breath and blew it out. "Yeah. You're right. I just knew all those things hurt and figured if I tried a little harder, he'd treat me like he did her."

Sandy nodded, then wrapped an arm around her and pulled her close. "I know. I found it hard to watch you struggle, but I figured you'd eventually outgrow it."

Linda's laugh felt like a gunshot. "Yeah. Well, news flash. I'm sixty-five. How much longer do you think it'll take?"

"I'd say you're almost there. At least you can talk about it. You know his feelings had nothing to do with you, don't you? He obviously let his memories of his first wife dominate his life. You couldn't have done anything to change that fact. He had to be the one to let go of the past and learn to live in the present. His loss."

"My loss too." Linda snuggled into Sandy's strong arms. "At least I had Mom. And you. Thanks for helping me see things a little clearer, Sandy."

"That's Dr. Porter to you." Sandy kissed the top of Linda's head and squeezed her. "Now the dogs have a question."

Linda inhaled with contentment. "What's that?"

"Are you planning to stay overnight, or do they get their place back?"

Linda startled from Sandy's arms. "Gosh. I almost forgot. Riley's spending the weekend with me, and I have to pick her up first thing in the morning. I better get home." She jumped out of bed.

"You obviously weren't planning to accept the lawyer's invitation to sleep with her, even if she'd had a chance to extend one."

Linda shook her head. "No. I guess not." She grinned. "Besides, if I had, I'd have missed this little talk with you, and I wouldn't have done that for anything." She pulled on her coat and waved. "Don't get up. I'll let myself out. Thanks a million, for everything."

As Linda drove down the deserted country road toward town, she glanced up at the moon. It looked so stark and cold, but the sun still warmed and lit part of it. As she neared her house, she turned down the street where Bree lived, then slowed.

Who'd parked in the driveway at almost eleven? *God. No. Don't let it be*...Ann. And no lights on in the house. What on earth?

Linda's heart abruptly felt as cold and cratered as the waxing moon that rode across the sky. If only it were the dark of the moon so she couldn't see how much her hands trembled as she finally drove home. Her dad had always preferred Ann, and obviously Bree did too.

CHAPTER TWENTY-ONE

B ree woke up early, happier than she'd been in years. The earth seemed to have shifted back onto its axis after wobbling for decades.

She peeked into the guest bedroom to make sure she hadn't dreamed what had happened last night, but no. Tousled blond hair covered one of the pillows, so Bree tiptoed downstairs and began to prepare breakfast.

As she laid four strips of bacon in a skillet, she silently thanked Linda for teaching her such a basic skill. Linda! How was she doing? Bree had been so caught up in her own affairs she'd completely forgotten about how Linda might be reacting to the news about her father. She picked up the phone. Linda seemed like the type who'd get up early, even on Saturday.

"Uh, hello."

The groggy voice told her she'd misjudged. "Sorry to wake you. I just wanted to touch base and see how you're doing. You'll never believe what happened—"

"For heaven's sake, Bree. It's six o'clock."

Bree had never heard Linda use such a sharp tone. "Sorry. I'll talk to you later. We haven't seen each other in several—"

"Got to go. 'Bye."

Bree glanced at the phone as she placed it back in its charger. "What on earth?" she muttered to herself. Linda must have had a rough night. She shouldn't have called her so early.

"Bree. Where are you?" Ann called from upstairs.

"Down here in the kitchen. Ready for some coffee?"

Ann wandered in, still wearing Bree's T-shirt, her hair uncombed, her feet bare.

"I sure am." She stretched and yawned. "Wow. I haven't slept so well in years. Do I smell bacon frying?"

Bree clicked her Keurig on.

"Yep. Linda taught me how." She beamed, feeling like a gourmet chef who'd just prepared a soufflé. "She said the secret was to keep the heat low and cook the bacon slowly. And I've got biscuits baking."

Ann inspected the K-Cups in Bree's carousel and chose a Dark Magic one.

Bree grinned. "Ah. Extra bold. I should have known. Suits you to a T. Here's a cup."

Being able to tease Ann as if they were friends felt so good. She stopped. They *were* friends. Who would have thought, after all this time, such a miracle could have happened? Her feelings for Ann, as murky as a sewer for fifty years, had suddenly transformed into a clear mountain stream sparkling in the sunlight.

She walked over to the stove and turned the bacon strips as Ann fixed her coffee. The smell of bacon and coffee combined into a pleasant duet, accompanied by the baking biscuits. Bree had dreamed of such a scene forever, though she'd pictured a long night of lovemaking beforehand. But being friends was almost as good, if not better. She and Ann had obviously been destined to follow different paths, and Bree had wasted fifty years denying reality. Just as she had denied Brett's death in a senseless accident.

Her chest suddenly cramped.

Ann looked up from her coffee. "Hey. You okay?"

She took a deep breath and exhaled slowly. Then another one.

Ann put her mug on the white tile counter and wrapped an arm around her. "It's fine. You're fine."

Bree's legs threatened to give way, but she managed to reach the nearby square breakfast table before she sank into a chair. Putting her head down onto her crossed arms, she sobbed.

Ann rubbed her back. "Just let it all out, Bree. Cry as much as you need to."

Brett was actually dead, and she needed to let him go. She was fine. Ann had said so. And just as she thought her tears would end, another round of grief hit her. Finally, she smelled the acrid odor of burning bacon and hiccupped to a stop.

She jerked her head up. "Ann. The bacon." By now it was smoking, so they dashed around raising windows and fanning the smoke outside before it triggered the smoke detector.

"Shit," Bree exclaimed. She exhaled loudly. "Now I'll have to start all over."

"That's right." Ann gave her a fierce hug. "And that's a good thing. We all need to start over occasionally. Let's just hope the future's better than the past."

Bree nodded, and relief spread through her like the warm ribbon-cane syrup she planned to heat to sweeten her biscuits with.

❖

Linda felt as cold, cloudy, and gray as the late-November day promised to be. Winter hadn't even officially begun, but she wanted to just stay in bed until March. Well, maybe February. When it came, she'd need to go outside and trim the roses to jump-start their inevitable cycle of pushing out new branches, producing leaves and buds, and finally bearing deep-red roses.

She rehashed the disasters of the last twenty-four hours. Last night she'd innocently expected a wonderful dinner and a pleasant conversation with Tonda, who'd flattered and intrigued her for several months now. After that date fell flat, Linda had naively checked on Bree, who'd bewitched her for almost as long as she could remember. But no, her sister Ann—make that her half sister—no, her stepsister had apparently recaptured Bree's heart.

Only the interlude last night with Sandy, indisputably her aunt, had temporarily lifted the chill that now filled every pore of her body. She pulled the covers up to her nose, glad it got light so much later now than it did in the summer.

Bree had called, sounding far too radiant, and Linda had rebuffed her.

Linda's birth dad hadn't wanted her, and her adopted dad had preferred Ann, his real daughter, as did Bree. Linda pulled the covers over her eyes and went back to sleep, hoping she didn't dream anything. It would more than likely be horrible.

❖

"What's wrong, Granny?"

Riley had acted more subdued than usual this morning after Linda had picked her up. She hadn't even bothered to put on her play clothes yet. She'd just plopped down on the couch and watched Saturday-morning cartoons in her purple flannel pajamas.

"Nothing, sweetie. Why would you ask that?"

"Because you don't act the way you usually do."

"And how's that?"

"Oh, you know. Thinking up fun stuff for us to do."

"I'm sorry. Sometimes grownups get sad, just like you were that day when we transplanted those amaryllis."

"Oh, the little baby ones. I remember."

Linda ran her fingers through Riley's uncombed hair. "Why don't you run get me the brush, and I'll see what I can do with all these tangles."

As she brushed, she thought about Patrick. Silly that hair color could make such a difference. So Ann was a blonde like her mother, whom Linda's stepfather—she tried out the new word—had apparently never quit loving. She recalled how his eyes had sparkled when Ann walked into the room. Oh, he never did anything cruel to Linda, but he just didn't come alive around her the way he did around Ann.

"You're sad, aren't you?" Riley asked, even though she faced away from Linda.

"How can you tell, baby girl?"

"I can feel it, Granny. Kids know more than you think."

Linda finished with Riley's hair and set the brush on the arm of the big chair they sat in. She hugged Riley to her for a minute. "I know. And I'm glad we can tell each other what we're thinking about and feeling."

Maybe if she'd known the real situation between her parents, she would have been surer of who she was and what she wanted.

She sighed as Riley jumped to her feet and began to gear up for the weekend. "I'm feeling better now, sweetheart. How about you run dress and then help me make some decorations to put on the tables for Thanksgiving? Your aunt and her girlfriend are flying home from Chicago to be with us for a few days, and we need to make everything look special for them. Okay?"

"Okay, Granny. What do we do first?" Riley seemed back to normal, and Linda felt a little better than she had since Bree had exploded her world with the bombshell about her parents.

CHAPTER TWENTY-TWO

Linda straightened the house after Riley left Sunday afternoon, lonelier than she could ever remember. Was Ann still at Bree's house, celebrating their apparent reunion? Since late Friday night when she'd spotted Ann's car in Bree's driveway, Linda's mind had taken her places she'd rather not visit, and not even her morning meditations helped.

She flopped down onto her leather couch like Riley had done yesterday. With Thanksgiving practically here, she had a million things to do, but she just wanted to sit and stare at TV.

The phone rang, and she plucked it from its cradle as if it were a baby pitching a tantrum. "Hello."

"Hey, sis. Ready for Turkey Day?"

"Not really. But I will be." Since when had Ann shown any enthusiasm for a family holiday? She rarely showed up, and when she did, she came late and left early.

"I've ordered a Greenberg turkey to be delivered Wednesday."

"What? How big?"

"Oh, the one that feeds twenty to thirty people."

She did a quick mental count. Her three children and their spouses, four grandchildren, Sandy and Ann and herself. "I expected thirteen or fourteen."

"Oh. I invited Bree and her mother, and Carolyn. And maybe a few others. Is that a problem? Bree and her mother plan to make some pies, and Carolyn volunteered to bring a big fruit salad and rolls. Okay?"

Linda slumped back into the couch. Not only had Ann confiscated Bree and Sarah, but she'd taken charge of Linda's Thanksgiving celebration as well.

"Linda? You there?"

"Sure you don't want to have the meal at your house?" Linda tried to keep the resentment from her voice.

Ann didn't slow down. "No, thanks. I'm not as good at that sort of thing as you. By the way, Bree told me about Dad."

"She did? Why—"

"Don't be mad at her. I wormed it out of her the other night."

Linda choked on her tears.

"I'm glad she told me." Ann's tone sounded unusually soft and sympathetic.

"Yeah?" Linda couldn't force out another word. At least she hadn't slammed the phone down in a rage.

"I always felt bad that Dad favored me, and furious at how much better Mom liked you than me."

Linda's tears dried up, and she sat up straighter. "You realized Dad liked you best?"

"Hmm-huh. I always sensed it. And on some level you must have too."

"But Mom didn't like me more than you."

Ann's laugh sounded harsh. "Of course she did. But I never gave her a chance to like me as much as she would have. Dad gave me enough attention."

"What do you mean?" Linda didn't trust her.

"How about we call it even? After all, you have a fascinating mystery in your life. If I were you, I'd hop on the next plane to Paris and try to find all my long-lost siblings and their offspring. Maybe they'd act nicer to you than I ever did."

Linda relaxed into the sofa cushions and chuckled. "You know, I might just do that. Want to come along?"

Ann laughed. "Sounds like fun, but I have my hands full right here. Good talking to you. See you Thursday with turkey in hand, if not sooner."

As Linda lowered her phone, her head spun. How could she make it through Thanksgiving with Ann and Bree celebrating their reunion right in front of her? She had to talk to someone or she'd burst.

❖

"What do you think, Sandy?" Linda stroked Zoe's soft coat, who'd immediately cuddled up next to her and rested a paw in her lap. Cowboy covered Sandy's lap as she leaned back in her oversized burgundy recliner.

"You're sure keeping my life interesting lately, Linda. Without you, I'd never have known what a little Peyton Place this town was."

"Watch it. You're showing your age. I was younger than Riley when *Peyton Place* was popular."

Sandy brushed away the comment with one hand. "Doesn't matter. People will always sneak around to do what they want, no matter who they hurt. And don't try to change the subject."

Linda ran her fingers through Zoe's coat again and began to relax.

Fidgeting in her chair, Sandy seemed to have caught the agitation Linda had just shed. "I'm stunned that Helen got pregnant by a stranger and had to get married." She tossed the Sunday paper onto the floor. "I never suspected a thing."

"Well, you'd have been about Riley's age. You probably didn't even know where babies came from."

"Ha. When you grow up on a farm like I did, you know all about that." She picked up Cowboy's ear, then let it drop. "I probably just wasn't interested in what the grownups were talking about. I was outside all the time playing like a wild creature."

"Yeah. I can imagine that."

"I'm sure the news about your parents was a shock, but has it changed anything?"

Linda shifted her weight. Zoe's head was beginning to get heavy. "It's strange, but things seem better between Ann and me now."

"Better how?"

"With everything out in the open, it's like we can both understand what was happening and why and finally let it be. That's a relief."

"So what's bothering you now?" Sandy nudged Cowboy, who scooted over a bit.

Linda suddenly flushed all over, and it wasn't from holding Zoe. "It's Bree. I thought we had something special, but then Ann showed up and everything changed."

"So the old sibling rivalry is still alive and well?"

"I'm afraid so. When I saw Ann's car there late Friday night, I went to pieces."

"And you haven't heard from Bree since?"

"She called first thing the next morning, but I told her it was early and—"

"How did she sound?"

"Excited. That's what got me, especially when she said, *You'll never believe what happened.*"

"What had happened?" Sandy roused Cowboy and made her jump down.

"That's just it. I don't know. I cut her off, so she never had a chance to tell me. Whatever it was, it had to be about her and Ann, and I didn't want to hear it."

"What if she'd just won the lottery or had a wonderful dream about you or—"

"Okay, I get it." Now Zoe jumped down too.

"Do you?" Sandy stood up and stretched. "I'm hungry. Want a sandwich?"

"No, thanks. You go ahead." Linda sat in silence after Sandy left the room.

"Do you remember what we discussed about magic several months ago?" Sandy said from the kitchen.

"I'm not sure. You've told me a lot of things about it." Sandy didn't realize what a novice witch Linda was.

"Magic doesn't create the changes you're trying to make." Sandy's words floated into the room.

"You mean I can't just wrinkle my nose like Samantha the witch used to do on *Bewitched* and get what I want?"

"Exactly." Sandy emerged with a peanut-butter sandwich and a glass of milk. "Sure you don't want something?"

Linda shook her head. "I'm fine."

"Remember what I'm about to tell you." Sandy set her glass on an end table and sat down next to her.

"Okay. I'll try."

"The changes you want have to come from inside you. That's the basis of magic. Got it?" Sandy took a bite of her sandwich.

"Maybe. But how do the changes happen?"

Sandy chewed, then swallowed. "You have to put yourself in a position where what you want can occur."

"That's still kinda vague."

"Okay. Let's just say, theoretically, you'd like to have some type of romantic relationship with Bree."

Linda glowed with heat and nodded. "Uh-huh. Theoretically."

"Yesterday morning, she was excited and wanted to share something with you, but you didn't want to listen. In fact, you cut her off. Was that an example of opening yourself so what you want with her can take place?"

Linda shook her head again. "No. Hey, your sandwich looks good. Okay if I make myself one?"

"Of course. Go ahead." Sandy picked up her glass and took a long drink of milk.

"What should I have done?" Linda called from the kitchen as she spread a glob of crunchy peanut butter onto a piece of wheat bread.

"You tell me," Sandy called back.

"Shared her excitement? Listened to her even though I was afraid what she'd tell me would hurt?"

"That's it. You expected the worst, so you got it. You haven't heard from her again, have you?"

"No." Linda placed another slice of bread on her sandwich and slid it onto a paper plate. "And I probably won't if I don't call her. But what does not hearing from her have to do with magic?"

"I've already told you. Magic comes from inside you."

"Yeah. And?"

"Well, it happens when you harness the amazing power of your spirit."

Linda poured a tall glass full of milk, its coolness tempering the heat their discussion of Bree and magic had provoked. "And how do I do that?"

"If you want something, you have to play the game. But you also have to accept and enjoy both the times you win and the times you lose." Sandy lowered her empty glass as Linda settled beside her on the couch again. "You just need to practice using your energy to make the changes you want in your own life and even in the world around you."

Linda took a bite of her sandwich. "How? Go play the slots in Shreveport?"

"Might help you loosen up. But closer to home, you're already doing your daily visualization, right?"

Linda nodded, her mouth full.

"Okay. Now I want you to cast a spell."

"Cast a spell?" Linda almost choked on her sandwich.

"Yes. To set the mood, burn some incense or a candle with a certain fragrance you like. Then focus on what you want to occur and state your wish exactly."

"And it'll happen?"

"Yes. If you want it enough. Just make sure it's what you want."

"You're sure?"

"Yes. Your ritual will help you focus your thoughts and intentions, and focusing on something long and hard enough will cause results." Sandy looked thoughtful. "I remember dating a man who wanted to become rich. He always told me that if you wrap yourself around a stock—he was interested in Pennzoil at the time—and consider it a winner, it will be."

"But he was forced to research companies like Pennzoil so extensively he could tell if they would make money. Right?"

"To some extent. And he did become a rich man."

"So why didn't you end up with him?"

"He got too wrapped up in making money instead of in me."

Linda laughed. "So he achieved what he wanted but ended up lonely."

"Not necessarily." Sandy seemed to be really serious about the subject. "Maybe he eventually found someone who loved money as much as he did, but that wasn't me. Like I said earlier, follow the advice you've probably heard all your life. Be careful what you wish for."

Linda finished her meal and stood up. "And on that note, I'll take my leave. Thanks, Sandy. For everything. You're my hero."

"No problem, kiddo." Sandy wrapped an arm around her and squeezed. "What do you want me to bring Thursday?"

"Some kind of casserole? Just let me know in a day or two. Did I tell you Ann's bringing a Greenberg turkey?"

"My God. It's a miracle. Or perhaps magic."

The twinkle in Sandy's eyes made Linda feel better than she had since last week, before she'd learned about her dad. Maybe she'd take Sandy's advice and try a little magic.

CHAPTER TWENTY-THREE

Linda knocked on Sarah's door at Silverado. "Yoo-hoo. Anybody home?"

"Sure. Come on in."

The faint odor of oil paints and turpentine greeted her.

Sarah stuck her brush in a jar of paint thinner and pushed her red walker over to her recliner. "It's good to see you, Linda." She eased herself down. "I've missed you."

"I'm sure the aides here are taking care of you. I gave them a special lesson but thought I'd stop by and check." She knelt, then pulled up Sarah's pants leg. "Ah. This looks better every time I see it."

Sarah sat back after Linda finished. She seemed more rested and alert than she had since she'd moved in here. "Are you thinking about going back home now?" Linda sat down in the chair reserved for visitors, grateful for the new, more comfortable one.

Sarah shook her head. "No. I don't want to risk another fall. Besides, I can't ask Bree to give up her job and move in with me. And I'd rather be here than hire sitters."

"I understand. I haven't seen Bree in several days, but I suppose she's probably getting ready to leave for Chicago. I hope she's enjoyed her visit."

"Oh, I'm not sure when she's leaving. She's found a beautician she likes at Foxx III, and she and Ann seem to have rekindled their friendship. Evidently Ann talked her into going to Dallas, shopping, today."

Linda's throat clenched and she stiffened. She'd been right. Bree and Ann had gotten back together, and Bree wasn't in any hurry to leave because of that.

Fragments of Sandy's advice about magic suddenly ran through her head. *Magic comes from inside us. Cast a spell. Play the game. Have fun. Focus!* Could she possibly affect Bree's decision? Could she visualize Bree wanting to stay because of her?

"By the way, Bree told me about my birth father last week." Linda kept thinking about him, and Sarah had actually met him. "What was he like?"

Sarah sighed and leaned back, as if she needed some support. "I'm glad Bree decided to let you know. We've lived with secrets like that for too long." She stared at Linda as if gauging her ability to accept the truth. "From what little I know, he was a wonderful man. He and his French wife seemed very much in love when I stayed with them in Paris. They both appreciated literature and the arts, and they seemed to enjoy each other's company immensely."

"So why would he be unfaithful to her?" Linda had already asked herself the question a million times.

Sarah rubbed the velour fabric on the arm of her chair. "We'll never know. Perhaps we're capable of loving two people passionately at the same time, but usually we have to choose which one we'll be loyal to. I don't doubt for a minute that he loved your mom too. He was that kind of man."

Linda relaxed back into her chair. "You're sure?"

"Yes. I knew his mothers well and admired them tremendously. I'm certain they set a wonderful example."

"They were lesbians, right? Bree said they were named Molly and Jaq."

"Oh yes."

"I'd love to have met them," Linda said. "What did they look like?"

"When I knew them, Jaq's dark hair was graying at the temples, and Molly's red hair was turning white." She stared at Linda. "In fact, it eventually turned the same pure white yours is becoming. She'd probably recognize you as her granddaughter."

Linda's heart raced. "I wish I'd known her. Not that I didn't love the grandmother I had, but…"

Sarah laughed. "You sound exactly like Molly. Always sweet and considerate."

Linda flushed. "But I bet she wasn't a total wimp, like I tend to be."

"You're not a wimp." Sarah shook her finger at Linda. "And she definitely wasn't. She could have stayed here in Texas, but she followed her heart to be with the woman she loved. That wasn't a small thing here in this part of the country almost a hundred years ago. You're more like her than you realize."

Linda straightened up in her chair, then stood. "Thanks for saying that. But say, I heard my sister invited you and Bree to spend Thanksgiving with us."

Sarah smiled. "Oh yes. I appreciate you having her ask us. Bree's talked me into helping her make some pies. I plan to sit and let her do all the work. How about a pecan and a chocolate?"

"That sounds wonderful. I'm sure we'll all enjoy them. I'll make a cake and some chocolate candy, so we should have the sweets covered." She grinned. "I'd love to see Bree hustling around the kitchen."

Sarah got up and headed toward her canvas. "I'm looking forward to it. And if I don't see you before then, I'll definitely see you Thursday, pies in hand."

Linda waved, and as she left Sarah's room, she felt stronger. She'd definitely follow Sandy's advice. If her grandmother could do what her heart desired all those years ago, surely Linda could try to do the same now.

CHAPTER TWENTY-FOUR

Bree unloaded her mother's walker from the cargo area of her mother's Lexus SUV. It was a tight fit but easier to load into than the trunk of her Mustang. "I bought everything you put on the list for the pies," she said as she unfolded the walker and positioned it so her mother could grab the handgrips as soon as Bree helped her out of the SUV.

Sarah surveyed the yard as she started walking toward the house. "Looks like you need to call Miguel to come rake all these crepe-myrtle leaves, Bree. And he needs to pick up those branches over there."

"They just fell the other day, during that storm. I'll ask him to come next week, after the holiday weekend."

"Don't put it off too long. You know how picky the neighbors are."

"I won't, but let's get you inside. This wind's chilly." They headed for the nearby garage.

Bree was glad the housekeeper had come yesterday. The house was immaculate inside, so her mother shouldn't have any complaints about it.

"Why don't you sit at the table?" Bree suggested. "That way you can see everything I do while I make the pies. Want something warm to drink?"

"That sounds good. How about some hot tea with lemon?"

How strange to be orchestrating the activity in the kitchen for a change. Bree felt stiff and uncomfortable, and her mother probably did too.

After she settled Sarah in the most strategically located of the chairs, she clicked the Keurig on and fixed each of them a cup of tea.

"Sit down, Bree. Let's talk a minute before we start on the pies."

Sitting felt more familiar. How many hours had she spent here after school, doing her homework, barely aware of what her mother was up to? They'd rarely, if ever, just faced each other and talked.

"What's going on between you and Linda?"

Bree almost spit out the drink of tea she'd just taken. "What?" She set her cup down. "Nothing's going on."

Sarah sipped her tea as calmly as if she'd just asked her about tomorrow's weather forecast. "Are you sure?"

"I haven't even seen her since last week in the library, when I told her about her real father."

"How did she take the news?" Sarah lowered her cup and scrutinized her.

"What do you expect? She was surprised and upset. A little distant maybe."

"Have you talked to her since then? That was, what, last Wednesday or Thursday?"

"I thought she might want some time to process the news, but when she hadn't called by Saturday morning, I phoned her. She was unfriendly, so I decided she must not be ready to discuss it yet." She tried another drink of her tea. "Her invitation to Thanksgiving dinner surprised me, but I guess she's feeling better. Why do you want to know? Have you talked to her lately?"

"Yes. She dropped by Monday to check on me, while you were in Dallas. She said she hadn't seen you lately and thought you might be going back to Chicago. She said she hoped you'd enjoyed your visit. Have you?"

Bree set her cup down with a clatter. "Yes. A lot more than I expected. But why would she think I'm going back? You've just been out of the hospital a full week."

"You are still gainfully employed, aren't you? If you're not, you must have a lot of vacation time accumulated." Sarah put down her cup too and looked around. "I'm hungry. Do you have anything to snack on?"

Bree jumped up, eager to escape her mother's third degree, if only for a minute. "Sweet or salty?" She strode over to the pantry and pulled out a couple of boxes.

"Bring me both." Sarah bit into one of the small, round, salty crackers first. "Hmm. I like the crunch of these."

What was she up to?

Then she tried one of the rectangular, larger cookies. "And this is good too. Sweet. Which do you prefer?"

Why was Sarah fixating on these snacks?

She didn't wait for Bree to answer. "Have you seen much of Ann lately?" Sarah asked, out of the blue. Had she missed some of her medication today?

"Uh, yes. I told you she dropped by Friday and even spent the night and that we went to Dallas."

"Did Linda know?"

"I doubt it. I also told you I haven't seen her since last week, and when I talked to her Saturday, she almost hung up on me."

"Hmm. I wonder." Sarah picked up another cracker and crunched into it. "There might be more sisterly rivalry between Linda and Ann than you and I are aware of. I'm glad we'll be around them tomorrow. Maybe we'll be able to figure it out."

Bree gave up trying to follow her mother's reasoning. "I wish I could understand what you're driving at, but shouldn't we start on those pies? I don't want to show up empty-handed."

Sarah finished her tea and pushed the plate of snacks away. "We can't have that, can we? Now go get out the flour, salt, and cooking oil, and I'll show you how to make a piecrust."

"Yes, ma'am." Bree jumped up, relieved. Her mother was talking in riddles.

❖

Maureen's plane wasn't due in Tyler until 4:20 p.m., but sometimes the flight arrived early. Sure enough, Linda had just pushed through the glass doors into the reception area when Maureen and her partner Terry bounded toward her, each pulling a small suitcase.

They gave her a huge hug, then followed her outside. "Love your new spinners," Linda said as they stowed their cases—Maureen's pink and Terry's lime-green—into the back of her CR-V.

"We wanted you to be able to spot us in a crowd, Mom," Maureen said as she crawled into the front seat and left the backseat for Terry.

As they sped through Tyler, they briefed her on their news. "I assume you're having a crowd of people over for Thanksgiving tomorrow," Maureen said. "What can Terry and I bring?"

Linda glanced at her. "You know you don't have to bring anything."

Terry chimed in. "But we want to."

"Oh, okay. What if you two buy some Chinet paper plates and plastic utensils? That way we won't have to spend all afternoon and night washing dishes."

Maureen nodded. "That's easy. How about stopping by the store on the way in? I assume everything will be closed tomorrow."

"Sure. I'm expecting about twenty people."

"Wow. Why so many?" Maureen glanced at her. "Not that I mind. I'm just curious."

Linda shrugged and turned into the Kroger parking lot, crowded with last-minute shoppers.

"I'll run in and pick out the stuff, Maureen," Terry offered. "You stay here and visit with your mom."

Maureen blew her a kiss. "Thanks, sweetie. Don't buy out the store."

"She's really thoughtful, isn't she?" Linda said as Terry walked away.

"Yeah. She's the best. I'm lucky to be with her."

"I'd say she's lucky to be with you too." Linda squeezed Maureen's forearm. "Y'all doing okay?"

Maureen smiled, her eyes still on Terry as she disappeared into the store. "Couldn't be better. What about you? Found anybody special yet?"

Linda squirmed. It was strange to be having this discussion with her daughter, who not that many years ago had come out to her and spent hours talking about her busy dating life.

"Not yet. I did have quite an experience Friday night, though."

After she described her disastrous date with Tonda, Maureen laughed. "I bet she's hot, Mom. You could probably have some good times with her, but she's apparently not the type you're interested in."

"You're right. In fact, I wasn't planning to tell you this, because it may be over before it even gets started, but I really like one of the women who's coming over for Thanksgiving tomorrow."

Maureen stared at her. "Who?"

"I doubt I've ever mentioned her. I had a crush on her when I was a teenager. She's been living in Chicago and has been here almost a month now. We've spent quite a bit of time together, but things are up in the air between us now, and she'll probably be leaving soon. I'm trying not to get my hopes up."

"So you invited her to spend a major holiday with us? Smart move, Mom."

Linda laughed. "I know. But I didn't invite her. Your aunt Ann did."

"Ann? Oh no. When did she show up again?"

"Oh, you know how she flits in between husbands. I even thought she'd found one here, but evidently she decided against him. I have no more idea how long she'll be in town than I do about Bree—"

"Bree? Bree Principal?"

"What? Do you know her? How?"

Maureen raised a brow. "Mom. Every lesbian in Chicago knows her—at least knows her reputation. She's an old-school player, a love-'em-and-leave-'em type. She'd probably make your date last Friday night look tame."

Linda's heart suddenly felt as frozen as some of the turkeys she'd seen in the grocery store earlier this week. "Where'd you hear that?"

"Gossip. I've never actually met her. We run in different circles. She's very private, very selective. But I've heard whispers about her, and I remembered her name because she's supposedly from this part of Texas." She grimaced. "Not that she'd ever admit it. I've also heard she doesn't sound like it either, like she's ashamed of being from down here. That's one reason I've never even tried to meet her."

"Are you sure we're talking about the same person?" Linda asked, but Maureen's comment about Bree purposely losing her East Texas accent rang true.

"No. But if she's going to be there tomorrow, I'll sure check her out. I won't put up with anyone like her breaking my mom's heart." She looked as ferocious as Riley had that time she'd threatened Bree, but then she glanced out the window and smiled. "Here's Terry."

"That didn't take long," Linda said as Terry opened the back door and loaded several bulging plastic bags onto the seat.

"No. I got lucky. The express lane was empty."

"Well, let's go home, girls. I have a big pot of chili waiting for you two. I know how much you like it."

"You got that right, Mom. And I'm starving."

Maureen had sounded so much like Bree just then that Linda's heart thawed a bit. If what Maureen said was true, thank God she hadn't become too involved with Bree.

She sighed. Which would she rather have—a frozen heart or a broken one?

CHAPTER TWENTY-FIVE

Linda had just finished eating a light breakfast with Maureen and Terry when the phone rang.

"Hey, sis. Thought I'd come over a little early and help you get ready for the big event. What time would be good for you?"

"You don't have to do that, Ann. I can press Maureen and Terry into service." Linda didn't know whether Ann's sudden friendliness pleased or depressed her.

"No. I mean it. I've sloughed off on holidays enough. Let the girls rest. They're supposed to be on vacation."

They did seem a little tired. "Okay. I'm sure they wouldn't mind just lounging around."

"Great. Since we're supposed to eat at two this afternoon, how about I show up at noon, turkey in hand?"

"That should work. See you then."

This was certainly a first. What was up with Ann?

Exactly at noon, a sleek black Lexus pulled into the driveway, and Ann unloaded a large UPS box from the front seat.

Linda hurried to the back door. "You haven't even opened the box yet?"

Ann shook her head. "I'm not totally helpless. I refrigerated it yesterday and let the turkey sit out all morning."

"It should be perfect. Let's find a platter."

After they settled the turkey on the dining-room table, Ann looked around. "Nice decorations."

Linda stared. Ann rarely noticed anything creative she'd done, much less complimented her. "Thanks. Riley helped me. They're not professional, but we enjoyed making them."

"That's what counts, isn't it?" Ann followed her into the kitchen. "Now, just tell me what to do."

Maureen and Terry had greeted Ann when she arrived, but after half an hour, Maureen said, "Looks like you two have it covered here, Mom. Okay if Terry and I take a quick nap before company gets here?"

"Sure. Go ahead."

Ann hadn't stopped working, but after the girls left the room, she said, "We need to talk."

Oh, my God. Linda had dreaded this moment. Could she bear to hear why Ann had undergone such a radical personality change practically overnight? However, she'd followed Sandy's advice lately by trying to focus on what she wanted rather than cut herself off from what she feared might happen.

"Okay. Let's take a break."

They sat down at the breakfast-room table, and Ann said, "You've got to have noticed my sudden holiday mood."

"Yes. I wondered about it but figured you'd tell me what caused it when it suited you."

Ann nodded. "I'm giving myself several days to make sure I'm not jumping the gun this time."

Linda gritted her teeth and forced a smile. Yes, Ann had spent the night with Bree almost a week ago. "That's smart."

"I've finally found someone who seems to love me even with all these wrinkles and my little potbelly." She patted her stomach and giggled.

Linda's smile almost iced up her cheekbones, but she held it. She felt glad for Ann, who'd never really seemed happy before now. But why did Ann's newfound joy have to destroy hers? A deep sigh welled up from deep inside her.

"That's all I get? A sigh? Don't you want the details? Aren't you happy for me?" Ann faded like an aging rose, which hurt Linda.

"No, no—I'm thrilled for you. Tell me all about it." Linda had never uttered two more painful sentences, but she chose to listen to her better angel.

"I'm truly in love, for the first time and for the right reasons. I want to spend the rest of my life with Carl and—"

"Carl? What do you mean?" The sun seemed to have emerged and began to thaw Linda's frozen smile.

"What do you think I mean? That I could find somebody else to fall for in such a short time? We've been engaged for at least a month now. Even I don't work that fast."

"No...I..."

"Aha." Ann's grin appeared teasing yet sympathetic. "I bet I know."

"Know what?"

"You thought I've been talking about Bree." She took Linda's hand and squeezed it. "Look at me. That's why you've seemed so down in the mouth lately, isn't it?"

"Why, I..."

"You can't fool me. You care for her, don't you?"

Linda's smile melted, and she let it fill her face. "Yes. I can't help it. But—"

"But you're not sure how she feels about you. Right?"

Linda let her head drop. "Right."

"I can't help you there. From all indications, she's very fond of you and has enjoyed your time together a lot. But you'll need to talk to her. I can't think about anything right now except Carl. He's been so patient with me."

As Ann raved about Carl, Linda listened with half an ear. Hopefully, Ann's sixth marriage would be a double charm.

But how could she get Bree alone and find out how things stood between them? Maybe, as Sandy said, magic actually worked.

From the moment Bree strolled though the front door wearing an orange sweater and brown jeans, Linda couldn't keep her mind on anything or anyone else. The two of them seemed to exist in an iridescent bubble, a glistening membrane that kept them from straying too far apart and filtered everyone else out.

After everyone piled their plates high with the food laid out on the Corian counters, the youngsters migrated outside to enjoy the unpredictably balmy, springlike weather. Even Sarah finally moved to one of the tables on the back patio and sat in the warmth of the sun.

Linda thought of the safe picnic area she always visualized in her daily meditations, but the dad who'd adopted her morphed into her biological father, Patrick. Sandy was the only other person here who used to go to those picnics, but Linda's new family gathered at her home today supplanted the one of her childhood.

She and Bree sat at opposite ends of a long table, and neither said much, the bubble cocooning them. Did Bree feel it too, this womb-like sensation? Or did Ann? No. Ann was too wrapped up in Carl, who sat beside her like he'd just won the Kentucky Derby, listening as Ann chattered. Only Sarah seemed to detect the fragile membrane that cradled Linda and Bree, and she never stopped smiling as she sat there in the sun.

Sated from turkey and casseroles and hot rolls and sauces, Linda rose and walked inside to sample the desserts.

"You look wonderful today, Linda." Bree spoke so softly Linda barely heard her amid the hubbub from outside.

"Thanks. It's because you're here." She cut a slice of pecan pie. "Did you really make this?"

Bree's grin made the warmth of the sun spread throughout Linda. "Yes. I'm learning all types of new things. But I've missed seeing you lately. Are you all right?"

Linda watched the vein in Bree's right temple pulse. She could practically see the blood pounding through it.

"May I come back later, after everyone has left, so we can talk?" Bree gazed into Linda's eyes so intently Linda opened her mouth to say yes.

"Mom. Oh, here you are. You haven't introduced me to your friend." Maureen stood there like an Amazon warrior, staring at them.

The iridescent bubble burst, leaving Linda exposed to the demands of hospitality, of motherhood, of friendship. "This is my friend Bree, from high school. Bree, my daughter Maureen, visiting from Chicago."

Bree seemed to shake herself from a daze as Maureen held out her hand. "So glad to meet you, Bree. Mom mentioned that you live in Chicago too. I bet you're missing big-city life."

Linda suddenly felt furious at Maureen for destroying the connection she'd been absorbed in, the magic she'd help create between Bree and herself.

Bree nodded, apparently awake from their mutual dream state too. "Actually I'm not missing it at all. I'm tired of its fast pace and the cold weather."

Then Terry glided up behind Maureen and wrapped her arms around her waist. "Where's my slice of chocolate pie, sweetheart?"

"Sorry. I got distracted." Maureen's eyes softened as she cut into the pie and placed a piece gently on a plate. "Good to meet you, Bree." She put the knife back down with a clang.

Linda hoped that only she had caught the slight curl of Maureen's lip as she glanced at Bree before she walked back outside with Terry.

The afternoon passed in a whirl of games, conversation, and laughter. As she and Bree pitched horseshoes with the young people, it was as if they were magnetized, trying to see how close they could come to occupying the same space. Their hands grazed each other as they moved from one end of the playing area to the other.

Later, Bree and Maureen batted a Ping-Pong ball back and forth across an old green table as if jousting for Linda's favor, but Maureen finally conceded the victory to Bree and wandered off with her arm around Terry.

And when they all played Mexican Train, Linda sat as close to Bree as possible, jostling her arm as she laid a domino on the table.

The afternoon wore far too quickly into dusk. "I need to get back to Silverado and take my evening medicine," Sarah told Bree and Carolyn, who'd driven them to the celebration in her big Lincoln.

After preparing plates of leftovers, Linda watched her family and friends trickle away, waving good-bye. Even Maureen and Terry deserted her, citing a movie they wanted to see, and friends of Maureen who'd asked them to visit. They wouldn't be back until late, they called. Don't wait up.

Her hands immersed in soapy water, washing the remains of the pans and serving dishes, Linda held on to the warmth of the day, her connection with Bree, until the moon began to rise.

She walked to the back porch, standing there and watching it peek over the tree line, a bite of it gone after last night's fullness. She seemed to be falling from a great height, air rushing past her, silence surrounding her. She wanted to embrace the glowing moon, clasp it in her arms, force it to stay full forever.

But then a car door slammed, and she was certain it was Bree. She drifted toward the old Mustang, to the woman who stood beside it gazing up at the almost-full moon, as if also caught in its spell.

❖

As Linda neared, emerging from the dark backyard like a glowing spirit from another dimension, Bree thought it might finally happen. The grazing and jostling of arms all afternoon, the sensation of wanting to occupy the same space had made Bree want to kiss Linda more than she'd ever wanted to touch her lips to another woman's. The craving had pulled her back here like a kite on a string being reeled in. She had to kiss Linda or she'd fly apart in the gale buffeting her.

She stood and waited, unsure what to do with her arms, which begged her to wrap them around Linda, to pull her close. Linda had enchanted her, banished everyone but the two of them from the otherworldly state they'd languished in all afternoon.

Suddenly, headlights shone around Bree, cast her shadow on the ground in front of her, made her doubt her very existence. The sound of an engine roared like a jungle creature. "Mom. I forgot my wallet."

Bree wheeled from the giant, white, smiling moon, from the woman drifting toward her, to the bright headlights blinding her, the suspicious face glaring at her.

"I thought you'd left. Where's my—"

Linda called from the darkness. "Maureen. Why are you here? I thought you wouldn't be back till late."

"We hadn't planned to, but it looks like you need a chaperone. What's going on with you two?"

"Nothing," Linda said.

Everything, Bree thought.

"Bree just came back to eat a turkey sandwich with me."

Maureen's eyes glittered like obsidian.

"She's a player, Mom. I warned you about her," Maureen said, her voice loud, filled with venom.

"Maureen. Watch yourself."

"I don't want you to get hurt." Maureen ran through the front door into the house and quickly emerged, holding her wallet like a trophy. "We're just going to the store. Be back in half an hour."

"Come on." Terry called from the idling SUV, her voice a welcome sound as she claimed Maureen, tried to urge her away.

Bree stood riveted to the driveway as Maureen gunned the motor and pulled out onto the highway with tires squealing.

Linda ran to Bree. "Don't pay attention to her. She's still young enough to think everything's either black or white."

A cloud covered the moon. Bree just stood there, rigid, feeling transformed into a pillar of salt. "She's right, you know. I used to be a player."

Only the sounds of the night joined them as they stared at one another. The hush was so palpable, Bree could have sliced it like a piece of pumpkin pie. Her heart beat in her temples. They throbbed until she feared they might explode. The membrane that had surrounded them most of the afternoon reappeared, squeezed them into a shrinking space.

Linda looked toward the highway, toward the spot where the car had sped away. The angry sound of the engine still echoed in the still night, and she paused. Then she breathed in like a baby tasting her first gulp of air. She toddled toward Bree, and Bree held out her arms.

They kissed. The taste of Linda entered her, flowed through her. She sampled the sweet and salty depths of Linda's lips, her moonlit cheeks and neck. "We better take this inside," she whispered. "What will the neighbors say?"

Linda kissed her back. "I really don't care, but I do have to live here. Maybe we should pay a little attention to them." They paused at the steps, arms entwined, and gazed back toward the waning moon.

"A little attention, but not too much, okay?" Bree kissed Linda's hand, drew her to her side as they headed inside. "How about that sandwich you promised? Or can you think of a better way to pass the time before your irate daughter roars back here?"

"I'll fix you one to go. I'd rather use my mouth for something else during the rest of our precious few minutes."

They practically fell on the couch together, clutching each other like they were drowning. The womb-like membrane enclosed them again, creating an oasis of sensation and escape. Minutes dissolved as they flowed together.

Bree reluctantly broke away. "I hate to say this, but Maureen should be here any minute, and I don't think she'd be too happy to see me. Any chance we can continue this tomorrow?"

Linda shook her head, looking almost dazed. "What incredibly bad timing. The girls and I plan to spend all day shopping and going to the casinos in Shreveport. And they've already made reservations for tomorrow night at some fancy restaurant there that everyone's talking about."

Something constricted inside Bree, made her almost nauseous.

"Don't look at me like that. I need time to make Maureen realize how much you mean to me. And to be sure she knows you won't hurt me." Her level gaze was like iron. "You won't, will you?"

"Not if I can possibly help it." She took Linda's hand and pressed it to her heart, praying she could keep her promise.

Linda squeezed slightly, and Bree's breasts pulsated with longing. "How about Saturday night? We're going to game night at Don's, in Tyler, but I'd love for you to go too."

"*We*? Your plans include other people? I'd rather be with just you."

Linda smiled. "Yes. You'll have to charm Maureen, and the other people we'll be with are very accepting. Then after I put Maureen and Terry on the plane Sunday, you should have me all to yourself—within reason."

"I'd rather be without reason. But if you say so, I guess I can wait that long. Now where's that sandwich? I need to make a quick exit. Don't want your daughter to challenge me to a duel. She has a few years on me."

After one last, long kiss, Linda jumped up, fanning her face with her hand like a teenager. "You're right, but don't underestimate yourself. You're still in pretty good shape."

Bree watched Linda slice turkey with something resembling contentment. She could grow very used to this woman.

CHAPTER TWENTY-SIX

S aturday night, they approached a stone fortresslike structure
dominating a hill, and Linda placed her hand on Bree's thigh.
"Let's stop here for a few minutes."

Bree wheeled her Mustang into the crowded parking lot. "What
is this place? It looks like it could withstand a barbarian invasion."

"This is Fresh, our local answer to Whole Foods Market. I
promised Maureen we'd meet her here. She wants me to help her
choose some pastries for game night."

"Oh, were we supposed to bring something?"

Linda waved a hand toward the backseat. "Don't worry about
it. I brought enough for both of us. I think Maureen just wanted an
excuse to visit this place."

Inside the high-end grocery store, Bree glanced at the rows of
produce. "This does remind me of Whole Foods. Even the prices
aren't that different from the ones in Chicago."

"Correct." Linda waved to a young man busily replenishing a
pile of beautiful organic tomatoes. "The surrounding area is Tyler's
new elite community. There's practically no vacant land left in the city
to build a home on, so new subdivisions keep pushing southward."

Maureen and Terry strolled up. "Fancy meeting you two here."
Maureen barely glanced at Bree. "We got lost in traffic. It's not easy
to keep up with a vintage Mustang." She glared at Bree now and took
Linda's arm. "Where are those pastries you told me about, Mom?"
Before Linda could reply, Maureen steered her toward another part
of the store.

Terry strolled along beside Bree. "Don't pay any attention to her. I don't know which she's more jealous of—your relationship with her mother or your car. It irked her to have to drive Linda's CR-V, though she'd never admit it."

"My relationship with Linda? What does she think's going on?"

"That you've seduced her and plan to leave her high and dry when you get tired of her and go back to Chicago."

Bree stopped to look over the variety of seafood displayed in a refrigerated case. "Is my reputation that bad?"

"Yep. Evidently you've been a busy lady."

"Not that busy. I've just lived a long time, so I've had plenty of opportunities to make more mistakes than I like to remember. And I'm also not that easy to satisfy." Bree wandered past the meat cases, admiring the lean cuts there.

Terry snorted, as if in surprise. "At least you're honest. I can see how you earned your reputation, and I'm not trying to flatter you, but you've aged well."

Bree glanced at the tasteful displays of wine they strolled past now. "How can I convince Maureen I don't have dishonorable intentions toward her mother?"

"Do you?" At this end of the store, cases of freshly cooked dishes for takeout surrounded them.

Bree paused to examine an open bar that displayed olives of many sizes, colors, and shapes. "I'm not sure." She picked up a small plastic container and filled it with large black ones. "I've known Linda a long time, which I can't say for any of the other women who helped me gain my reputation."

Terry raised an eyebrow. "So?"

"I plan to know her a lot longer, so I don't intend to jeopardize our friendship."

"That's what it is? Friendship?"

"Are you Maureen's proxy?"

"Self-appointed. Believe me, my questions are mild compared to the ones she'd be pelting you with."

Bree filled a second container with small green olives. "Okay, that's fair. And yes, I think friendship is at the top of the list right now. But Thanksgiving night…something happened, and honestly, I might be tempted to tell you about it, if I could."

"What do you mean?"

"I don't really know. I'm out of my depth, exploring new territory, and frankly, it's scaring the living daylights out of me. But the way I feel about Linda...well, let's just say that when I realize what my intentions toward her are, I'll let Maureen know before I consciously do anything to hurt her mother. Is that fair?" She filled a third dish with large purple Kalamatas.

Bree held it out, and Terry took one of the olives. "Umm. That's so good. And I think your offer may satisfy Maureen, though I can't speak for her. But I'll convey it, and we'll just have to wait and see."

Bree balanced her three containers in a neat stack and looked down the aisle to the right. "Speak of the devil—"

"Hi, sweetheart." Terry left Bree's side and joined Maureen, who was carrying a white bakery box. "What do you have there?"

"Some of the most divine-looking pastries." Maureen gazed at Terry with pleasure, and then they walked on toward the checkout counter, their heads almost touching.

"What was all that about between you and Terry?" Linda asked, frowning slightly as she joined Bree.

"Just a friendly chat." Bree grinned. "Your daughter's certainly crazy about you."

"Why do you say that?" The muscles in Linda's face gradually relaxed. "Oh...she had Terry talk to you about...us. I wonder how much they saw the other night when they caught us in the driveway."

"Enough, evidently. She must be very intuitive. I've been given fair warning. So with them and my own mother breathing down my throat, not to mention little Riley, I'm going to be forced to give up my evil ways and be a good girl." She tried to keep her expression carefree but wasn't sure she succeeded.

Linda took her arm, and they headed toward the exit. "And how do you feel about that?"

Bree blew out a breath. "I'm not sure. Uncertain, excited, scared as hell."

"The big, bad adventuress scared?" Linda lightly elbowed her.

"I never thought I'd admit it, but yes, I am. And did I mention confused?" Bree put up her hand to push through the heavy glass door.

"That, I'd believe." Linda chuckled. "Now you better back up and go pay for whatever's in those containers, or you'll have to add arrested for shoplifting to your list."

Bree laughed and did exactly as Linda suggested.

❖

"Where to now?" Bree asked as they sat in the Fresh parking lot.

"Just head across the highway into Hollytree. And make sure Maureen and Terry follow us. We're almost there."

Two-story brick houses of a variety of styles lined both sides of the streets they twisted and turned through, each house dominating the small lot it sat on. "So this is the subdivision I've heard so much about."

"This is it."

"Sarah's mentioned this neighborhood occasionally, but I had no idea it was so large, and so posh."

"Yes. Don's house is one of the smaller ones, but it's a gem." Linda pointed. "There it is, on the left. Just pull into this circular driveway behind Lou Anne and Kay's Camry."

Linda rang the doorbell, and Don immediately appeared and pulled her in with a hug. "Hi, pretty lady. So good to see you again, Bree. And who else did you bring?"

As Linda introduced Maureen and Terry, Bree stood looking at the grand piano that filled the small room to their right. To the left stretched a shining formal dining table and chairs, backed by a large china cabinet bursting with crystal glassware.

"Here are your name tags." Lou Anne stood by the table. Evidently she and Kay shared hosting duties of this game-night event with Don.

"Come on in and meet the others," Kay said.

An assortment of people, young and old, clustered around a long granite-clad bar dividing the small kitchen from the breakfast-room area. Linda placed the platter she'd brought on the bar and uncovered it to reveal generous slices of ham. A plate of assorted cheese slices and several bowls containing chips and dips sat nearby.

"Do you have a dish for these olives?" Bree asked Don, who seemed to be everywhere.

"Of course. These look scrumptious. And those pastries Maureen just handed me are to die for. I see they're all from Fresh. Nothing but the best, I always say."

Bree loaded her plate with the snacks everyone had contributed, then wandered into the adjoining living room. There she paused in front of a lit curio cabinet filled with porcelain figurines and Swarovski crystal pieces, all dust free. She made a mental note to discuss the collections with Don later.

On a side wall of the living room stood a desk covered with framed photos, all showing a younger-looking Don with an older, kind-looking man. "That's John," Linda said, appearing beside her. "He's Don's partner who died a couple of years ago, the one who played the grand piano you were looking at when we got here."

The photos showed the two men enjoying themselves on cruise ships, at clubs, and at restaurants, always smiling and obviously very much in love. "Don must miss him so much." Bree was just beginning to realize what life could be like with someone she cared for. She couldn't bear to think of losing someone so special, like Don had.

"Oh yes. He was devastated. But do you remember the young, dark-haired produce manager I waved to in Fresh?"

"Yes. He seemed nice."

"Well, Don told me that he and John had agreed that if either of them died, the survivor would date him. And that's what Don has done."

"Interesting—and how's it going?" Bree glanced around the immaculate, beautifully furnished room, warmed by the heat from the fireplace on the far wall.

"Let's just say Don hasn't gotten over John's death yet."

"How sad. At least he feels like opening their beautiful home to their friends once a month."

"Yes. We all appreciate him. And who knows? Maybe he'll find someone else someday." Linda sighed.

Suddenly, a tall, dark-haired woman appeared nearby and held out her hand. "Hello. I haven't met you yet. I'm Rosemary."

"This is Bree," Linda said. "Rosemary's one of our straight allies. Bree's visiting from Chicago."

"Really?" Rosemary burst into a smile. "My daughter and her partner live there, on the northwest side. Do you know them?"

Bree grinned. "I'd need a little more information, but I doubt it. I'm on the south side of town and rarely get out of my neighborhood."

"Well, my daughter is a lot younger than we are, and she says the same thing. Sometimes I think we have a larger, more active community here in Tyler than people in a lot of big cities do."

"From what little I've seen so far, I tend to agree," Linda said. "Come on, Rosemary. I want to introduce you to *my* daughter. She and her partner live in the same part of Chicago as yours and might possibly be acquainted. If not, maybe they could all meet each other."

Bree was introduced to more people than she could ever remember, many of them gay men ranging from eighteen to eighty. A retired nurse named Sheri and her on-again, off-again partner stood out because they both liked to read and seemed full of life and up for just about anything.

Slowly, people began to drift toward the two round folding tables set up in the living area or to the large dining table. A collection of board games was stacked in one corner of the living room, and as people gathered, they began to choose games.

"Hey, Linda. Do you and Bree want to play Rummikub with us?" Kay asked.

"Sure, if it's okay with Bree."

The four of them sat at a small folding table, and Lou Anne opened a case filled with game pieces. Then each of them chose fourteen small tiles from the large group lying facedown the table and arranged them on her own plastic rack.

The game moved quickly, and Bree easily caught on. Lou Anne made some complicated moves, though Kay distracted her once by asking, out of the blue, "Don't you think my honey looks sexy in red?" Lou Anne became so flustered she missed an obvious play. Bree seemed to try her best, but Lou Anne ended up winning almost every game.

After four games, Lou Anne and Kay stood up and stretched. "I'd like to buy a copy of your book," Bree told Lou Anne. "I've intended to ever since Linda told me about it."

"Of course." Lou Anne seemed delighted. "I'll run get one from my car and sign it for you."

Just then Maureen wandered in from the dining room and picked up a can of Dr Pepper. "Having fun, Mom? What's this game?"

Bree stepped over to refill her plate, seeming to steer clear of Maureen, who'd barely spoken to her all night.

Linda was explaining the basics of Rummikub to Maureen when the doorbell rang. "What kept you so long?" she heard Don say. "I thought you'd decided not to show up."

Linda froze as Tonda entered the room, arm in arm with him. "You know I wouldn't miss game night for the world, Don." Immediately she zeroed in on Linda and sailed over and planted a big kiss on her lips, as if they were an item.

"Hi, Tonda." She didn't know whether to look at Maureen or at Bree, who'd both gone as rigid as she felt.

Maureen stared, then walked up to Tonda. "Hello. I'm Linda's daughter, Maureen. Should I know you?"

Tonda tossed her head and stared Maureen up and down. "I'm not sure. Should you? Or would you like to?"

"I doubt she's interested in anyone," Bree said, "since she seems to be content with the woman she's living with." With a gesture, she indicated Terry, who'd just wandered in from the dining room.

"That's right," Maureen said. "I have exactly what I want, and I think my mom's following my good example." For the first time that night, she met Bree's eyes and smiled.

Don swooped in and took Tonda by the arm. "Now, now, girls. Don't be catty. In fact, I want to show you the new shirts I bought the other day at Macy's. Come on." He winked at them as he led Tonda toward the other part of the house.

"Thanks, Bree," Maureen said. "I think I'll stay here and try whatever you're playing. Want to join us, Terry?"

"No. I'm enjoying the game in the dining room. You go ahead."

Just then Lou Anne walked in carrying a signed copy of her book, and Bree paid her. "Kay and I usually like to play hostess and circulate. Does anyone else want to play Rummikub?" she asked the ones nearby who were finishing their game of Imaginiff.

"No, thanks," several of them said.

"I'd love to." The person Linda least wanted to hear from had apparently returned. "Thanks for showing me your new clothes, Don, but I really did come to play." Tonda paused. "If these three lovely ladies don't mind."

"Of course they don't." Don's eyes twinkled. He seemed to enjoy the electric current racing through the room.

Linda gritted her teeth. It was a game, she told herself, even if she did feel pulled in three directions.

Maureen's eyes flashed. "Come on, Tonda. Let's see what you're made of."

Bree remained silent as she carefully chose her fourteen tiles one by one.

Linda scooped up a handful and glanced at the clock. Eight forty-five. Only fifteen minutes until the party officially ended.

❖

"Pass," Linda said, and drew a tile.

Bree focused on her tiles. What luck. Three of them were number thirteen, so she easily produced the required thirty points.

Tonda straightened in her chair and laid down a run of ten, eleven, and twelve, all red. "Pass," she said, her smirk irritating.

Maureen frowned. "Pass." She picked a tile from one of the piles scattered around the table.

Bree added a red nine to Tonda's run and passed to Linda, who had to draw again.

After two more rounds, Maureen finally had enough points to enter the fray, though her smile didn't bother Bree as much as Tonda's expression of triumph had. Her casually possessive attitude toward Linda infuriated Bree. Was that how Maureen saw *her*?

But Bree hadn't blatantly entered a room full of people and kissed Linda like she owned her. Only the moon had witnessed the kiss she and Linda had shared on Thanksgiving night, and if anything, their kiss owned Bree. She still trembled when she thought of the beauty, the wonder, the sense of rightness she'd felt.

Tonda's kiss had seemed to demean Linda, reduce her to a prize she used to show everyone how desirable *she* was. Bree refused to do that, though she'd been guilty of doing the same thing so many times in her past she shuddered to think about her dreadful behavior.

"Damn it, Tonda. I wanted to play there." Maureen had muttered so quietly Bree wondered if anyone else heard her. But Bree would have said exactly the same thing, in the same tone. Maureen locked eyes with her, and Bree knew Maureen realized the difference between the two kisses she'd recently seen her mother receive.

She sighed, relieved she didn't have to battle Maureen's hostility as well as her own guilt about her past cavalier treatment of women.

"Can you believe it?" Linda asked. "I can finally lay down." Her tray overflowed with tiles, which she slowly, methodically placed on the table. "And I'm out," she announced quietly.

"What?" Tonda said. "I don't believe it. You won? Are you sure?"

"Of course. You can check if you want." Linda held up her empty tray.

"Congratulations, Mom. What an upset. I'm proud of you."

"Me too, Linda." Bree didn't know how, but Linda had managed to put Tonda in her place and reconcile the bad feelings between her and Maureen with only one simple game of Rummikub.

Who was this quiet, kind woman who drew Bree to her more inexorably every day?

❖

"I enjoyed myself tonight," Bree said as she pulled up into Linda's driveway. "Thanks for inviting me."

"I'm glad you could go. And even more happy you and Maureen seemed to mend your fences."

"You can thank Tonda."

"She obviously has a high opinion of herself, thinking she can lay claim to me on the basis of one date, which I cut short."

Bree chuckled. "I don't want to sound like I'm defending her, but I can understand why she'd act like she did."

Was Bree teasing her? "What do you mean?"

"She obviously finds you irresistible. And she's not the only one."

"Oh, she's not?" Linda gazed at Bree's face in the moonlight. So their kiss the other night hadn't been a fluke. She leaned toward Bree, drawn by an attraction she couldn't control.

Suddenly Bree maneuvered her hand under her sweater and held her breast as if it were a football she'd caught for the winning touchdown.

"Whoa, girl. What do you think you're doing?"

"Uh, I thought…after the way we kissed the other night and the way I can't get you out of my mind—"

"That I can't wait to fall into bed with you?" Linda pulled away, disappointment flooding her like a cold shower.

"Then why did you invite me to go with you tonight?" Bree looked as if she couldn't believe she'd been rejected. "Haven't you been interested in me all along?"

"Maybe so. But possibly I'm interested in the ideal you I've hero-worshipped for so long."

"And I've disappointed you, huh? Don't you know I'm made of flesh and blood, not moonbeams? Do you think lesbians are somehow less human than straight women?"

Linda rested her head in her hands. What had she expected of Bree? Their kisses the other night had been so beautiful, so transcendent. They were the stuff of fairy tales: the prince waking the sleeping princess, true love's kiss. A fumbling hand on her breast in a sports car seemed so crass. She could have that with a man, with her first lesbian lover, with Tonda. Somehow she'd thought Bree would be different.

Raising her head, she asked, "How can someone as old as I am be so naive?"

Bree looked surprised. "I suppose that's one reason I'm so attracted to you. And now you have to go and be honest and direct as well as naive. That's a fatal combination for someone as jaded as I am." She took a deep breath. "Tell you what. I'll try to control the raging-beast side of me if you'll give me another chance. I honestly care for you, but frankly, I'm used to more action."

Linda smiled. "Did you forget that we're in the South, and everything's way slower here than it is up North in the big city? I need a steady diet of moonbeams and roses, nights of sharing our dreams and fears, before I feel comfortable jumping into bed with you."

Bree drew back, as if digesting Linda's words, her right hand clenching the steering wheel. "So you expect a Southern-belle courtship?"

Linda took Bree's hand and massaged it. "Not at all. In fact, just the opposite. I want us both to be sure we've faced all our own demons and will treat each other as equals." She let go of Bree and turned to face her squarely. "I'm sick of having men and women act like I'm a sweet little buttercup they can pick and set around for decoration."

"Any ideas how to change that dynamic?" Bree reached out, probably to tweak Linda's cheek, but pulled her hand back.

"As a matter of fact, I do. I'd like for you to read one of the books I recently loaned you."

"That sounds easy enough. Which one?"

"Starhawk's *Dreaming the Dark*."

"Why that one?"

"Do you recall the subtitle?"

"No. I just glanced at the book."

"It's *Magic, Sex, and Politics*. She believes people have confused sex with domination, and that's exactly what I want to avoid in all of my relationships, especially one with a lover."

"So you'll give me a chance if I read the book?"

"If you really absorb it, yes."

Bree was intrigued. "Any chance of a good-night kiss to seal the deal?"

Linda laughed. "You're incorrigible. And remember. I expect a full report on the book, but don't rush. It offers a lot to digest."

Bree pulled Linda into her arms and breathed in her fresh fragrance. How could this woman simultaneously feel so soft and solid, so fairylike yet grounded? As she pressed her lips against Linda's she forgot everything except the way the moonlight gilded Linda's hair.

CHAPTER TWENTY-SEVEN

H ave you ever had your cards read?" Linda asked Bree as they sat holding hands on Linda's couch. A log crackled in the fireplace, which gave off a steady, warm glow against the chilly December wind howling outside.

"You mean by one of those fortune-tellers who advertise on a neon sign stuck in front of their low-rent houses?"

Linda frowned. "What an elitist remark. But you've always been a snob, haven't you?" She softened her words with a kiss on Bree's palm.

"Guilty as charged, ma'am. Care to elaborate on my transgression?"

"I'm sure a lot of those so-called fortune-tellers are fakes just out to make a buck, but when I see one of their signs, I can't help but think of the way men have systematically robbed poor people, especially women, of their power and their land for centuries." She sighed. "Many of those fortune-tellers you look down on would probably have been wealthy, powerful women today if men hadn't gained control of the matriarchies that once ruled the world."

"Sounds like you've taken Starhawk's philosophy to heart."

"Of course. By the way, how are you coming along with *Dreaming the Dark*?"

"I skimmed it, but then the epilogue made me slow down. I always admired the Renaissance, but Starhawk puts it in a totally different perspective by explaining why so many millions of witches were killed at the time."

"Yes, and I didn't tell you, but Sandy was in Starhawk's coven in California awhile. That's one reason I feel so connected to her philosophy."

"Interesting. I'll peruse it more slowly now. It's just been a couple of days. Anyway, you asked me about reading cards."

"Yes. I meant Tarot cards, and you don't have to visit a fortune-teller to have them read."

Bree put her arm around Linda and pulled her close. "You mean we can have one come join us?" The scent of fresh herbs made Bree nuzzle Linda's hair. Being around this woman was more invigorating than anything Bree had ever experienced. Returning to Chicago became less tempting every day.

Linda gently stroked her cheek, then kissed it with a soft caress. "No, silly. And that's the kind of remark I'm trying to help you stop making."

"Sorry. I have a lot of bad habits when it comes to the way I've treated women."

"Well, I just happen to have a deck of Tarot cards and a guide to their meaning. In fact, we could read each other's cards, in private. I'm not expecting any visitors tonight."

"I can think of something else we could do in private," Bree murmured, conscious of Linda's lips still near her cheek. "It resembles reading in braille but requires absolutely no cards or any other type of props. Not even clothes." Bree flushed all over, certain the burning logs weren't the cause.

Linda pulled away slightly. "Not yet." Petals seemed to close over her flower-like face. "I told you I want to be more sure of whatever's between us before we take that step. Sorry for acting so prudish, but it's too easy to stay stuck in old patterns."

Now Bree stroked Linda's cheek. "I never thought I'd say this, but I do understand. And we can wait as long as it takes. In fact, I'm glad we didn't discover each other earlier in our adult lives. I'm not really as horny as I may seem. Age actually does calm the raging hormones, but it leaves us with a steady glow that more than compensates for the sound and fury of youth."

"Hmm. You're a poet." Linda's face seemed to open again.

"I'm just trying to understand and express my feelings as truly as I can, so I'm glad to have time to sort them out. If these Tarot cards can help, let's do it. Read the cards, I mean."

Linda chuckled. "Okay. Don't move. I'll be right back."

Bree burrowed into the couch. What did Linda have in store for her now? She listened to the logs crackle in the fireplace. Whatever it was, she was sure she'd enjoy it.

❖

On her return, Linda cleared all the magazines and books from her coffee table and pulled a deck of oversized cards from a wooden box. "Have you ever seen any Tarot cards?"

"Yes. I even owned a deck years ago. A beautiful set of the Crowley cards." Bree shrugged. "But I never really got into them."

"Oh. Those are gorgeous, but evidently Crowley hated women, so I've steered clear of them. Sandy gave me this traditional set the women who wrote this book chose to use." She held up a tattered red paperback called *A Feminist Tarot*. "She said the deck's not perfect, but its symbols are powerful."

"Looks like you've used the book a lot."

"Yes. Reading my own cards helps me meditate and think through certain issues." Linda shuffled and cut the cards, trying to relax and clear her mind from the distraction of sitting so near Bree.

"What kind of problems?"

"Whatever I'm most concerned with at the time. Mainly situations I'm curious about and would like to explore. Do you have anything like that in mind?"

Bree grinned. "Like, what's going on between you and me?"

Linda couldn't keep herself from smoothing a finger down Bree's arm. "That's exactly what I had in mind."

"Good idea. How should I phrase it?"

Linda forced herself to quit buzzing physically and let her mind take over. "How about, what's happening between the two of us, and how can we make it a positive experience for everyone concerned?"

Bree nodded. "That sounds good. What do we do now?"

Linda handed her the deck. "I don't usually let anyone handle my cards, but you're an exception. So think about our question while you shuffle the cards."

Linda loved the way Bree's expression changed from flirtatious to serious, as if she were letting their question penetrate not only her mind but every part of her. She shuffled the cards slowly, several times, and handled them carefully, as if she were making love to them. Linda's mind began to drift from their question to the bedroom...

"Linda!"

"What?" She shook herself back to the living room.

"Have I shuffled them enough?"

"Oh. Sorry. Yes. Now, with your left hand, cut them three times to the left and leave them in three piles."

Bree did as instructed and watched as Linda put the center pile on top of the one to the left, then placed the combined stacks over the right one. Energy surged up through Linda's arms. Their question was a powerful and important one.

She gazed at Bree, who seemed as focused on the cards as she was. "Think of our question as I lay out ten cards. We can study them all for a minute and then concentrate on them one at a time. Okay?"

Bree merely nodded, her silence soothing and appropriate.

Linda took a deep breath, then exhaled slowly as she allowed the images on the ten cards lying on the table to come to her. "Wow. Your reading is really spiritual, Bree. And we don't have much control over its outcome."

"Why do you say that?"

"Because you have more Major Arcana, or trump cards, than anything else."

"Major Arcana?"

"Yes. The twenty-two most powerful cards in the deck, like Death and the Universe. And look. Your final card is actually the Emperor. Because it's a trump, you can't do much to change the outcome. You can only try to understand."

"Wow. I hope my reading's positive."

Linda took Bree's hand and smiled. "Me too. Ready to find out? I'm sure you're strong enough to do exactly what you want, in spite of what the cards say."

"Okay. Let's go." Bree picked up the first card Linda had laid down. "What do you see?"

Linda paused and let the image swirl around in her. "This card, the six of discs, provides the background of the question and the person who's asking. You've evidently become successful and act rather condescending toward people who were once in your situation."

Bree laughed. "In other words, I'm a snob, which you said earlier."

Linda blew out a breath, relieved Bree was being such a good sport. "Maybe. It also tells me you're in danger of forgetting your roots, of denying your culture or upbringing."

"Like getting rid of my Texas accent and rarely visiting my hometown, eh?"

"Yes. Also, though you're used to being successful, now you're a beggar, like the ones shown kneeling in this card. You need to swallow your pride and accept help."

"Ha. Reminds me of our clash over Mother's health care, when I called you an aide."

Linda's heart picked up its pace. "Sure you want to go on?"

"Positive." Bree ran her hand over Linda's hair, then touched her cheek. "I can take the truth. What's next?"

Linda sighed. Maybe reading their cards hadn't been such a great idea, but if the experience could destroy whatever was between her and Bree, she'd rather know now than later. "This next card shows the obstacles facing us."

"Is it a picture of Tonda or Maureen?" Bree chuckled.

"No, silly. Tonda was never an obstacle, though Maureen could have dealt us some misery. It's the Death card."

"Jeez. Now that's a doozy. And closer than I like to think about. Though it makes me appreciate the years we have left."

"It's actually not as bad as it seems." Linda took Bree's hand. "Granted, the skull-faced knight on horseback has power over everyone, even the religious figure praying to him, but the card traditionally symbolizes the end of a personal point of view and the beginning of a more universal outlook. The sailboat on the lake and the sun either rising or setting in the background suggest that interpretation."

"Hmm. Nice way to put it. We can't avoid death, or any other major changes, but we can broaden our horizons as it approaches."

"Easier said than done, but it's probably everyone's most common obstacle."

Bree looked back at the spread of cards. "What's this third one trying to tell us?"

"The best scenario you can expect in this situation, your ideal resolution, your goal." Linda picked up the ten of swords.

"Remind me what the swords stand for. And the star-shaped figures on the first card in my reading? You called them discs?"

"Discs deal with practical, down-to-earth things, such as money, home, and jobs. Your coming home and thinking about retiring certainly apply there. And swords represent the mind and the voice."

"So my third card, the ten of swords, pertains to my goal of understanding what's happening between us?"

Linda gasped as she studied the card showing a corpse lying facedown on the ground with ten swords plunged into its back. She picked up the book next to her and flipped to the interpretation. "This card signifies a ritual killing and a death that hasn't been dealt with," she read.

"Brett," Bree whispered.

"Yes." Linda stared at Bree's ashen face.

"Of course you could interpret the card more symbolically, like most people do with the actual Death card. But maybe one of your challenges about coming back home has been to finally accept and mourn Brett's death."

Bree stared at Linda. "Yes. That Friday you went to Tyler on a date, I came a long way toward doing just that. Strangely, Ann helped me through it, and I also mourned another death that weekend."

"Another death?"

"Yes. The death of my infatuation with Ann. I'm sure she felt as relieved as I did to see it end."

Linda felt as contented as she did while working in her flower bed on a warm spring day. The worst had passed between her and Bree—unless something else unexpected popped up. She looked at the next card, number four in the spread.

"What does the androgynous figure hanging upside down from a tree limb tell us?" Bree asked as she took a sip from the glass of ice water Linda had brought her earlier.

"The Hanged Man supposedly indicates the root of the situation. You've had a pause in your life, you've symbolically let the male part of your personality die, and you've reenergized your female side. Look how the figure's smiling. The card shows you've gained a lot of strength."

"So coming here turned my life upside down, and I'm a lot happier because of what I've been through? Makes sense and feels right. These cards are pretty neat."

Linda rested her head on Bree's shoulder. "Want to take a break, or are you good for another six cards?"

"Maybe a short one." Bree pulled Linda toward her and placed a soft kiss on her forehead. "This is for your amazing brain."

"Thank you," Linda murmured.

"And those eyes that don't miss a thing." Linda closed her eyes, and Bree kissed each of them gently.

Linda kept her eyes shut, anticipating Bree's next move.

"But especially these lips." Bree's breath was sweet, her lips forceful yet yielding as she pressed them against Linda's mouth and slipped her tongue inside her.

"I didn't do a relaxation exercise before we began your reading, but you've just found the perfect way to take care of my need." She sagged under Bree's touch, which energized her at the same time.

But just as quickly as Bree had initiated the welcome distraction, she pulled away. "Okay. Break's over."

Disoriented yet strangely alert, Linda opened her eyes to the crackling fire and the warmth of Bree's grin. She stretched and sank into the sofa cushions. "Can't we just sit here forever and kiss each other senseless?"

"That suggestion's hard to turn down, but you don't really want to get totally carried away…do you?" Bree looked hopeful.

"Now that you mention it…" Linda shook her head. "No, I would like to wait a little longer. If you don't mind."

Disappointment flashed across Bree's face but immediately disappeared. "I do mind. But that's another perk of growing older. I have more patience than I used to, especially when I know the wait will make what's coming even sweeter. Kind of like waiting for Christmas, only better."

"I don't know if I can hold out that long, but we'll see. In the meantime, where were we? And what was the question?"

Bree laughed and settled next to her, their thighs touching, which raised the temperature in the room considerably. "Us. What's going on between us and how we can make the best of it."

"Okay. The fifth card, the nine of wands, indicates your past relationships."

"What does a wand stand for?"

"Generally passion and specifically love of travel, ambition, career, athletics, competitiveness, restlessness, and charisma."

Bree pressed her hip against Linda's. "Wow, I've been busy."

Linda struggled to maintain her focus. "You have. But this specific card tells me you've needed to rest lately. You might have been exhausted before you came home, not really able to trust yourself to the people you were associated with in Chicago. You've needed to withdraw and to center yourself."

"You got all that from seeing a guy with a head bandage leaning on a leafing stick and standing in front of eight more sticks like it?"

"Well, I've studied several different sets of interpretations, but I've also read these cards for myself a lot of times. The more I read them, the more I see in them."

Bree nodded. "Impressive. What's the next one mean?"

Linda wondered what Bree wasn't telling her about her past life in Chicago, but she didn't want to pry, so she picked up the sixth card in the spread. "This one deals with the present and how it will impact your future."

"And?"

"The Queen of Cups is sitting on her throne, which features three Cupid figures. Water's flowing at her feet, and she's holding an ornate chalice decorated with angels and a cross."

"This is my first card in the suit of cups, isn't it?"

"Yes. It represents the emotions. Cups deal with our love life— romantic as well as familial and friendship. They also indicate our psychic powers."

"I've had one sword, one disc, and one wand, but after this cup, I have two more of them, plus another wand. Seems like I'm becoming more immersed in my feelings than in any other part of myself." Bree leaned back into the couch and took a deep breath. "Interesting."

"Yes. The Queen of Cups indicates that the mother usually passes important gifts to her daughter, especially the capacity for growth. The Queen is usually generous in sharing knowledge, insights, and ideas."

"So does the card point to my mother? She's certainly given both of us some important insights lately. And if I follow her example, I should live a long and healthy life."

Linda entwined her fingers in Bree's. "Without your mother I'd never have come to know and understand a part of my own mother that I never suspected. Learning about my birth father has made me look at myself differently. Your mom's special, and so is her daughter."

Bree cupped Linda's chin and kissed her with a blend of passion and tenderness that made Linda glad she was sitting down. She shook her head, trying to regain some type of rationality. "I've never spent so much time doing a reading and certainly never enjoyed one so much. Would you like to end our session early?"

"Love to, but would I have to go home?"

"'Fraid so. You're oh-so-very tempting, but if we don't stick with these cards, you know where we'll end up, don't you?"

"In bed?" The look in Bree's eyes could have melted cement.

"And I'm not ready. Or did you forget?"

Bree nuzzled Linda's neck and sighed. "No. But I hoped you'd change your mind."

Linda smoothed her hand down Bree's arm and sat up. "Well, I didn't. Would you like to see what the next card says about your attitude toward the question we're exploring?"

Bree's eyes still looked hazy, almost unfocused. "What's the question?"

"What's happening between us."

"I already know what I'd like to happen between us. I don't need a card to tell me."

"Do you want me to fix you a cup of strong, hot coffee to sober you up?" Linda produced her best fake frown.

"Do you really want me to?"

"What?"

"Sober up."

Linda thought about how dull her life had been before Bree had reappeared. "No." A sudden surge of uneasiness hit her. "I just want us to slow down a little before I jump in over my head."

Bree kissed her hand. "Your wish is my command."

Linda swatted her with her other hand. "Silly. Let's finish this before I toss you out the door."

"Okay. Whatever you want." Bree studied the next card in the spread. "Another cup. The ace. So what do you see in it, my lady?" Bree blew Linda a kiss.

"I see an outstretched hand holding a chalice from which water is overflowing."

"And what does it mean?"

"Your sensuality, creativity, and good feelings are pouring out of you. You seem very satisfied with what's happening between us."

Bree grinned. "You can say that again."

"This is a perfect place for this card to turn up. You're giving yourself what you need to make our relationship strong and happy."

Bree put her arm around Linda's shoulders. "What's left to say then?"

Linda flinched. The cards were telling her Bree was truly getting in touch with her feelings and the spiritual realm. But would she get up one morning and say she needed to fly back to Chicago and report to work? "You never know what the rest of the cards might turn up." Linda tried to hide her lack of total trust in Bree and hoped she'd succeeded. Maybe she was being overly cautious.

But Bree removed her arm and suddenly turned serious, and Linda was afraid she'd sensed her distrust.

"What's next?" Bree asked, her tone a bit too hearty.

"The final card of the Major Arcana, the World."

"And what does the World indicate?" Bree moved away slightly so their legs no longer touched.

Linda missed Bree's playfulness and their physical contact. "The factors that can influence our relationship, such as family and friends."

"And does the naked woman twirling batons mean what I think she does?" Bree waggled her eyebrows. Linda was relieved to see her discomfort pass. "And what do the figures in each corner of the card mean?"

Linda smiled. "The wreath circling the woman and the powerful figures in each corner symbolize the end of an era. A new phase of life is set to begin, probably something creative, symbolized by the dancing woman." She lightly touched Bree's hand. "This powerful card tells me the people we love probably view our new relationship as good for both of us."

"You think?" Bree sounded hopeful.

"Yes. Or possibly you've quit needing to play roles and have harmonized the various parts of your personality into a consistent identity."

"Now in English, please," Bree teased.

"You can finally be yourself."

"Accepted for who I am?"

"That's right."

"Wow." Bree grinned. "I like that. It's been a long time coming." She edged back toward Linda, who held up the ninth card.

"A second wand. Though you're really into your feelings, you're also trying to deal with your energy level."

"And?"

"Well, the Knight of Wands indicates you're an impatient, charismatic adventurer full of dramatic ideas. These qualities can help you attract followers into sometimes unstable, even dangerous situations that everyone may regret."

"And that's what I fear?"

"You need to answer that question."

Bree sat silently for a long moment. "I'd do anything not to hurt you, but I have such a bad track record I'm not sure I trust myself."

Her honesty touched Linda in a rarely visited part of herself. She gripped Bree's hand. "You can learn to trust yourself. I know you can."

Bree's dark-eyed gaze almost burned Linda. "Promise me you won't let me do anything we may both regret."

Linda stared back at her. "You're sure?"

Bree nodded.

"I'll do my best."

As Bree settled down, Linda laid her hand on Bree's thigh. "We'll be fine. Ready for the last card?"

"Sure. Introduce me to the Emperor sitting so grimly on his throne."

"Okay. The bloodred mountains and the animal skulls decorating his throne show he's gained his power through violence."

"What's he telling me about the future? That's the main concern of this final card in the reading, isn't it?"

"Yes. Absolutely." Linda tried to soft-pedal the meaning of this card, but she had to be honest. "The men in your life, the patriarchy, the institutions that have educated you and employed you, even the male parts of your personality, dominate you and have blocked your true emotions."

"That's clear, but what can I do about it?"

Linda took a deep breath. "Release them through loving sex."

Bree's grin almost split her face. "That's more like it. Okay, I'm ready."

"Down, girl. Remember what you just made me promise."

"What? I don't remember a thing."

"You can't fool me. Seriously, having the Emperor in this final position is quite a challenge. He represents your impatience and desire to control, but he usually shows that your life will soon change in a big way. You'll have to control yourself and learn to manage the emotions and creative urges bouncing around in you. If you can't, you'll probably run away again."

Now who was being harsh? Linda asked herself. She prayed Bree could break the patterns of a lifetime—she prayed they both could—but felt confident they'd work together toward that shared goal.

Chapter Twenty-eight

I'm so glad you insisted that we wait."

"Are you sure?" Linda wrapped her arm around Bree's waist.

"Yes. Even though it's been the three longest and hardest weeks of my life."

They stood together in Carolyn's large living room, a quiet island in the middle of a sea of murmuring locals.

"Are you ready? It's getting late." Bree glanced at her watch. "Sandy promised to have Mother back at Silverado by midnight."

"Do you think she'll turn into a pumpkin if she's late?" Linda rubbed her way up Bree's back, massaging it. She loved to tease this woman.

"There's no telling what those two might get into if we don't keep an eye on them. They'll be forming a coven at the assisted-living place before we know it." Bree's eyes were clearer and more full of energy than they'd been in high school.

"And that would be a problem…how?"

Carolyn walked over to them. "What are you two dreaming up?"

"Whatever we can. By the way, thanks so much for hosting this Yule Eve celebration tonight. I wish we could all stay here till sunrise and greet the new year together."

Carolyn suppressed a yawn. "Eleven o'clock on a weeknight is way past my bedtime, and I suspect quite a few of the others feel the same way." She glanced around the room, where the crowd had thinned considerably. "I'm amazed so many people showed up."

"Of course, a lot of them thought they were simply here to celebrate Ann and Carl's recent marriage and Bree's retirement and official homecoming. They would have been appalled to realize we were celebrating several other events as well."

"I think all those people have left, Linda, so we should assemble the coven before half of them fall asleep. Sandy said she plans to keep the ritual very brief tonight." Carolyn motioned to Sandy, who loudly cleared her throat.

"Fellow Wiccans and sympathetic others. Once, in California, I attended a Yule ritual on the beach. We all stripped naked and plunged into the freezing surf."

"Makes my teeth chatter just to think about it," someone called out.

"Yes, my teeth were definitely chattering, but the more we frolicked in the waves, the more alive I felt. I'll never forget that experience."

"So what do you have up your sleeve for us tonight, Sandy? Surely you won't ask us to try to top that."

"Actually, I want to announce another wedding—of two more people we love and respect."

Everyone glanced around the room, some with a knowing smile and others with blatant curiosity. Even Ann and Carl had elected to stay, though they stood on the fringe of the group.

"For several weeks Linda and Bree have been preparing for their union and at the last minute decided to make it official. Come on up here, you two."

As she and Bree stood in front of Sandy, Linda felt as if her heart were floating in the cold Pacific. It tumbled, it quivered, it rode the waves until it washed ashore at Bree's feet.

Sandy stood before them. "As an ordained minister, I'll preside at their marriage," she said.

Linda took Bree's hand, which felt as frigid as her own. What was racing through her beautiful head?

Sandy interrupted her musing. "Linda and Bree have written their own vows, and I promise to be brief."

Linda dropped her shoulders a bit when Bree squeezed her hand.

"Do you two pledge to do your best never to try to hold power over one another, as our society has too often taught us to do?"

She glanced at Bree and they replied, in unison, "We do."

"Do you promise to keep yourselves whole and balanced, to honor the power that exists within you, and to share it with one another freely and gladly?"

"We do."

"Are you willing to talk through every difference of opinion, to try to reach an amicable compromise, and to respect your differences?"

Linda turned to Bree and gazed at her strong features. Could she trust that Bree had changed enough to honor these vows? Could she trust herself?

After what seemed like an eternity, Bree said, in a loud, clear voice that emerged at the same time as Linda's, "Yes, I am."

Sandy stared at them as if seeing into all their hidden places. "Now I have one vow for the rest of you to respond to."

She addressed everyone in the room. "Do you all promise to support the union of these two women, to consider it sacred, and to defend it if and when others try to demean it?"

Hearing the voices of family and friends ring out in the affirmative made Linda's throat seize up. This simple wedding seemed so much more valid and meaningful than her elaborate first one had.

Sandy stood before them, strong and tall. "On this eve of Yule, the shortest day of the year, and by the power inherent in me, I am happy to confirm that you two women have joined your lives in this most meaningful of ways. May tomorrow be the first of many lengthening days full of growth and love, for yourselves, each other, and those of us who support you."

Linda slid a plain gold ring onto Bree's finger, and Bree did the same for her.

"When you look at these rings, let them remind you of your connection. I hope you will always be as happy and content as you both deserve. Blessed be."

Bree turned to her, beaming, and kissed her, and then the others formed a circle around them. The new ring on Linda's finger shone as brightly as Bree's did, and the sincere glow on the faces of all those in the room confirmed and strengthened her union with Bree.

"Congratulations," someone called, and everyone echoed the word as the energy seemed to crescendo. Linda felt well and truly married.

Sarah came up and put her arms around both of them. "My dear daughters. Welcome to the family, Linda. I can't think of anyone I'd rather see Bree spend the rest of her life with. Now I won't worry about her starving."

They all laughed, and Sarah turned to Bree. "And you, my darling, seem to have finally found who you are and what you want. My dream about you being stuck in the Renaissance makes sense to me now. In fact, I'm giving you two my painting of it as a wedding present."

Linda would never forget the way Bree smiled at her mother, even though she'd have to ask Bree about that dream. "Thank you. We're honored," she managed to say, in spite of her tight throat. "I could never find a better mother-in-law than you."

Sarah scoffed and shifted into her usual no-nonsense voice. "Well, I better go find Sandy. It's getting late. I'll probably sleep through breakfast."

"She'll never change, will she?" Bree asked as they watched Sarah herd Sandy toward the door.

"I hope not," Linda said. "After all, she produced the best daughter in the world."

❖

"Do you think we're silly for waiting until after we're married to make love?" Linda asked as they strolled to Bree's home, arm in arm under the cold December sky.

Bree stopped and looked up. "Do those stars seem distant and frigid to you?"

Linda turned her face skyward. "Of course they do. I'd hate to have to warm my hands by them."

"But think about it. Each one is a fiery ball of energy that would incinerate us if we wandered too close."

"Agreed. But what's your point?"

"This may sound corny, but we might have burned each other up if we'd slept together when we first discovered we were attracted."

"You must be a really slow learner, because I discovered my feelings for you fifty years ago."

"Ha. Who's the slow learner? I didn't get married, have children and even grandchildren, before I realized I loved women."

"But I didn't waste my time flitting from woman to woman like you apparently did. I stuck with my attraction to you all those years. Now top that." Linda wrapped her arms around Bree.

"I don't want to top that. I don't even want to top you, you wonderful woman," Bree murmured. "I don't want to do anything but taste every part of you, smell all your fragrances, touch every inch of your body, and hear your voice as I watch you fall apart."

"And you think you can make me do that, do you?" Linda squeezed Bree fiercely.

"I hope so. If you'll let me."

Linda seemed to melt. "I'll think about it." She glanced up. "Look at the moon. It should be full in a few days, probably by Christmas."

"That's how I feel. Almost full."

"Anything I can do to help you become completely full?"

Bree buried her face in Linda's sweet-smelling hair. "You know there is."

"Then why are we standing around out here looking at the moon?"

"I'm just waiting for you to say the word."

Linda's smile was lazy. "I've already said it. I trust you."

"Ready to go try out that new queen-size bed I had delivered today?"

"I'd sleep on the ground in a tent here in the backyard with you."

"I think we'd be a lot more comfortable in our new bed, though if you insist…" She pulled Linda toward the garage where the family's camping gear was stored.

"On second thought, we'd probably sleep better inside, especially since we plan to wake up to watch the sun rise. Have you set the alarm?"

Bree kissed her. "I was hoping we'd still be awake."

"You never know, given our advancing years."

"Ha. I feel younger than ever."

"I'll remind you of that in the morning."

"Okay. Ready for your wedding night?"

"I thought you'd never ask."

❖

Linda smoothed her hand over Bree's arm as they stood in her bedroom. "Here. Let me help you take your sweater off."

Linda's hands burned Bree where they touched her, but she stood rigid, staring into green eyes accented by the earrings she'd bought at the syrup festival. "Two months ago I would never have imagined this scene."

Linda circled Bree's waist with her arm and guided her to the edge of the bed. "And you haven't thought about it since Thanksgiving, when we first kissed?"

"No. I've tried to during the past few weeks, but I've drawn a blank every time," Bree admitted. "My feelings for you aren't like any I've ever had."

"Just let go."

Was an alien inhabiting her body? Bree asked herself. They should be stretched out in each other's arms, kissing like nothing else mattered. But suddenly, everything mattered…too much.

"Talk to me." Linda sat close to her on the side of the bed, gazing into her eyes. "Tell me what you're thinking, what you're feeling."

Bree heaved a great sigh. "I feel as bare as the old willow tree we just walked past. My leaves have fallen, and I'm shivering in the cold."

Linda continued to stare at her. "Do you realize how beautiful that tree is, stripped to its essentials, its graceful, unadorned limbs shining in the moonlit sky?"

"I can't get past my graying hair, my sagging breasts, and my spreading hips."

"I wish you could see yourself through my eyes. You're even lovelier now than the first time I saw you. Just in a different way. Believe me."

"I want to. But I still have a long way to go before I root out the self-hater inside my head that I've always listened to."

Linda's smile made Bree relax a bit. "We all do, especially we older models. Want to fight it together?"

Bree sighed again. "How do we begin?"

"Just breathe. Feel the air deep inside you, then push it out. I'll do the same." Linda took a deep breath too.

Bree's belly expanded, then contracted as the warm air circulated through her.

"That's it." Linda's voice sounded like it came from far away. "We're breathing the same air. Sharing it. That's as intimate as you can get. If you want, we can share any other part of ourselves in the same way. Until you're completely comfortable with your own body, you won't be able to share it fully with me. And vice versa."

"With all my experience you think I need lessons?" She nuzzled Linda's neck.

"I think we all need them."

Bree lay back and simply breathed, focusing on each breath. She tried to forget that the woman she hadn't been able to keep her hands off for the past weeks now lay beside her. She tried to forget everything except the fact that she was exactly where she had chosen, with the person she wanted to spend the rest of her life with.

She inched her hand across the soft expanse of comforter that separated, no, joined them. She didn't have to prove anything to Linda or satisfy her in a unique way. She could simply be, and let Linda be, and whatever they did or felt like doing would please them both. She didn't have to be anything or anyone but who she was at the moment.

"Better?" Linda whispered as Bree touched her cheek.

"Much. I'm looking forward to getting to know you, and myself, as fully as possible. Thanks for taking this journey with me."

Linda covered Bree's hand with hers and squeezed. "You're welcome. Believe me, it's my pleasure."

Bree rolled nearer and lay on her side, propping up her head with her hand. "You mean *our* pleasure."

Linda scooted within kissing distance. "Yes. That's exactly what I mean."

About the Author

Shelley Thrasher, world traveler and native East Texan, has edited novels for BSB since 2004. A PhD in English, she taught in college for many years before she retired early. She has published poetry, short stories, and essays, as well as one scholarly book. Shelley and her partner Connie, with their two dogs, cat, and parrot, live near Dallas, Texas. Her first novel, *The Storm* (2012), was a GCLS historical-romance finalist and a Rainbow Awards runner-up for best debut novel. Her second novel, *First Tango in Paris* (2014), is based on her travels abroad. In *Autumn Spring*, she returns to her roots in East Texas and creates a world populated primarily by older women.

Books Available from Bold Strokes Books

The Chameleon by Andrea Bramhall. Two old friends must work through a web of lies and deceit to find themselves again, but in the search they discover far more than they ever went looking for. (978-1-62639-363-9)

Side Effects by VK Powell. Detective Jordan Bishop and Dr. Neela Sahjani must decide if it's easier to trust someone with your heart or you life as they face threatening protestors, corrupt politicians, and their increasing attraction. (978-1-62639-364-6)

Autumn Spring by Shelley Thrasher. Can Bree and Linda, two women in the autumn of their lives, put their hearts first and find the love they've never dared seize? (978-1-62639-365-3)

Warm November by Kathleen Knowles. What do you do if the one woman you want is the only one you can't have? (978-1-62639-366-0)

In Every Cloud by Tina Michele. When she finally leaves her shattered life behind, is Bree strong enough to salvage the remaining pieces of her heart and find the place where it truly fits? (978-1-62639-413-1)

Rise of the Gorgon by Tanai Walker. When independent Internet journalist Elle Pharell goes to Kuwait to investigate a veteran's mysterious suicide, she hires Cassandra Hunt, an interpreter with a covert agenda. (978-1-62639-367-7)

Crossed by Meredith Doench. Agent Luce Hansen returns home to catch a killer and risks everything to revisit the unsolved murder of her first girlfriend and confront the demons of her youth. (978-1-62639-361-5)

Making a Comeback by Julie Blair. Music and love take center stage when jazz pianist Liz Randall tries to make a comeback with the help of her reclusive, blind neighbor, Jac Winters. (978-1-62639-357-8)

Soul Unique by Gun Brooke. Self-proclaimed cynic Greer Landon falls for Hayden Rowe's paintings and the young woman shortly after, but will Hayden, who lives with Asperger syndrome, trust her and reciprocate her feelings? (978-1-62639-358-5)

The Price of Honor by Radclyffe. Honor and duty are not always black and white—and when self-styled patriots take up arms against the government, the price of honor may be a life. (978-1-62639-359-2)

Mounting Evidence by Karis Walsh. Lieutenant Abigail Hargrove and her mounted police unit need to solve a murder and protect wetland biologist Kira Lovell during the Washington State Fair. (978-1-62639-343-1)

Threads of the Heart by Jeannie Levig. Maggie and Addison Rae-McInnis share a love and a life, but are the threads that bind them together strong enough to withstand Addison's restlessness and the seductive Victoria Fontaine? (978-1-62639-410-0)

Sheltered Love by MJ Williamz. Boone Fairway and Grey Dawson—two women touched by abuse—overcome their pasts to find happiness in each other. (978-1-62639-362-2)

Asher's Out by Elizabeth Wheeler. Asher Price's candid photographs capture the truth, but when his success requires exposing an enemy, Asher discovers his only shot at happiness involves revealing secrets of his own. (978-1-62639-411-7)

The Ground Beneath by Missouri Vaun. An improbable barter deal involving a hope chest and dinners for a month places lovely Jessica Walker distractingly in the way of Sam Casey's bachelor lifestyle. (978-1-62639-606-7)

Hardwired by C.P. Rowlands. Award-winning teacher Clary Stone, and Leefe Ellis, manager of the homeless shelter for small children, stand together in a part of Clary's hometown that she never knew existed. (978-1-62639-351-6)

No Good Reason by Cari Hunter. A violent kidnapping in a Peak District village pushes Detective Sanne Jensen and lifelong friend Dr. Meg Fielding closer, just as it threatens to tear everything apart. (978-1-62639-352-3)

Romance by the Book by Jo Victor. If Cam didn't keep disrupting her life, maybe Alex could uncover the secret of a century-old love story, and solve the greatest mystery of all—her own heart. (978-1-62639-353-0)

Death's Doorway by Crin Claxton. Helping the dead can be deadly: Tony may be listening to the dead, but she needs to learn to listen to the living. (978-1-62639-354-7)

Searching for Celia by Elizabeth Ridley. As American spy novelist Dayle Salvesen investigates the mysterious disappearance of her ex-lover, Celia, in London, she begins questioning how well she knew Celia—and how well she knows herself. (978-1-62639-356-1)

The 45th Parallel by Lisa Girolami. Burying her mother isn't the worst thing that can happen to Val Montague when she returns to the woodsy but peculiar town of Hemlock, Oregon. (978-1-62639-342-4)

A Royal Romance by Jenny Frame. In a country where class still divides, can love topple the last social taboo and allow Queen Georgina and Beatrice Elliot, a working class girl, their happy ever after? (978-1-62639-360-8)

Bouncing by Jaime Maddox. Basketball Coach Alex Dalton has been bouncing from woman to woman, because no one ever held her interest, until she meets her new assistant, Britain Dodge. (978-1-62639-344-8)

Same Time Next Week by Emily Smith. A chance encounter between Alex Harris and the beautiful Michelle Masters leads to a whirlwind friendship, and causes Alex to question everything she's ever known—including her own marriage. (978-1-62639-345-5)

All Things Rise by Missouri Vaun. Cole rescues a striking pilot who crash-lands near her family's farm, setting in motion a chain of events that will forever alter the course of her life. (978-1-62639-346-2)

Riding Passion by D. Jackson Leigh. Mount up for the ride through a sizzling anthology of chance encounters, buried desires, romantic surprises, and blazing passion. (978-1-62639-349-3)

Love's Bounty by Yolanda Wallace. Lobster boat captain Jake Myers stopped living the day she cheated death, but meeting greenhorn Shy Silva stirs her back to life. (978-1-62639-334-9)

Just Three Words by Melissa Brayden. Sometimes the one you want is the one you least suspect. Accountant Samantha Ennis has her ordered life disrupted when heartbreaker Hunter Blair moves into her trendy Soho loft. (978-1-62639-335-6)

Lay Down the Law by Carsen Taite. Attorney Peyton Davis returns to her Texas roots to take on big oil and the Mexican Mafia, but will her investigation thwart her chance at true love? (978-1-62639-336-3)

Playing in Shadow by Lesley Davis. Survivor's guilt threatens to keep Bryce trapped in her nightmare world unless Scarlet's love can pull her out of the darkness back into the light. (978-1-62639-337-0)

Soul Selecta by Gill McKnight. Soul mates are hell to work with. (978-1-62639-338-7)

The Revelation of Beatrice Darby by Jean Copeland. Adolescence is complicated, but Beatrice Darby is about to discover how impossible it can seem to a lesbian coming of age in conservative 1950s New England. (978-1-62639-339-4)

Twice Lucky by Mardi Alexander. For firefighter Mackenzie James and Dr. Sarah Macarthur, there's suddenly a whole lot more in life to understand, to consider, to risk…someone will need to fight for her life. (978-1-62639-325-7)

Shadow Hunt by L.L. Raand. With young to raise and her Pack under attack, Sylvan, Alpha of the wolf Weres, takes on her greatest challenge when she determines to uncover the faceless enemies known as the Shadow Lords. A Midnight Hunters novel. (978-1-62639-326-4)

Heart of the Game by Rachel Spangler. A baseball writer falls for a single mom, but can she ever love anything as much as she loves the game? (978-1-62639-327-1)

Getting Lost by Michelle Grubb. Twenty-eight days, thirteen European countries, a tour manager fighting attraction, and an accused murderer: Stella and Phoebe's journey of a lifetime begins here. (978-1-62639-328-8)

Prayer of the Handmaiden by Merry Shannon. Celibate priestess Kadrian must defend the kingdom of Ithyria from a dangerous enemy and ultimately choose between her duty to the Goddess and the love of her childhood sweetheart, Erinda. (978-1-62639-329-5)

The Witch of Stalingrad by Justine Saracen. A Soviet "night witch" pilot and American journalist meet on the Eastern Front in WW II and struggle through carnage, conflicting politics, and the deadly Russian winter. (978-1-62639-330-1)

Pedal to the Metal by Jesse J. Thoma. When unreformed thief Dubs Williams is released from prison to help Max Winters bust a car theft ring, Max learns that to catch a thief, get in bed with one. (978-1-62639-239-7)

Dragon Horse War by D. Jackson Leigh. A priestess of peace and a fiery warrior must defeat a vicious uprising that entwines their destinies and ultimately their hearts. (978-1-62639-240-3)

For the Love of Cake by Erin Dutton. When everything is on the line, and one taste can break a heart, will pastry chefs Maya and Shannon take a chance on reality? (978-1-62639-241-0)

Betting on Love by Alyssa Linn Palmer. A quiet country-girl-at-heart and a live-life-to-the-fullest biker take a risk at offering each other their hearts. (978-1-62639-242-7)

The Deadening by Yvonne Heidt. The lines between good and evil, right and wrong, have always been blurry for Shade. When Raven's actions force her to choose, which side will she come out on? (978-1-62639-243-4)

Ordinary Mayhem by Victoria A. Brownworth. Faye Blakemore has been taking photographs since she was ten, but those same photographs threaten to destroy everything she knows and everything she loves. (978-1-62639-315-8)

One Last Thing by Kim Baldwin & Xenia Alexiou. Blood is thicker than pride. The final book in the Elite Operative Series brings together foes, family, and friends to start a new order. (978-1-62639-230-4)

Songs Unfinished by Holly Stratimore. Two aspiring rock stars learn that falling in love while pursuing their dreams can be harmonious— if they can only keep their pasts from throwing them out of tune. (978-1-62639-231-1)

Beyond the Ridge by L.T. Marie. Will a contractor and a horse rancher overcome their family differences and find common ground to build a life together? (978-1-62639-232-8)

Swordfish by Andrea Bramhall. Four women battle the demons from their pasts. Will they learn to let go, or will happiness be forever beyond their grasp? (978-1-62639-233-5)

The Fiend Queen by Barbara Ann Wright. Princess Katya and her consort Starbride must turn evil against evil in order to banish Fiendish power from their kingdom, and only love will pull them back from the brink. (978-1-62639-234-2)

Up the Ante by PJ Trebelhorn. When Jordan Stryker and Ashley Noble meet again fifteen years after a short-lived affair, are either of them prepared to gamble on a chance at love? (978-1-62639-237-3)

boldstrokesbooks.com

Bold Strokes Books

Quality and Diversity in LGBTQ Literature

E-BOOKS

SCI-FI

MYSTERY

EROTICA

YOUNG
ADULT

Romance

W·E·B·S·T·O·R·E

PRINT AND EBOOKS